Falling for the Unwanted Billionaire

LILY CROSS

Contents

Chapter 1: Sterling

"Sterling, you have to drop everything you are doing right now and go help Edie!"

I'm on my way to Cape Town International Airport when I answer the phone call. New York is six hours behind, so I do a quick calculation in my head. "Good morning, Alice. A 'how are you' would be nice."

I could have looked at the U-Boat Black Swan Italo Fontana limited edition black diamond watch on my left wrist for the time, but I don't. South Africa is one of the most dangerous countries in the world for anyone who wants to flaunt their wealth or success, and I've never been one to take chances. Even sitting in the back of the private shuttle Emirates offers to all their first-class passengers, I won't risk it.

I keep my watch on New York time to combat jet lag—an old trick I learned during my stint as a Navy SEAL. Alice and Edie have been best friends for ages, but Edie Kruger hasn't made a blip on my radar for over fifteen years except when Alice mentions her in passing.

Alice ignores my criticism of her telephone manners. I can hear her huffing as she waits for my answer. "I can't divert my route," I tell her in a firm tone. "I'm carrying."

She only knows what I do for a living in the very vaguest of ways, but Alice knows the drill and she knows the code words I use for certain jobs. When I'm carrying a package for delivery, I go from A to B, and that's that.

Clicking her tongue with annoyance, she prepares to argue with me. "I know that, Sterling! But Edie just called me from CTI airport. She's desperate and needs help. I told her I would see what I could do. Can't you send one of your buddies from work? Get her on a flight to New York. That's all they need to do."

"Fine. I'll sort something out. But I'm doing you a huge favor here, Alice. You owe me one."

"You're the best person in the world! And I didn't need to ask how you were, because you always land on your feet, Sterling. You're like a jungle cat like that! Bye. Mwah, mwah."

For one moment, I turn the phone around in my hand contemplating whether I should kick this problem over to HQ for one of the assistants to sort out. Looking out of the tinted window, I see we're already approaching the Drop-Off Zone outside the First-Class passenger entrance.

I guess I'll have to grin and bear it and buy a ticket for Edie Kruger to fly to JFK myself. I'm here, so I might as well. As the driver pulls up to the curb, I unlock the case handle handcuffed to my wrist.

It might shock some people to know this, but making a big deal out of carrying something precious actually makes them a target for the dozens of conmen who prowl major airports. Pickpockets are so skilled and fast that some-times it's hard to catch their actions on CCTV after the fact.

At Lewis, Marshall, and Associates, we courier our cargo incognito. Leaning forward, I pat the driver on the shoulder. "Thanks, buddy." All my staff and service providers know how much I hate having someone open the door for me. "Check in my bag for me and then flick me a photo of the tags."

He nods and waits for me to exit before driving away smoothly. A hot fog of diesel fumes blasts into my face as I take my last breath of South African air before walking through the sliding doors. I keep my head down, not because I stand six feet five inches in my bare feet, but because that way no one can see my eyes moving from side to side as I clock anyone paying me too much attention.

Besides a few younger women doing double takes as I stride past them—I'm too used to that happening for it to make much of an impact on me anymore—I make it to the information desk without any problems.

I receive a typical South African customer service experience as I stand there. Made to wait while both women chat to friends on the phone without acknowledging me for a good ten minutes. If it was any other country, I would give them a piece of my mind. But out here in Africa, life goes at a slower, more relaxed pace.

Finally, one of the women pretends to notice me for the first time. "Help you?"

"Can you call Miss Edie Kruger to the desk, please?" It's not a question. The customer service woman sees something in my eyes that makes her jump right to the task.

Moving at a brisk pace, the clerk goes to make the announcement. I can't help but smile when I hear little Edie's name coming over the speakers. Alice loves her South African pen pal like family. I guess it was so much easier for the two girls to stay in contact once emails became common.

Leaning back against the desk with my elbows resting on the edge of the counter, I wait and watch for her arrival. At least, that's what it must look like. In reality, I'm scoping the crowds, watching for anyone interested in the case I have casually clasped in my fingers.

I'm carrying about one hundred million dollars worth of diamonds. The outer layer of the case is made of special carbonite alloy, which deflects X-ray and sonar penetration. I pass through all security checks without a problem. Commodities are better than cash when you want to make a deal in Africa.

I spot two pickpockets stalking through the masses of frequent flyers, but they're small time. They move to the ATMs to wait for those poor jet-lagged souls who need cash for a taxi and are too strung out to notice it when the cash and/or their cards go missing.

Suddenly, the two pickpockets get distracted. I don't blame them. The woman walking quickly across the marble floor is sensational in every way a female can be. She's tall enough to not have to bother with craning her neck to see over the milling crowd and blonde enough to draw the eye like a bright beacon.

Part of my job is to assess people and calculate if they are a risk. Hell, yes! This stunning beauty is a risk to any single man with twenty-twenty vision and a penchant for legs that go all the way up to paradise. Every cheesy cliché in the book jumps into my mind as she comes closer.

She's wearing a tailored white shirt with the top three or four buttons open. It gives me a glimpse of her sun-kissed skin and the elegant symmetry of her collarbones. The blonde has poise; I'll give her that. She moves with a certain kind of athletic assurance, which can only come from lots of exercise.

Her form-fitting pencil skirt is strictly business. Gray linen with a demure slit up each side. The cherry on top is the pair of black stilettos on her feet. My friend, Dan, likes to call that kind of footwear "Fuck me" shoes. The heels must be four or five inches high at least. They were designed for women to wear in bed because there is no way anyone could run very far in them.

My heart skips a beat as she changes direction and walks towards me. Throwing me an elusive smile, she plops her handbag down on the desk, tucks a strand of long blonde hair behind her ear, and leans over with her hands clasped. "Excuse me? Is this where I come if someone announces my name?"

Her voice is low-pitched, but sweet as honey. I'm dumbstruck. It couldn't possibly be....

"Edie Kruger?" She looks sideways at me as I say her name, sizing me up before committing to answer my question. She must like what she sees because she turns sideways after dragging her handbag closer. No one can leave their bags unwatched in South Africa. It gives me a better view of the round curve of her ass under the pencil skirt.

"Yah, I'm Edie. Did Alice ask you to come and help me?"

She leaves the question hanging, waiting for me to fill in the answers that only one of Alice's friends would know. "Alice Carter. Yep. She said you're in some kind of trouble and need to get to JFK?"

Throwing back her head, she gives a short yelp of laughter. "You can say that again!" Darting a dazzling smile in my direction, enough to make a grown man weak at the knees, she sticks out her hand. "Pleased to meet you...."

"Sterling." Her hand is cool and smooth as we shake. I'm so tempted to run my finger over her soft palm, but I manage to restrain myself. She isn't shy about looking me straight in the eyes as we stand closer together. For one golden moment, I see her acknowledge the introduction with a slow smile lilting on her lips.

Hazel eyes with flecks of green. No makeup, perhaps some mascara. She's got silvery fair hair, the kind that means everywhere else on her body will be blonde as well. I try hard to push that image out of my mind before I suggest we go get her sorted out with a ticket.

Pointing to my case, Edie asks me if I work for Alice Carter. "You came so quickly. One minute I was on the phone with Alice and the next moment I heard my name being announced. You don't sound local, Sterling."

I like the way my name sounds when she says it. She has a slight lisp— "Shter-leeng." God, it's so sexy. As we circumvent the queue, the usher lifts the red velvet rope for us to enter the hallowed First-Class desk serving Emirates Airlines. "Nope. I'm American and self-employed. You got lucky. I was one klick away from here when I got the call."

She shoots me an enigmatic look. "Yah. I got real lucky...."

I'm hoping Edie brought her passport with her because I don't want to hang around waiting for a private jet. "Passport?" I hold my hand out for it. After digging around in her shoulder bag, she gives it to me, another one of her quirky smiles turning up the corners of her mouth.

"I've never flown on an Airbus before. I'm so excited but nervous, you know?" She's interrupted by the check-in clerk. "And how will you be paying for this, Miss... Kruger?"

Edie opens her mouth to explain, but I grip her elbow and give it a squeeze. "Put it on my account, please. You have my details on file." Turning back to Edie, I explain. "It's an apex flight. We stopover in Dubai en route to New York."

The clerk's fingers dance over the keyboard with sharp taps. This part always takes a long time. Most passengers don't realize that the check-in staff are actually typing code into the computer linked to the mainframe. The Amadeus Service Hub is the platform most airlines use. Bookings and special requests are made in real-time and shared with every server all over the world.

That's how flight attendants know which passengers need help with infants or vegan meals—because of the codes on their tickets.

Suddenly, it dawns on me. I have the chance to spend the next nine hours with Edie Kruger thirty thousand feet up in the air! "Stop." The check-in clerk looks up, startled. "Yes, sir? Is anything the matter?"

I glance over at the stunning woman standing next to me. My mind is made up. "We're going to need the upgrade to first class."

"The upgrade?" The clerk makes double-sure before she goes back to the booking.

Edie clutches my arm with excitement. "You're upgrading me to first class? Oh, Sterling—I think I've just died and gone to heaven!"

Chapter 2: Edie

The phone in my hand vibrates with another text from my best friend, Alice Carter. One word and lots of emojis. My throat constricts with tears of relief as I read the word: Sorted!

My childhood playmate has come through for me. I want to hug her so hard. Riffling through my large shoulder bag, I check that I have everything I need to flee: phone, passport, makeup holder, driver's license, pocketbook. I have just enough money left on my credit cards to pay for an economy flight to New York.

"Will Miss Eddy Kruger please come to the information desk?" Close enough. That's me. Holding my handbag close to my hips after zipping it closed, I hustle to the location with the large 'i' sign hanging above it.

My heart skips a beat when the man leaning against the information counter desk says my name. Walking to the desk, I couldn't help but notice him right away. Tall, dark, and handsome much? You bet. And while brooding, good-looking, muscular men are kind of a dime a dozen in South Africa, this man is unique.

His dark-brown hair is cut so that he would never need to brush it when he wakes up. A simple short back and sides with a bit of length on top. As I smile up at him, he runs his fingers through his hair in a sweet, nervous gesture that I find incredibly endearing.

I'm not short— I'll admit to being nearly six feet tall in heels—but I have to tilt my neck back to look at him as we stand close together to shake hands.

His laser-blue eyes seem to stare into my soul as we connect. This man is the epitome of the rugged, outdoors type. The opposite of what you would expect to see in someone who works with computers.

There's a uniform break at the bridge of his nose, which gives his face an intense, almost predatory expression, like an eagle looking for a nice, soft mouse to eat. One corner of his mouth slants up—I guess that's as close as he's going to get to a smile.

His eyebrows seem to be pressed together so that a permanent crease has formed in the middle. Is he scowling? Then I realize he's summing me up, inspecting every inch of my face and body, but not in a creepy way. It's more like he's used to being naturally cautious.

With our introductions out of the way, he seems to accept my authenticity. He hustles me over to the Emirates First-Class desk. I guess he must be one of Alice's husband's business associates. Jack Carter's company does data analytics. Nice work if you can get it because it sure must pay well for them to be jetting around first class.

Running away on an Emirates Airbus kind of has a nice ring to it. But before I can ask the clerk how much an economy-class ticket is, Sterling steps up and upgrades me. I'm shocked, and maybe just a little bit excited. I've never flown first class before in my life. When I grab his arm,

I feel the rigid muscles underneath his jacket sleeve and dare I say it, get even more excited.

He handles my joy pretty well. "Let them handle the rest of the check-in, Edie. I think it's time I took you to the lounge."

His long strides mean I have to walk really fast to keep up with him. My heels clack on the marble as we approach the elegant attendant standing behind the front desk at the lounge entrance. She doesn't even ask to see Sterling's ticket. We get ushered straight through to the dark, sophisticatedly scented interior.

I hope I'm not gaping, but this place is the last word in high luxe, every bit as marvelous as the finest five-star hotel. A staff member steps forward. "Good morning, Mr. Sterling. How may we help you today?"

Sterling turns to me and my tummy does that little flip again. "Have you eaten breakfast? Or would you like a massage at the spa?"

"Do you want to have breakfast?" I don't want to be the one to force him to sit opposite me whilst I scarf down croissants. "I mean, it couldn't hurt for us to go and see what's on offer, could it?"

He gets it. I'm only going to be doing this once in my lifetime, so I might as well see what's on offer. "Breakfast it is," he says, shooting me another one of those quirky, lopsided grins, "but I warn you—they serve amazing food on the flight as well."

Giving in to temptation, I hook my hand over the arm he's got angled out for me to hold on to. "Look at me," I tell him, "and please don't tell me that I don't need a lot of feeding. I'm starving."

Sterling takes me up on my offer and looks at me long and hard. All the way up and down. It's a good thing that I'm so suntanned, or else he would see me blushing. "Why haven't you been looking after yourself?" is all he says as the server shows us to a table for two and takes our orders. "It's not that you need to eat a healthier diet—I can see you haven't been sleeping well either."

As if it is the most natural thing to do in the world, Sterling stretches his arm over the table and runs his finger down the side of my cheek. His touch is light, and there is a faint hint of calluses on his fingertips. It feels so good; my body can't help but react.

Like magic, I relax. My breathing slows down. I give a long sigh and close my eyes. "Yah, you're right. I feel as if I could sleep for a real long time, Sterling."

"A hundred years. Isn't that how the fairy tale goes? Sleep until you get woken up by a prince's kiss?"

That makes me giggle. "Are they even allowed to tell that story anymore? He doesn't ask her permission, you know."

He shrugs his broad shoulders. "Sometimes a man's got to step up if a woman needs him to break a bad spell."

"That actually makes a lot of sense, Sterling." Glancing down at his left hand, a check for a wedding band. His tanned hands are large and suit his big frame. Why am I imagining them moving lightly over my stomach and down-wards?

I'm a tea and toast breakfast person. Sterling and I settle into a comfortable silence as we eat. He's busy with an exotic-looking fruit salad and I'm finished already. Making sure that the ringer is turned off first, I risk bringing out my phone.

Flicking straight to my social media, I interrupt his meal.

"Sterling. Is that your first or last name?" I want to see all of his posts—and get a better idea of who this tasty beefcake really is.

He doesn't even look up. "My work doesn't allow an online presence."

"Ooookay." I accept that. Social media has become a bit of a data-sharing nightmare over the last few years. "So, what is it you do again?"

The scowl is back. "Like I said. It involves me not having an online presence." Short and sweet. I have to give him credit for drawing a line.

My phone has not stopped vibrating since I picked it up. Sterling notices but doesn't comment. I guess Alice's husband must have filled him in on a few details. Like why I had to run away from my dream wedding.

***

I have sacrificed everything to appease one insatiable, despotic man who acts like he's a god.

Like the good little meisie kind that I always try to be—that is what Koos Van der Hoff calls me, his "girl child"—I am prepped and perfect, and ready to walk down the aisle.

South Africans have never bothered to shake off the strict, narrow mindset that has ruled over the country since the Victorian era. Like a trail of Hansel and Gretel breadcrumbs, the same game must play out for every generation.

Meet a boy, in high school or during university, date the boy (but only once you have your parents' blessing), and move into a small apartment when we are both old enough to know the long-term consequences of "shacking up" together. Then it's all rapidly downhill with engagement, wedding, honeymoon, and kids following closely behind.

That's how it has been for the last two hundred years, and nothing must rock the boat. I played by these rules because I knew it would make my parents happy. I attended a private boarding school and passed my exams with honors. Moving on to university, I met Koos at a rugby game and we started dating pretty soon after that.

We moved in together after I graduated. I started working for the Save the Rhino charity organization. And after a diligent five years of being hounded to get engaged, I finally said yes when Koos brought up the subject again.

But I knew in my heart that it was the wrong move. Maybe it made sense to Koos when he was sober enough to think about it, but it made no sense to me. You see, the problem with that relentless trajectory of getting hitched is that it didn't factor in the stone-cold truth. My future husband-to-be is a bully and a violent drunk.

Everyone called us the perfect couple. Koos works on his parents' vineyard in Stellenbosch, a famous wine-growing area outside of Cape Town city. But the moment that diamond ring was on my finger, it felt like a noose tightening around my neck.

Koos's idea of getting ready to become a married couple was to force me into a joint bank account, but one where only he has control of what goes out. "You must give notice at that shitty job of yours, meisie kind," he would slur after his fourteenth brandy and cola evening sundowner cocktail. "You aren't going to have time for that nonsense when the babies start coming."

I am passionate about animals and adored my work. As an NGO, the charity could only offer me a basic salary, but I loved bouncing out of bed in the mornings and going to work. The crusade against poachers and illegal hunters is a constant battle in one of the poorest and most violent countries on Earth.

The violence when Koos got drunk was cyclical. A slap or a push. Blaming it on me the next day and then crying for forgiveness. Only for the whole thing to begin again the next time he needed a scapegoat.

There was no chance for me to dump him. In our small community—the rapidly dwindling group of people who choose to hang on as the country experiences a seismic shift in power and wealth redistribution—leaving your partner is not an option. "You broke it, you buy it," is how folks explain the strange custom of sticking it out with the man who takes your V-card.

But when Koos stumbles into the bridal suite at the One and Only Hotel, swearing up a storm because he wasn't allowed to smoke in his room, I can't hold back.

"Koos!" My mum and bridesmaids scatter. They don't want to witness a fight. "You're not allowed to see me in my wedding dress!"

"Fuck you, man," he slurs. "When I drink, I like to smoke. Fuck this place."

It's not even nine o'clock in the morning and he's already drunk on Bucks Fizz. The moment he slams the door, I wriggle out of my frothy lace gown. With shaking hands, I put on the outfit I arrived in last night. After a quick glance in my handbag, I checked that I had everything I was going to take with me on our Seychelles honeymoon.

I head for the exit. I don't look back as I climb onto the airport shuttle bus. Finally... I'm free.

Chapter 3: Sterling

Of course, I notice her phone blowing up, but I'm not going to step into those muddy waters. The last thing Edie Kruger must need right now is someone demanding that she justify her actions.

"What?" she notices me quietly observing her. "Have I got toast crumbs stuck to my mouth?" Reaching for the stiff linen napkin on her lap, she rubs it across her lips. I'm almost mesmerized by her luscious pout.

I shake my head. "Nope. I was thinking about if we had time to go get a massage at the spa."

Immediately, her expression changes to one of delicious anticipation. "I really hope so. When do we have to start walking to the gate?"

Leaning closer, I tell her that boarding for First-Class passengers happens from the lounge. "This is where you get to wave goodbye to South Africa, Edie. But don't stress about missing the massage. They offer them onboard as well."

With a spontaneous gesture, she reaches for my hand. "Thank you. I—"

Giving her hand a protective pat, I want Edie to know there's no need to thank me. "Save it up for when you see your friend on the other side." I see the steward approaching us out of the corner of my eye. "Shall we board? It's time."

As we're escorted through the plane entrance, I see Edie's eyes get wider and her pretty mouth becomes an "O" of wonder. But she doesn't embarrass herself or me by making a big deal out of it. I have to admit that it's truly entertaining seeing my world through her eyes. Maybe I take some of it for granted because it's been my life for over five years.

Emirates first class is indescribably luxurious. Each seat is its own private suite. Once the automated privacy doors shut, the passenger is in a capsule of bliss. Besides having its own minibar, snackables, and Bulgari amenities kit bag, the suite has a widescreen TV and reading lamp as well.

Settling into my chair, I place the case on my lap. The clerk has booked Edie and me opposite one another so that we can chat across the aisle without having to turn our heads sideways. She gives me a thumbs-up sign and shivers just a little but as she wiggles in the chair. "Ooh, Sterling. This is so cool. But I'm not going to thank you again, cause I can see it makes you uncomfortable."

I bow my head to acknowledge her remark. Giggling as she wiggles around in the wide leather chair, she darts me a naughty look. "Maybe you could use a bit of discomfort in your life, y'know? Doesn't all this luxury get boring sometimes? I mean, aren't you worried about having to rough it in the boondocks if push comes to shove?"

We lock eyes across the aisle. "No, Edie. It does not." If only she knew how often I find myself bouncing over dirt roads in an old Land Rover with only an AK-47 assault rifle to protect myself with. I change the subject.

"So, what are your plans for when you get to New York?"

Her buoyant mood changes on a dime. It's like I stuck a pin in a balloon. She gets serious, pleating the handle of her bag with nervous fingers. "Umm... I think I just need to get there first. I don't want to plan too far ahead. I might jinx it."

Damn, but whoever she is running from must have really done a number on her. Edie goes from happy-go-lucky to hesitant in an instant. In typical gallant Emirates style, they have given her my window seat while I get the one facing the dividing wall. Kicking her sexy shoes off, she folds her legs at an angle and stares out of the window for takeoff.

The slits in her skirt crease and lift as she faces away from me. I'm not worried about her negative body language. I can tell she has a lot on her mind. A serene flight attendant passes silently down the aisle, her face reassuring as she makes a few suggestions about how to tighten the seat belts. Everyone in first class has the announcements and information updates feature muted as they glue themselves to the latest sports game or financial news update.

I almost forget I have one hundred million dollars worth of diamonds sitting on my lap as I get a glimpse of Edie's underwear. I'm not one to follow fashion trends in lingerie, but there's something about whisper-thin, transparent silk stockings that arouses me.

The way she has her knees bent lets me see that special gap where the stockings end and the smooth tanned skin of her thigh begins. As I feel myself stiffen, I move the case on my lap to hide how fast the blood has rushed to engorge my cock. Fucking little Edie Kruger, Alice's best friend from her schooldays, is all I can think about.

Her toenails are painted marshmallow pink. They are pinched into a point by the stocking seam. As she stares out the window and sighs, she moves her toes, flexing them against the soft silk casing. I'm bursting with rampant excitement. With just one glimpse of her sexy lingerie and thigh, Edie had brought me to the edge.

The moment the seat belt sign goes off, I stand. Edie turns, looking up at me as if she doesn't want to be left alone. "Restroom." I jerk my thumb towards the galley, hustling down the aisle with the case pressed against the front of my pants.

I get there just in time. Sliding the lock, I throw the case down onto the vanity and place my hands on each side of the basin. Staring at my face in the mirror, all I can do is shake my head. "Damn—"

I try to block out the image of her curled up on the seat with her round ass facing me and her long, blonde hair falling over her shoulders. I guess I have two choices. I can masturbate and try to regain control of myself that way, or I can splash my face with cold water and go back out there.

This is what you wanted. You planned this. From the time you saw Edie walking to the information desk at the airport, you were strategizing a way to get her alone and fuck her as hard as you can. Don't deny it.

I make my decision. Seeing as we upgraded to first class together, I'm not going to wimp out and beat myself off all alone in a restroom. I want to fuck Edie Kruger with every inch of my ten-and-half-inch cock. Reaching for the case after drinking a bottle of mineral water, I go back out there.

Her privacy door is closed. No, wait. It's open a crack. She has the lights on inside and she's removing the tight items of her clothing. I linger just out of her line of sight, blocking anyone else's view and unmoving.

Unbuttoning her shirt slowly, she shrugs out of it, letting it fall onto the seat. She's braless underneath, her pert breasts and nipples puckering as they sense the change in temperature. The tight areolas are a delicate pastel rose pink, contrasting beautifully against the two white triangles of pale skin delineating her bikini tan.

As she unzips the pencil skirt, I get an eyeful of her lingerie—a white lace suspender belt clipped to those transparent silk stockings that drove me so crazy just now. A narrow band of white lace panties cover the plump mound and hug her delicious round ass.

Edie bends down and starts unclipping the stockings. Then she rolls them down to her ankles one by one and pulls them off. Flexing her toes, she slides her feet back into her stilettos. Unhooking the suspender belt and shoving it into her bag, she shimmies back into her skirt and shirt.

From what I saw of her body, she looks frail, like some tropical bird that has lost its way and spent way too much time looking for a way out of the trap. It's given her a coltish appearance, all long limbs, hip bones, and even a few visible ribs.

My desire is tempered with compassion. I feel intensely protective of her. Who stood by and watched while she lost sleep and weight?

Only when she sits back down do I go to my suite. When she hears me sitting down, she presses the button and reopens her door. "Travel sick?" she peeks around the edge of the door as it slowly opens.

That gets me laughing. If only she knew how many cargo transport planes I've rattled around in. "No... I was checking out the showers. I might have one later on."

She sizes me up. "Won't your head bang the ceiling? I mean, you're so big. Will you fit?"

"Amazingly enough, Edie, I do. They take all sorts into consideration when they design these planes, you know."

Making a stand, Edie shakes her head. "No way. If you had an online media profile, you would know that one of the biggest complaints about air travel is that most people don't fit the seats."

"Did you know that only three percent of the Japanese population is categorized as over-weight? If companies allow their employees to gain weight over a certain restricted waistline measurement, they are fined. And Japan has the second longest life expectancy of nearly eighty-five years."

Giving a squeak of amusement, Edie taps the end of her nose and then points at me. "Which country has the longest?"

This is easy for me. A lot of my clients live near the south of France. "Monaco. I think they kick you out there if you don't live to be over ninety."

Edie shakes her head. "That doesn't count. It's technically not a country. Monaco is a principality. And they all travel around in private jets anyway."

I give her statement some thought. "Maybe you're right."

The flight attendant comes down the aisle. I pushed my bell for service. "Can we have a bottle of Dom Pérignon, please?" Again, it's not a question.

"Vintage or non-vintage, sir?"

"Vintage."

"What year?"

"Nineteen-ninety-six."

The flight attendant disappears and comes back with two demis of the best Dom Pérignon vintage. They are exact replicas of standard champagne bottles except shrunk down to half size. I notice a sad, wistful smile lilting on Edie's lips. "You've had it before?" I point to the label on the bottle. She shakes her head. "No. It just reminded me of someone—I mean, something."

After a half bottle of champagne, the sad look on Edie's face is gone. She's back to her normal bubbly self, making daring remarks in an almost teasing manner. Raising her glass towards me, we clink rims across the aisle.

"Here's to my knight in shining armor. My hero, my savior, my desperado coming to save me in my darkest hour!"

"I think you've had enough to drink, Miss Edie," I tell her off in a mock-strict tone. "You realize it's still officially morning?" I glance at my watch. The glitter of black diamonds catches her eye. "I've never seen a watch like that before. Where did you get it?" She demands to know; the champagne has lifted her up and made her bolder.

"It was a gift." The U-Boat Black Swan Italo Fontana limited edition is actually a payoff. An Eastern European oligarch gave it to me after running up a securities exchange bill with the firm.

Her enticing hazel-green eyes blink at me. "From a lover?"

Time stands still for a moment as a silent communication passes between us. It's official. Edie Kruger wants to fuck me.

I shake my head in the negative. "No such luck. Edie, do you know the airline carries casual wear for passengers who prefer to travel light? Wouldn't you like to change into something a little more comfortable?"

Reaching across the aisle for me to clink my glass with hers one last time, Edie drains hers and then stands up. "I'm off to have a shower."

Slipping her feet back into her stilettos, Edie paces like a gazelle down the aisle. My eyes follow her, and I'm glad I did. As she reaches the shower facilities, I see her turn back and give me an alluring wink.

After a discreet wait of five minutes, I follow her to the shower.

Chapter 4: Edie

Fingers crossed Sterling takes the hint. I'm steaming with repressed sexual expression. I've only ever been to bed with one man in my entire life and most of the time it was hit and miss, at best.

That's what happens when two sexually inexperienced people get together and decide to hash it out as best they can. Koos and I never had a sex life, per se. We had a mattress where he would lie sprawled out drunk and I would press my legs together and writhe with frustration next to him.

I've never had an orgasm where another person was involved in helping me attain it. And now

I'm ready to wash away that stain of frustration forever.

The shower is a haven of spacious elegance. Sculptured smooth white surfaces and a small space to hang clothes and change. Biting my lower lip, I turn with my back to the wall and wait, my hands locked behind me to hide how nervous I am.

One tap and I know it's him. Sterling. Activating the sliding door, I let him in. He's removed his tie and the top two buttons of his stiff linen shirt are undone. He smells divine as he presses against me. Like fresh cotton and well-worn leather. Without taking his eyes off me, he puts the black case he always carries around with him on the shelf.

"Are you sure about this?" Our bodies are pressed so close together, that I have to tilt my head way back to look him in the eyes as I reply.

"Yes."

That's all he needs to hear. His strong hands slide around my waist and we kiss. The way my body reacts nearly knocks me off my feet. A slow, sensual warmth floods my pussy, making me feel heavy with desire.

The sensation of his kiss is perfect because it's not too intrusive. I feel his tongue brush over my upper lip before he moves his mouth down, where he does the same thing to my lower lip. It's gentle, almost caressing. His hands grip me tighter as I can't resist seeing what kind of effect our kiss is having on him.

Brushing my fingers lightly over his crotch, I get some idea of how rampant he is. His cock jerks with impatience when it feels my touch. He's huge, but in proportion. The man is tall enough to handle all of that gorgeous girth and length, believe me.

I can't help gasping with excitement as his fingers lightly brush over my nipples. I don't have to wear bras because of my cup size, but I never knew how fantastic it could feel to have my breasts stroked with such urgent intent. Grabbing one of his large hands, I press it against my breast, so that he knows I want him to massage me roughly.

I'm swept away by all the gorgeous possibilities fucking this man is offering me. Leaning back against the wall gives him room to explore me like I know he wants to. "Take off your clothes," he growls, staring at me from underneath his dark brows. "Leave the shoes on."

God, it thrills me when he tells me what to do. Now I know I can relax and let him take control. Slowly, I unbutton my shirt as he watches. Then I turn to face the wall, which allows him to pull the zipper of my skirt down.

I can feel his intense gaze burning into me as my skirt falls to the ground. My panties are completely transparent. He must have a full view of my ass. He slides his hand under the diaphanous fabric and cups my ass cheeks, before moving down. As his thumb presses in between the groove of my ass, his fingers slot deeper and find my pussy.

Of course, I'm wet. Sterling must be really turned on by what he feels because he pushes against me as his fingers probe deeper. Nuzzling my neck, he murmurs gruffly, "I'm going to tear these off you—because the thought of you walking out of here with nothing on under that tight skirt of yours makes me so hard."

Turning me around, he removes my shirt gently, allowing his fingertips to trail erotically over my skin. Then using two hands, he rips the silk panties as if they are made of candy floss. He steps back to admire me. I love the hunger in his eyes.

And then, just like that, he releases his cock from his underwear. Hauling it out of his zipper proves to be quite a mission because it's so thick and rock-hard. And then there's the sheer size of it. I almost come just from the way his cock jerks every time he looks at me.

We don't need words to explain how badly we both want this. As if I weigh no more than a feather, Sterling picks me up. I wrap my legs around him, and he allows me to find my comfort zone. At first, I find the sensation of his big prick rubbing against my clit beyond amazing, but the more I run my tight snatch along him, the more I want him inside me.

Throwing my head back, I grind on his shaft. "OH, please, give me more," I moan softly, aware that flight attendants and passengers are only a few feet away from us, behind the soundproofed door. He knows I'm ready. Lifting me up, he lowers me back down onto him, inch by inch.

As my wet pussy envelops him, I can feel his knob expand. Immediately, some internal part of my body begins to pulse. It's as if he has the ability to reach and explore all the undiscovered areas connected to orgasms inside me. Crushing his mouth with my lips, I manage to gasp. "I... I think I'm coming."

He holds me still, allowing the throbbing need to build up to a crescendo of passion. Flicking the shower on to drown my moans, Sterling thrusts balls deep inside me as I come off with shuddering, explosive intensity. He comes too, which must have hit that special spot inside me again because I can't stop coming.

The shower cubicle is full of steam and the extractor fan is making quite a commotion. As the exquisite tremors subside, I am brave enough to look at him. We are eye to eye, and he shows no sign of tiring out of holding me. My thighs relax and he lets me stand, only letting go when he is sure I won't collapse to the floor.

Adjusting his shirt and zipping up, he kisses the top of my head and murmurs. "See you outside, Edie. Don't be too long." Taking the case, he leaves.

The rest of the trip is a blur. Not because I drank champagne, but because we can't keep our hands off one another. We go to the private bar for a mocktail or two—Sterling won't let me have anything more alcoholic to drink because of the dehydrating effects—but it's hard to focus and sit still. I'm swept away with my head in the clouds, and can't get enough of him. Whenever I think about his hands clasped around my waist as his cock thrusts deep inside me... I'm flying.

He can read the need in my eyes. While the rest of the First-Class passengers snooze behind their sliding doors, Sterling shows me how to turn my seat into a bed. This time, it's my turn to be the driver. He lies down on the seat as I hitch up my skirt and straddle him.

He's so big, I have to angle forwards and tilt my hips back because I can't handle the deepest penetration imaginable. Leaning over him, I ride his cock to my satisfaction, sliding up and down as his hands cup my ass. "I want to see you with no clothes on," I whisper into his ear as I move closer for another kiss.

Giving my lower lip a delightful nibble with his teeth, all he does is shoot me another one of his dangerously cute lopsided grins. My stomach flips as my clit builds towards another orgasm at breakneck speed.

Exhausted and completely satiated after having to hold back my screams of pleasure, I fall onto his chest. We lie there for a long, sweet moment, just letting our bodies adjust back to normal. Then clenching my pussy to make sure no cum drips out, I move to the side.

It's too tempting: I run my hands over his chest, my thoughts in chaos as to how daring and carefree being upgraded to first class has made me. "That... was... wild." I really have no words to describe how hard he made me come. Emotions bubble underneath my calm exterior.

I'm slightly shy at how crazily abandoned I acted, but not enough to not want it to happen again. And again and again. "I'm tempted to take another shower...."

Sterling traces a line down my arm with one finger. "No can do. We've started our descent already. The flight attendants are going to start coming through to square things away just now."

I'm curious. "How do you know? I mean, we can't be much more than two-thirds of the way there."

"Edie, an Airbus has to begin the descent when it's still two or three countries away from its destination. It's so big, and it's flying at such an extreme speed, that's the only way it can avoid a sharp drop in the nose angle."

I can't help it. I pout, tossing my hair back over my shoulder. "But I don't want this to end." He gives my shoulder a comforting squeeze. "Don't worry. I'm sure there will be plenty more upgrades in your future."

That makes me sit up. "That's not what I meant." I point to him and then tap my chest. "I don't want this to end."

This man makes me feel brand-new, reborn, and more full of life than I even believed was possible. I'm only being honest when I tell him I don't want it to end.

Grabbing the small, black case off the entertainment desk, he sits up too. "Who says anything about this ending? But I have to check my DMs and straighten up. We don't want to look fucked when we land, do we?"

I swat at the black case with my hand. "Live a little, Sterling. Let's stop over in Dubai and continue this awesome interlude in a hotel." I give him my best "little girl with big, begging eyes" look. I'd be lying if he didn't look tempted, but his willpower is stronger than mine.

"Edie, you can't miss your connecting flight to New York. I have business in Dubai and can't laze around in bed all night. Go to New York. Like I said, this won't be your last upgrade. I promise."

Frustrated and coming down off that champagne hard, I fail to see the common sense in this. I think I know what a brush-off looks like by now. I've experienced hundreds of them from Koos when he's too drunk to do anything but snore.

Folding my arms and huffing, I turn to face the windows. "Fine." When he leaves, it feels empty and cold. All that's left behind is the faint aroma of sex and expensive linen.

Riffling through the overnight bag the steward gave me, I find a disposable panty and wriggle it over my legs.

Screw you, Sterling. I hope I never get upgraded with you again!

Chapter 5: Sterling

I can see that she's unhappy, but I can't allow myself to be diverted from the job at hand. It feels like since I first laid eyes on Edie Kruger, I lost control of a very important part of me. And right now, I'm not sure if that part is my cock or my heart.

Like every Emirates experience flying first class, switching connections is made incredibly easy. An electric cart is waiting for Edie the moment she disembarks and enters the duty-free area. I'm exiting, going on through customs and Dubai; this is where we must go our separate ways.

"Alice says she's booked a driver to wait for you at the gate at JFK, Edie," I tell her in a firm voice, trying hard not to sound too brutal. She's hurting and fragile, unsure if she can make this last segment of the journey on her own. "He'll be holding a placard with your name on it. Just remember to keep an eye out for him as you pass through customs, okay?"

I called ahead to make sure Edie's visa was fast-tracked. She's flying under a British passport, but her permanent South African address would have counted against her if I hadn't pulled some strings.

She's looking downhearted and scared. Tipping her chin up with one finger, I force her to lock eyes with me. "You can do this, sweetheart. The world is your oyster, believe me."

"But Alice's family will be strangers to me, Sterling. And I might have to be forced to be nice to that creepy little brother of hers, Buck. Is he still hanging around, do you know?"

"Did he hang around last time?" I want to know. I hate the thought of her being frightened.

She gives a reflex shudder. "Ugh! The problem with Bucky is that I can't discuss how much I hate him with Alice because she always takes his side and defends him. She's my best friend, but she just doesn't want to listen to reason as far as her creepy little brother is concerned."

I laugh. "It can't be that bad, can it? Give him a chance."

Edie shakes her head with obvious loathing. "No can do. Can you text Jack and ask him if Buck has resurfaced from whatever slime pit the creep has been living in, please?"

This time, I don't bother hiding my laughter. "Ah, Edie. You make me smile, you know that, don't you? But he's harmless, I promise. I can't message Alice's husband and ask him such a weird question. So, play nice when Buck resurfaces again."

"When? I don't like the sound of that one bit. Me and Buck—" She inhales slowly and then breathes out fast, letting her anger go with it. "—we don't see eye to eye."

Her loathing makes me reassess her unnatural hatred for Alice's brother. "Look, Edie, I can't help it if Buck is still around. Just watch out, because there is a one-hundred-percent chance that you are going to be seeing him again. And probably very soon too. He's your best friend's family, for God's sake."

She gives me that gorgeous pouting smile again. "I guess I'll have to just grin and bear it then." I see her eyes dart over to the golf cart driver who is sitting behind the wheel with a blank look of disinterest on his face. It makes me wonder how many passionate hellos and goodbyes he must have witnessed over the years.

I place my finger over her lips when I see she's about to say something. "Don't say goodbye to me, Edie Kruger. I hope we meet again very soon."

Giving my fingertip a sharp nip with her teeth, she shakes her head before going to sit on the golf cart. As the man presses the acceleration pedal, the transport begins to move slowly away. When she is almost out of earshot, Edie waves. "Thank you for the upgrade, Sterling. Have a nice life. Goodbye!"

Shit! She was pissed with me this whole time! Damn it! I should have rebooked her ticket and spent the night with her at the Burj Khalifa. For one glorious minute, I think about sprinting after the golf cart, but my priority must be the case of diamonds. I can't help but notice that she never looks back once as the golf cart turns the corner.

That's how it has always been with my life for the last five years. Business before pleasure, every time. I head for customs with the case lightly clasped in my hand. A few flashes of my ID and I don't even have to use passport control—my details have already been scrutinized and entry permitted.

Truth be told, I can't wait to get this case out of my hands. A black uniformed driver is waiting for me in the meet-and-greet lobby. "Mr. Sterling? The prince sends his regards. Please follow me."

Dubai is a pleasure to see, as usual. Traffic moves at a sedate pace as passengers and drivers sit in air-conditioned serenity on the immaculately wide freeway. I glance up at the dozens of tall minarets everyone encounters no matter where they stay in Dubai. The only minaret-free zones are the airport and the beach.

I manage to suppress my callous amusement as I remember how shocked I was on my first visit to the city. The hidden loudspeakers at the top of the minarets blast out high-decibel calls to prayer every half hour of the day.

Starting at dawn and continuing well past midnight. My penthouse suite was not so soundproof as to stop the solemn calls to prayer from penetrating into my bedroom. Giving up after one and a half days of it, I asked for a plain room in the basement.

The Ruler ordered that no Dubai resident should ever be more than a fifteen-minute walk from a mosque at any given time when the call to prayer is sent out. So, there are a lot of mosques—and a lot of minarets with amplified speakers at the top of them.

There are three security checks before I reach the palace entrance. Retina scanning, fingerprinting, facial recognition, the whole nine yards.

I am asked to wait in the antechamber while the aide goes to alert the prince about my arrival. Aware of how precious my time is, His Highness arrives swiftly. Breezing into the room wearing a pristine white Kandura robe, leather thong sandals, and the obligatory red checked keffiyeh, the prince nods his head to greet me as I bow my head.

Respect and etiquette don't change much from country to country, but I am well-versed in how to address my clients. "As-salam alaikum, Mr. Sterling." The prince keeps his eyes locked on mine, even though I know he wants to look down at the black case in my hand. The greeting of "peace be with you," and the polite reply of "and upon you be peace" are standard good manners.

I'm lucky to have the prince as a client. He's remarkably chill when it comes to making a deal with people he trusts. Eastern Europe could learn a thing or two from these guys.

"Wa alaikum as-salam," I say the words in a neutral tone. This is not a friendly get-together; this is business. As the prince sits down on a custom-made couch, I step forward and present the case to him with both hands held out. He takes it slowly, keeping a cool facade, even though I can sense his anticipation.

"Did our friend keep his side of the bargain?" The prince wants to know as he presses his fingerprint on the case's lock. There are only three people in the world that case will open for, and I'm one of them.

"Yes, Your Highness. The first shipment of oil docked before I left Cape Town. The other nine tankers will follow in due course. There is no paperwork linking the transaction to you or the other party."

The South African politician who contacted me once he agreed to the deal also invited the prince to come and hunt whatever endangered species he wanted on his game ranch. But I would never pass along such a disgusting offer. South Africa has enough problems with the extinction of Big Game animal species because of poaching without me adding to it.

The prince nods politely. "Tell me, did the man have any idea of the real value of the stones?" As he's speaking to me, the prince opens the case and lifts the false bottom. A flash of light splits into a million fragmenting sparkles as one hundred million dollars worth of cut diamonds sucks up the light spectrum and spits it out as rainbow prisms.

There is every kind of fancy diamond represented in the case, and not a single one of them is smaller than a man's thumbprint. Pink, red, canary yellow, green, light, and dark blue—a riot of shimmering colors brightens the walls and ceiling.

The layer underneath the fancies contains even bigger blue-white diamonds. Digging in my pocket, I pass the prince a professional jeweler's loupe, a magnification device that makes it easier to spot flaws and inclusions in the stone. I lean back and wait as the prince inspects each one.

Halfway through, the prince asks me if I would like something to drink. I shake my head. "No, thank you." Neither of us can leave the room until both of us are satisfied the deal has been completed to the client's satisfaction. If I did want a drink, no servant would be allowed inside at such a crucial juncture anyway.

There's a tinkling fountain running in the corner of the room. It's very soothing. I nearly drift off to sleep on the soft armchair. Now that my part escorting the stones to their new owner is over, I can relax.

Like a shock to the system, an image of Edie flashes into my mind. She's standing in the shower cubicle, wearing only her black stilettos and bending over with her back to me. Her hands are braced against the wall, her long blonde hair streaming down the long column of her spine.

I'm unzipping my pants, in a fever of haste as my willpower is pushed to its limit. I fight to stop ejaculating as I take myself in hand. First, I want to touch her, take pleasure in the way her pussy grips my fingers as I slide them inside the tight, wet slit...

"Sterling?" I jump a little bit as I become aware of my real surroundings. The prince is staring at me. Shit. I hope it wasn't obvious what I was fantasizing about! "Yes, Your Highness?" Retrieving my phone out of my jacket pocket, I pretend I am calculating my travel costs in my mind.

"Would you consider taking a stone by way of payment? These are one of a kind, after all," he says, gesturing with his hand over the case of diamonds, "and the resale value of just one would be incalculable."

I'm about to negate the suggestion when my fantasy rears its head again. Yes. There was a thin band of white on Edie's ring finger on her left hand. Whoever she was running away from had put a ring on it to try and seal the deal.

Shifting forward to the edge of the armchair, I nod to the prince. "Now that you mention it, Your Highness, I might like to take another look at the collection. Thank you."

Chapter 6: Edie

I sleep like a log all the way to New York. For a moment, I worry about how the upgrade doesn't feel the same without Sterling traveling with me, but I try to eradicate that concern with ruthless determination as I allow exhaustion to overwhelm me.

While he definitely wasn't trying to use me—I went into the encounter with my eyes wide open—Sterling did take advantage of the fact that we would probably never see one another again. I suppose that is what made us so open to having sex the way we did. There was no need for us to be on our best behavior when saying goodbye forever was only a heartbeat away.

He didn't even offer me his phone number! Whenever I tried to ask Sterling about himself, he shut me down! If he was so worried I would try to slide into his DMs, he should have just said so.

I'm way too proud to beg. I got what I wanted out of him and that should be enough. I couldn't think of a more effective way to wipe all the memories of my ex-fiancé out of my system than to get sublimely fucked by the mysterious and oh-so-gorgeous Mr. Sterling.

The driver is waiting for me outside the Arrivals exit; an Emirates staff member escorts me all the way through Port Authority, guiding me to the electric-powered carts and carrying my duty-free bags for me. I bought a change of clothes in one of the athleisure wear-label shops in Dubai.

I feel comfortable and relaxed as I climb into the town car. The driver holds the door open for me and I thank him with a wide smile. The longer this goes on, the farther away from Koos I get and that makes me happy.

The car glides slowly through traffic, only fully stopping once we reach a long, shady canopy and carpet runner stretched across the Fifth Avenue sidewalk on the Upper East Side. My best friend, Alice Carter, comes from affluent parents and then married into even more affluence.

But her husband, Jack, is the last word when it comes to being a city slicker. I think his version of hell must look like any rural area with no cell phone tower in sight.

"Ma'am?" The concierge steps forward, holding his hand out for my case. Shaking my head, I gesture for him to go on ahead. "It's just me, I'm afraid. Mrs. Alice Carter is expecting me. Edie Kruger."

The man recognizes my accent. "As in Kruger-rands?" he asks with a grin. That makes me laugh. I have the same name as the famous gold coins produced in South Africa. "I wish! I can't even afford a silver dollar at this stage of my life, but watch this space. I plan on making it big in the Big Apple."

I have no problem making the statement. I've always been an optimist. I think that might be obvious to anyone attempting to marry someone they don't love anymore—only an optimist would be so deluded as to think things might get better once a ring is on their finger.

The elevator pings as I reach Alice's floor. She's waiting for me outside the door, jumping to hug me the moment it opens. "Edie! You daredevil! I can't believe you finally got up the guts to dump that oaf!"

Hustling me into the entrance to her apartment, Alice wants me to dish once I have some tea and cookies inside me. "You lucky thing," she says in an admiring tone as I demolish three cookies, "I've had to start cutting back since I had Noah."

She pinches her midriff and then pokes mine. "Ugh! Edie, you're still reed slim. I hate you."

I open my mouth but then snap it closed again. I can't believe that I was just about to say, "That's what Sterling says; he says I'm too slim." It's time for a rapid change of topic.

"Speaking of Noah, where are the wee imps? I can't wait to see my goddaughter again." Gabriella Carter, eight years old, is my god-daughter. Alice and I always meet up twice a year at my parents' safari game lodge. It gives me a chance to escape Koos's constant surveillance and check in with my friend's darling kids. Noah is her boy, six years old.

They love the game lodge and the wild game park. One of Noah's first words was "monkey," which turned out to be very suitable considering his behavior.

"Oh God, girl, don't ask." Alice leans back on the couch with a defeated sigh. "They both go to school during the week now, which gives me a bit of a break. But Jack is beginning to favor homeschooling, for some insane reason. As if I could teach them Mandarin and French!"

"Tutors?" I suggest. I adore children and love it when I get the chance to show Noah and Gab-by around my parents' game reserve. "I would have thought you had room here for an au pair and a housekeeper."

Alice acknowledges this. "Yes, but I won't have female staff living within five yards of my husband if I can help it. I mean, look what happened with Jude Law and Arnie. Is there something sexy about live-in help that I'm missing?"

Jack Carter is not exactly a Hollywood star. I haven't had much contact with Alice's husband since they got married. The wedding was held at The Ocean Club in the Bahamas. I was a bridesmaid, and the Carters were so kind as to fly me out there and put me up.

After making the usual jokes about me coming from the South African bush boondocks, Alice's parents left me mercifully alone. They can be a pill when they want to be.

The first time I got to meet Jack was during the pre-party. A short, balding man with glasses tapped me on the back. "Edie? Hey, I'm Alice's fiancé. Pleased to meet you."

Holy moly! Alice must have photoshopped the shit out of the images of her boyfriend that she sent me. Jack is, and always has been, the archetype of what a data analytics guy must look like. But from the looks of this uptown apartment, he treats my friend like a queen. Which is what every woman deserves, no matter what her partner looks like.

"So, is it okay if I stay here?" My voice pitches upward as I check with my friend. I want to be sensitive to her fears and jealousies. For some reason, she's always been petrified of someone wanting to steal her husband away from her. Alice's reasoning was this: if Bill Gates managed to find someone willing to have an affair with him, there was every possibility of the same thing happening to Jack.

She hugs me again. "Of course it is! I know you don't find Jack attractive, and goodness knows you are beautiful enough to find someone even richer. For the life of me, I never understood why you settled for Koos."

I shake my head, running my fingers over the velvet cushion I have hugged in front of me. "Alice, it was awful. Right from the start, it sucked. I never told you this before, but you know how hard it is for someone to have more than one partner in our culture. Once Koos popped my cherry, I was duty-bound to stick it out."

Another thing I never told Alice was that the stigma of dumping Koos might have affected my parents' and the game lodge. My actions would have long-term consequences for them if I failed to get my side of the story told first.

"You can't throw a stick in Cape Town without hitting someone who thinks the sun shines out of Koos's ass. When you play rugby or sport professionally over there, everyone treats you like an idol, even after you retire."

Alice shrugs. "I hear you. It's the same here as well." Slapping my thigh, she stands up. "Come on. Come and help me make dinner. I know you love to cook."

In South Africa, everyone who can afford it has lots of staff to help them in the home. It's the socioeconomic, responsible thing to do and one of the hardest traditions for people to understand. Every housekeeper, maid, gardener, and cook hired to work in the home, has a family they are able to support through their job. It's most definitely not because the homeowners are lazy.

Koos insisted that our housekeeper make all of the meals at our house. He liked the conventional South African food she always prepared: steak, roast potatoes, rice and beans, glazed carrots, and lots of brown gravy. I've always been more of a 'salad as a main meal, please' kind of girl.

"Ooh, goody! Can we make that broccoli, pomegranate, and bacon salad we both like? Mum still serves it at the game lodge."

"You bet!" Alice leads the way into her ultra-sophisticated kitchen. "But if you ask me, you have to set your standards a bit higher. Koos might have been a 'big man on campus' when you met him at university, but he peaked early. Honestly, I've seen the change in the photos you sent me. He's getting all jowly with a pot belly. That's why I told you I couldn't make the wedding—I couldn't handle watching my best friend throw her life away."

Pulling myself up onto one of the stools at the breakfast nook, I nod glumly. "Fuck! That reminds me. I have to arrange for all the wedding gifts to be returned." Burying my face in my hands, I don't want to even think about the pushback from what I did yesterday. And that includes that awesome fuckfest I had on the plane. Thank goodness Alice hasn't pressed me too much about my flight.

"I'm here for you, Girly-oh," Alice calls me the pet name we used to call one another when we were young girls. I was "Girly-oh" and Alice was "Whirly-oh", a poacher-fighting pair of superheroes. Together, we were the "Whirly-oh-Girly-ohs." What can I say? We had active imaginations.

I was twelve years old when Alice came to stay at my parents' lodge for the first time. Her family was there on a safari vacation, traveling from the Hamptons to the Western Cape of South Africa, because seeing the Big Five game animals—elephant, buffalo, rhinoceros, lion, and leopard—was on Alice's dad's bucket list.

We took one look at each other and became instant besties. I had to be the most stupid-looking girl in the Southern Hemisphere then. My face was covered in brown freckles, and I wore gold-rimmed glasses that made my eyes look enormous. My hair grew straight down my back like flat, dried wheatgrass; the chlorine from the pool always turned it green.

I was a beanpole, with no sign of breasts coming in and flat as an ironing board. To me, Alice seemed to be effortlessly sophisticated and mature. She was blossoming and buxom, with her teeth neatly restrained by an invisible retainer and her spots carefully hidden underneath thick bangs.

"Hi," we said shyly after our parents introduced us. "Would you like to see my pet duiker?" I suggested.

"What's a duiker?" Alice asked as we walked to the fenced-off enclosure together. I explained. "It's a miniature antelope only found in Africa. I raised Dickie myself. Our game warden found him injured on the trail and brought him back here."

"How did he get injured?" Alice wanted to know as we patted Dickie's nose and fed him carrots.

I took a guess. "Lion, maybe? Or a leopard. Whatever it was, it was large enough to take his mother. He was so small when Mpo found him, I had to feed him milk all the time."

Alice looked at me. "Edie, you are by far the most interesting person I have ever met."

I shook my head and turned red. "No way, man. I just live in an interesting place. There's nothing special about me."

Alice was prompted to warn me. "You're just shy. Watch out for my family. We're a loud-mouthed bunch. They like to call it teasing, but honestly, sometimes I think it borders on rude!"

"Jislaaik!" My eyes got wide. "I don't think so. Your family is wonderful. It must be amazing to live in America!"

Putting her arm around me, Alice started walking me back to the lodge. "What does 'Yis-like' mean?"

Searching for the best way to translate the word, I told her. "It means happy or sad, angry, or admiring—anything, really. I will also accept 'yussis' and 'yis' if you want. I think it's the best first word you could learn."

Alice had darted me a compassionate look. "Once you get to know my family better, Edie,

I think you might be saying that word an awful lot...."

And it turned out, she was right.

Chapter 7: Sterling

The last thing I want to do after my meeting with the prince is to stay at the Burj Khalifa on my own. I can't think of anything more depressing than to hang around my suite for the rest of the evening, mooning over how much I miss Edie.

The cool, calm way she dismissed me from her thoughts the moment I rejected her suggestion that we spend some more time together, turns over and over in my mind like a stuck movie reel. It's the first time a woman has ever treated me with such playful disdain. Was she just using me to flush out the toxic energy that had chased her all the way into my arms?

Suddenly, I'm invigorated. Alice owes me a favor big-time after I came through for her like that. It's about time I checked in with HQ anyway. Ducking my head as I step into the prince's private transport, I tell the driver to take me back to the airport.

I get busy on the phone the moment the car pulls out of the driveway. "Dan...." My business partner will want to know if the mission was completed to the client's satisfaction. "...have we got anything or anyone hanging east of the Atlantic? Or can I grab some R and R?"

A clatter of keyboard keys lets me know Dan is checking. "Fraser is inbound. Clint is waiting for confirmation. You're good to go." My partner lets the official tone drop for a moment. "R and R? Since when did you find the need for that?"

He acts all mystified and with good reason. I have nothing tying me to one place and I take full advantage of this. I've always found the nomad lifestyle appealing, and I have no family to lock me down.

"Long story." I never discuss my personal life with anyone. Period. "What's still on the books?"

Dan taps on the keyboard again. I hear his nostrils blowing into the audio receiver as he clamps the phone between his shoulder and his ear. "Okay. Don't get too cozy during your vacation, because E. E. wants to deal with N. A."

I can barely hold back my sigh. Another country in Eastern Europe wants to "exchange goods" with a country in North Africa. That means I don't need a crystal ball to tell me there will be a long, dusty journey bouncing in a Jeep in front of me.

"Roger that." My response is always the same. It's not like I have anyone waiting for me at home.

"Roger," Dan says, "over and out."

I disconnect the call and slide my phone back into my breast pocket. All my suits are custom-made for me and have hidden compartments for phones and keys. I like to know that if I get into a fistfight, I don't have to worry about my stuff getting lost.

My thoughts go back to Edie immediately. Damn it. After drumming my fingers on the seat with irritation, I take out my phone again.

Jack. Thanks for that intel. It was golden. I'm headed home. What's the temperature like on your side?

A brief wait for Jack's reply. I thank the driver. I'm back at the airport, but this time I won't be flying Emirates. The prince always lays on one of his private jets for my use whenever our business is concluded.

The flight attendant is waiting for me inside the hangar and she escorts me to the stairs. My phone vibrates as she helps me settle into one of the cream-colored leather seats. It's Jack.

It's all golden here too. Thanks for helping out. Al was over the moon to know that Ed finally kicked that sentient baboon fiancé of hers to the curb. We couldn't be more pleased.

Jack's code names for his wife and her best friend are Al and Ed, short for Alice and Edie. He can be a prickly customer sometimes, but he's okay once someone gets to know him.

I mull over the last sentence in the message. So, Edie kicked her partner to the curb? No wonder she was heading for the hills as fast as she could go. I type back.

I'm not too busy now, actually. Please keep me in mind if you plan a night out.

Jack bounces right back to being his usual acerbic self. No way am I taking my two brats to Kochi! It's my wife who owes you. Deal direct.

I take his advice and message Alice directly. My ETA is 9 a.m. Then it's time for me to call in that favor you owe me. Flick the Kochi booking details over to me for tomorrow evening. No later than 8, please.

She messages back fast. How did you know we were going to Kochi tomorrow evening?

My fingers fly over the screen. Call me gifted that way.

I wait. A few moments later, the phone pings. Kochi, 8 p.m. 10th Ave, Hell's Kitchen, New York.

Sometimes, there are really great payoffs to having my job. Reclining my seat, I close my eyes as the jet flies me back home and nearly half a day back in time. It's afternoon here, but I'll be landing at Teterboro at breakfasttime. Perfect.

***

It's not easy for me to relax. It's my natural state to always be on guard and ready for action. But after pulling nighttime sentry duty for weeks at a time at the start of my training, I learned ways to combat insomnia.

I went from school straight into the Navy, fresh and raring to go at seventeen years of age. I had already gained all the necessary qualifications to be accepted into the Marine Corps—I didn't even have to think before applying. It was just expected of me that I would enlist. Armed combat was what I excelled at and there was no use pretending that I was destined for any other life.

Besides meeting the rigorous mental and physical standards required by the recruitment board, I had my high school diploma, passed the Armed Services Vocational Aptitude Battery test (known as the ASVAB in all the military academies) with flying colors, and aced the medical and fitness.

There was no question that the Armed Forces was where I was always headed. The only question was for how long? I kept hearing that a four-star general rank might lie ahead for me in the future, but that was not what I planned for myself long-term.

After four years of active duty—boot camp, military occupational specialty (training to become an expert in my field—which was armed combat and weapons), and two years at my duty station—I reported to my fleet as a highly disciplined, unbelievably effective, lethal combatant.

But after two tours of duty, a lifetime of shuffling between command posts or pushing papers around at the DoD didn't really appeal to me. I knew then that I was never going to make the leap from NCO to officer. It helped that the captain in charge of my unit had the same idea.

"Marine, I hear you're thinking about opting out of the unit?" He added "at ease" before I could shout back my answer. No NCO would ever dare reply to an officer without standing ramrod straight and barking out the correct response.

Dropping my salute, I stared at the wall. "Yes, sir!"

The captain looked me up and down. "What brought about the change of heart? You like the thought of civilian life?"

I locked eyes with him. "No, sir, Captain Marshall, sir. I'm going private."

We all knew what that meant. I wanted to branch out, and work privately, but still in the capacity of a soldier. Soldier of fortune. Mercenary. Freelance gun for hire. Call them what you like, there's a lot of money to be made running ops outside of government control.

Captain Marshall stepped back and beckoned me to follow him. "So, you're not ready to cash in your pension just yet? I had you down as the sort of man to use Uncle Sam's dime to go to university." Enlisted men get the chance to attend college and have the government pay the tuition fees if they need a qualification to set them up in civilian life.

The captain had access to my files. He knew my IQ. So did I for that matter, but I had relied on my physicality for so long, I had no desire to trot off and study for a degree. I liked being the master of my own destiny and carving out my own way in the world.

He took my silence as a no. "I see here that you and your family don't see eye to eye. You haven't spoken to them for ten years?"

"No, sir. Twelve years, sir." My parents were stiff-necked martinets who sold my childhood away on a whim and a tantrum. I could never forgive them for that.

Captain Marshall grinned slowly and steadily. "Twelve years. Whew, boy, you sure can hold a grudge. Listen, I might have a spot open for you on the other side. I'll contact you."

There was no need for us to exchange numbers as if we were a couple of non-combatants. I knew that Captain Dan Marshall would get hold of me once I was discharged. Six months later, we ran our first op as civilians.

It was a delicate business and done on a shoe-string budget. A Russian oligarch's ex-wife had done a runner to Switzerland and taken his watch collection with her. There was no way we could bully our way into getting the items from her without causing an international incident, so I charmed her into showing me the collection instead.

There was a big difference between barging into her high-security Geneva apartment with guns blazing and being invited up to her room. I followed the ex-wife to her favorite nightclub and then sat drinking champagne at the table opposite.

I still had my Armed Services haircut and a half-suntanned, half-pale forehead after years of wearing a cap, but I was built like a brick shithouse and horny as a sailor on fleet week. I was cocky enough to know this would work after I pitched the idea to Dan.

It wasn't long before I got the invite. "Madame wishes to know if you would care to join her at her table, Monsieur?" the server asked me politely. Two dates later, Madame had her wrists tied securely to the bedposts while I walked out of the room with the watch collection.

She cursed me in a muffled voice behind the silk scarf I used as a gag. "Your husband sends his regards, Madame." I didn't feel bad about what

I was doing. Some relationships function best in the dog-eat-dog setting.

Did I fuck her to get her to trust me? You bet I did. I'm a ruthless man when I want to be, and fulfilling that contract meant an avalanche of work started coming in. And Dan and I receive ten percent off every single one of them.

I remember catching the flight back to New York afterward, sitting all cramped in economy class with my knees almost parallel to my ears.

"May I offer you a seat in first class, sir?" the pretty little flight attendant asked me, fluttering her eyelashes in a very flirtatious way.

Actually, I fucked that pretty little flight attendant too. But once I stepped out of her downtown apartment door, I forgot all about her.

So will someone please tell me why I can't get Edie Kruger out of my mind?! She's the first woman I have ever met in all my almost thirty-one years who refuses to fade from my memory. It's frustrating and worrying at the same time.

Why do I find her so captivating? Ever since she disappeared on that electric cart after verbally flipping me the bird, I can't get her out of my mind. Her handful-sized, perky breasts. Her long, coltish legs. That hair, that smile, my God!

I can't wait to see her again tomorrow night. I hope Alice's bloody family is not there to fuck things up....

Chapter 8: Edie

Honestly, Alice's family is hard to take. I know I should try harder to love them, but I can't. Her parents are brash and louder than any pair of retirees have the right to be. And don't get me started on her brother, Buck. He's a complete weasel.

But the whole caboodle is on their way to meet us at this fancy restaurant tonight, so all I can hope is that a nice distraction happens to take the focus off me. Alice has offered to lend me one of her dresses, but I don't know if that is going to work.

"I didn't think it was possible, Girly-oh," Alice says, shaking her head, "but I think you've gotten even taller."

We're in the master bedroom together, flicking through hangers in the walk-in closet. I'm losing hope of finding anything wearable, though. Alice is shorter than I am and has way more curves. Gabby comes in and sits down on the bed.

"Mom! You should have taken Edie to a boutique. No way is she going to fit into anything you have on the rack."

Alice sighs, going to slump down on the bed next to her daughter. "Gabs is right. Can't you wear that skirt and shirt combo again? It's not evening wear, but no one will judge you—plenty of Manhattanites go there straight from the office."

I'm about to concede when something on the shelf catches my eye. "Hang on... what about this?" Taking the white silk tunic dress and holding it under my chin, I smooth the fabric over my torso. "It could work. I can wear my stilettos and borrow some of your Chanel bling to amp it up."

Alice looks at the tunic with a jaded eye. "It's not fair, Girly. That dress reaches halfway down my calves, but on you, it's a mini. But yeah, you're right. It could work."

The sheath dress is a basic one-size-fits-all loose-fitting tunic tube. Gabby, Alice, and I fuss around with belts and jewelry until it looks acceptable. I like what I see in the mirror when I turn to look at my reflection.

The white silk is divine, clinging to the more prominent parts of my body like spilled milk and contrasting nicely with my tan. Once it's belted just below my waist, the hemline hits midthigh, but I reckon I can pull it off. It's basically just two pieces of thin silk sewn together.

Alice mutters unhappily about my big feet. "Honestly, you could waterski on those feet of yours without bloody skis! What size are you? An eleven? But I'm not sure if those black stilettos of yours go with the ensemble."

It's a pickle. Once the top part of the dress sensually falls off one of my shoulders, the black shoes ruin the whole effect. "You need gold sandals, Edie!" Gabby insists, "Mom, maybe Edie could fit those gold strappy slip-on flip-flops you bought for our holiday in Mexico? They don't have a back strap."

After opening and closing over sixty shoe boxes, we find the gold thong sandals. They are a bit wide, but long enough not to cut the soft heel of my foot. Alice and Gabby stare at me with critical eyes.

"Take off that jewelry," Alice ends up saying. "What you need is a thick gold band on each wrist and a thin gold choker."

"And her hair must be in an updo, Mom," Gabby chimes in, "piled on top of her head like I do with my Barbie." Gabby claps her hands together. "Oh, Edie! I'm so glad you're here. It's like having my very own live Barbie doll living in the house with me!"

A spritz of Clinique's Aromatics elixir down my back and I'm ready. "I can't believe I left so much stuff behind," I tell Alice as Jack holds the door open for us as we head for the elevator. "I feel naked without my darling Coco Mademoiselle. Thank you for lending me your stuff, Whirly-girl."

Jack answers on his wife's behalf. "Sure. Save your raptures for later, Ed. And just remember to keep that smile plastered on your face for Al's family. What's the expression again? Grin and bear it."

"Didn't you invite some of your workmates to join us?" Alice reminded her husband. "I got texts from some of them saying they would be seeing us there."

Jack shrugged. "I might have mentioned it on the group chat, yeah."

I keep my head staring at the floor all the way down, through the elevator, and to the town car. I don't want Alice and Jack to see how upset I am. Her parents are hard to swallow, but that rat of a brother of hers, Buck, is just a bratty bully with an attitude problem bigger than the national debt.

Steeling myself, I get ready to meet the family.

Before the car can pull away from the curb, there's a rap on the window. After a nod from

Jack, the driver buzzes down the glass. An elderly man is bending down, grinning into the dark back interior of the car. "Hey, Jack. Aren't you going to introduce me to your guest?" He points at me in a kind of insolent way and gives me a wave. "Hey there, gorgeous. I'm Alf Cohen. Two floors up. Pleased to meetcha."

I notice Gabby and Noah giggling in the kids' seats facing me. Jack rolls his eyes. "She's too old for you, Alf. She's almost thirty. Nice try. Bye."

Alice turns to me with a wry smile. "You've just gotten your first taste of the famous New York rudeness, Girly-oh. You better get used to it."

"Who was that guy?" I want to know as the car slowly joins the traffic. He was so confident of me welcoming his friendship, I find it hard to believe someone could be so forward. In South Africa, suspicion and hatred are the only emotions people have for one another outside of their own social groups and cultures.

"Him?" Jack laughs. "Only the wealthiest dude in the building. Sold his Blockbuster and Radio Shack shares in the late nineties to invest in Amazon and Apple. He loves your type of woman, but I'm afraid you missed the boat. Alf likes them young."

"Jack!" Alice is outraged. "Don't say such things! My best friend is not the sort of woman to go from the heart-wrenching decision to walk out of her wedding, only to hook up with the first guy she sees!"

Jack apologizes to me. I really wish he hadn't. I'm blushing in the dark, hoping the city lights sliding by outside the car don't show my discomfort. An aching pang contracts my tummy as I remember Sterling fucking me so hard in the shower.

Patting my knee, Alice comforts me. "I know you don't see eye to eye with my family. I'm here for you if you want to talk."

I shake my head and stay silent. No words can describe my feelings of hatred for Buck.

Leaving her parents to drink lots of gin and tonics by the swimming pool, my new friend, Alice, and I go walkabout the game lodge. We are officially tweens. Thirteen and all the problems that come with it are in front of us.

We bonded over boy bands and teen heartthrobs and now we want to explore my small South African world together. It's the Noughties. Twilight is huge. There's nothing to watch on television anymore because Friends wrapped its final episode four years ago, and I have a secret.

"I can't believe you have a wild animal as a pet, Edie," Alice marvels as we flap our rubber flip-flops through the dust. "Let's go see Dickie and feed him."

My secret is bursting to get out. I'm young and naive enough to believe that a secret shared is a secret solved. "Later, Alice. I have something important I want to tell you."

My friend's eyes got big. "Ooh, Edie. How exciting. Well?"

Staring ahead of me while I summon the courage, I blurt it out. "I like your brother. I like Bucky. Do you think he likes me?"

Alice's brother is older than she is, and she tries to always stay out of his way because of his tendency to tease. But to twelve-year-old me, he is the world. I think I can see past his long, greasy brown-blond hair, spotty cheeks, and skinny torso, all the way to the angel I believe him to be inside.

Buck attended a progressive school in New York—one that allowed him to express himself. That means he was allowed to run around like a monkey in a fruit factory and everyone said his bad behavior was because he had "a creative soul."

The next thing I know, Alice goes flapping off to tell her brother about my crush. I tag along so I can control the narrative, but also so that I can be there when Buck turns to look at me before holding his arms open wide for me to run into for my first kiss....

The reality is different. "Bucky, come over here—" Alice bends over to catch her breath.

The lodge grounds are extensive, and we've been running under the full glare of the African sun.

Bucky is standing with one of the game rangers and two other young boys who like to hang around. The ranger is showing the boys how to throw sand in the air to see which way the wind is blowing. They are preparing to go to the rifle range to practice shooting at long-range targets.

He comes over when his sister calls and the other boys head over to the shooting range, but I can see there's a devil of mischief in his eyes. Alice whispers in her brother's ear and points at me. I wait with bated breath, but I wait in vain for a positive response.

Buck's eyes crease with mirth and he bursts out laughing once my vicarious message has been delivered. He runs to follow the other boys to the rifle range. "Hey, dudes! Wait for me! You'll never guess what!"

I'm frozen with horror and embarrassment for a good few minutes while Alice looks at me with sympathy in her eyes. My hopes shattered, all

I can do is chase after him. He mustn't tell the other boys. I have to live with those boys and go to school with them after he has gone. Where's his pity?

As I barrel around the corner of the tall, grass fence called a boma, heading towards the rifle range as fast as I can, I hear a shot followed by a soft thump in the dust. I see my pet duiker, Dickie, collapse to the ground, blood pumping out of a hole in his chest.

When I look up, I see Buck staring at me, a rifle in his hands.

***

"We're here, Edie!" Gabby pokes me. "Were you looking out for tourist attractions? Can we go to the MOMA together? I love coming downtown. All Mom ever lets me do is walk in the park!"

Jack tells his daughter to hush or else he will tell the driver to turn around and go back home, and then Gabby won't get to see her favorite uncle.

I don't want to get out of the car. I really don't. I have never forgiven that fucking psycho for what he did. I swore vengeance on him all those years ago, and it boils like bile in my stomach. He scorns my sweet tween crush and then shoots my miniature antelope. How dare he?

"How big are these work colleagues of Jack's, Alice?" I mumble under my breath so that Jack can't hear us. "I might need to hire one of them to beat up your brother."

Alice laughs. "Ha! Good luck with that. Let it be, Girly-oh. I promise you'll enjoy yourself if you let go of the past."

As our party enters the premises, the first thing I see is Alice's parents perched at the counter. They give me an exuberant wave. "Hey there! How are your folks? Come and tell us about South Africa. Is it still a shithole?!"

South Africa gets a little bit more dangerous and poorer every year, but no one likes to be reminded of that if they live there. I shake their hands politely. "Howzit, guys. My folks are well, thank you." It is the standard South African greeting. "Howzit" when saying hello, and "howzat" when something good happens during sports.

Alice pushes me forward. "Isn't she gorgeous, Mom? I can't believe she decided to get married instead of coming here to work as a model or become a movie star like Charlize Theron. Gabby calls Edie her 'Barbie doll.'"

I'm about to deny resembling anyone other than myself when I'm cut off.

"Here's Bucky," Alice's dad says, smiling and waving at someone behind my back. Gritting my teeth, I turn around.

It's the man I fucked in first class. It's Sterling.

Chapter 9: Sterling

I watch Edie's face as everything she now knows begins to fall into place. Alice called her brother to help her best friend. I was the man standing by the information desk as Edie answered the announcement. And it was gormless Bucky Lewis who fucked her so hard in the showers and in her private suite.

Yes, I was an asshole when I was a kid, but I was punished harshly for it. Yanked straight out of my progressive high school in central Manhattan, I was thrown into one of the most prestigious military academies in the world and left there to rot.

Only, I didn't rot. I flourished. Turns out, the strict discipline and punishments meted out there was just what I needed. My dyed blond hair was cut off. My skin cleared up after all the outdoor exercise, fresh air, and wholesome food, and I bulked up.

In fact, the trouble Edie Kruger got me into turned out to be the best thing that could have happened to me. From the moment she pointed her hysterical, accusing finger at me, it allowed my parents to take action. They had been muttering about "stern measures" and a "regimented environment" for a long time.

With Edie's parents threatening legal action and news coverage, my mom and dad jumped at the chance to get me out of their lives for as long as it took for me to regret ever having laid eyes on Edie Kruger. That skinny blonde with braids, big eyeglasses, and a flat chest stared daggers at me after she came pelting around the corner. I'll never forget it.

I can't say I blame her. Like I said, I was an asshole. Losing a pet can be hard, but she got her revenge on me. I got beaten to a pulp for the first few years at military school. Only when

I reached the age of sixteen did I grow tall and muscular enough to fend off the seniors.

That's how I got my nose broken and my eyebrow scar. I was walking to my dorm, minding my own business, when I got jumped. Apparently, a bunch of bigger boys blamed me for the sergeant handing out extra-long parade exercises that morning.

All I could do—I had learned enough defensive positions by then—was to curl into a ball and try to cover my face. But a real hard kick in my kidneys made me arch my back in pain. That was all my persecutors needed. The moment I removed my hands from my face and grabbed my lower back as the agony surged through me, they got me good.

They didn't even bother bending down to punch me out. One boot to the middle of my face was all it took for me to say "bye-bye" to daylight. That's how a football must feel before a placekicker tries to punt the ball upfield.

When I regained consciousness, the doc told me I was lucky to have a live brain. "Thank the Lord for that thick skull of yours, Cadet! Too bad about your face, but at least you're fully functional."

I went from pretty boy to rugged with lightning speed. As soon as the nose splint came off and my dental work was complete, I was knocking on the sarge's door, asking him to train me. "What specialty?" The sarge raised an eyebrow as he asked the question, looking me up and down. I hadn't reached my full height yet; I still had a lot of growing to do.

But I didn't hesitate. "Turn me into a stone-cold killing machine in hand-to-hand combat, sir. And set me up with a trainer during school vacations too—I ain't never going back home again."

And I never did. It took a hell of a lot of reaching out to me before I was ready to forgive and forget. Making a name for myself in the dark ops business might have had something to do with it. It's hard being pissed with someone when they were instrumental in making you successful.

And that was how I thought about Edie Kruger too, all the way up to the time I saw her walking towards me at the info desk. It's amazing how fast a man can have a change of heart when a girl turns into a stunningly beautiful woman. I'm honest enough with myself to admit that.

Suddenly, the message Alice passed on to me at the safari lodge nearly seventeen years ago began to make a whole lot of sense. "Do you like Edie, Bucky? Do you want to be her boyfriend?" I had laughed with embarrassment then, but I'm definitely not laughing now.

Edie looks absolutely gorgeous, like some kind of a Grecian goddess. Aphrodite, or Venus, for sure. The white silk of her dress hugs her figure. When she moves, I get a glimpse of her nipples as they press against the fabric. Even though I dream about her every night, it falls short of how sexy she is in real life.

Edie has the longest legs, and every inch of them is smooth and tanned. Even when she's not wearing heels, she can pull off combining flats with evening wear. Her hair is up, which suits her. It gives me the opportunity to imagine myself kissing her long, elegant neck.

I go say hello to my godson. "What's up, Noah? How's school going?"

He gives me a quizzing look. "I wish Edie was my godmother, Uncle Buck, but I guess I'm stuck with you."

All the adults make that raucous laughing noise. The one that means they find the child's remark amusing after downing a couple of drinks. Jack, Alice, my parents, and Jack's workmates begin chatting amongst themselves.

But Edie doesn't join in the laughter. She's shooting daggers at me from the end of the counter. I wish I could say that her pouting glare makes her less alluring, but I'd be lying.

Alice stops whatever she's saying to our mom and beckons me over. "Do you want me to tell Edie that it was you who orchestrated her flight to New York? It might help melt the ice between you. Water under the bridge, and all that."

I grin. "Oh, she knows. I don't think she's ready to forgive me yet."

Mom interrupts. "Shoot! Is anyone even talking about that incident still? It's ancient history. It must have been over fifteen years ago, at least. Go and make it up to her, Bucky." She gives me a push in Edie's direction.

"How did Edie seem when she arrived, Alice?" I want to know if Edie had a change of heart halfway here. Had she mentioned the man she met on the flight? I know how women talk to one another—always whispering about how their men measure up.

Alice shakes her head. "I don't think she knows you helped out, Bucky, I really don't. She was carefree as a bird when she arrived. Edie only got upset when I told her my darling brother would be joining the family meal." My sister smiles and pats my arm. "Are you regretting that terrible decision you made during our family safari? Edie's grown up to be a real head-turner. Ha!"

I don't bother responding to the taunt. I leave them to dig into the first dish of Koshi goodness and move down the counter. I've never been the kind of man to sweep things under the rug and I'm not about to start now.

Edie is surrounded by three of Jack's work colleagues. One of them turns to me as I approach. "Hey, get in line, Stern-ling! You know the rules—whoever buys the drink, gets to talk to the girl."

"Oh, you mean the rule you guys used when you were pledging for your frat? I think I must have been in boot camp when you all agreed to that."

Edie doesn't even look at me when she says, "You call him Stern-ling? That makes me smile."

One of the wiseacres standing next to her chimes in. "Well, that can only be a good thing, because old Stern-ling here never does!"

They all laugh uproariously. My facial expression doesn't change. I wouldn't be much good at doing undercover work if I took offense at any little thing. The server appears at Edie's elbow the moment she drains her glass. "Vodka martini with a twist. That's what you're drinking, isn't it?" I ask Edie.

Those guys should have been paying more attention to how fast Edie was knocking back her cocktail instead of trying to needle me into backing off. She takes the drink, obviously not wanting to cause a scene, but she doesn't look at me or thank me.

I wait. The three guys all stare at one another and then over at me. They can read their future in my eyes. "Well, it was nice meeting you, Edie. Any friend of Jack's is a friend of ours...."

One by one, they leave to go sit at their table by the wall after placing their business cards on the counter in front of Edie's martini. I take their spot. "Alice thinks we should clear the air between us, Edie. I'm sorry for what you had to witness that day, but it was so long ago. Let's be friends again."

She puts her empty glass back down on the counter so fast the lemon rind twist spins. "We were never friends, Bucky, so don't start getting your hopes up about that happening."

Edging around me, she stalks to the back of the restaurant, only stopping to ask a member of the waitstaff where the restroom is first. Whipping around, I go after her. I manage to catch hold of her arm before she disappears inside. "Talk to me, Edie! We have a connection.

You can't deny it." My voice comes out in a low growl.

She's relentless. "That's not the way I remember things."

"You can't hold it against me that I had work to do in Dubai. I knew I would be seeing you again, but I wasn't ready to tell you my family's pet name for me."

I can see the thought crossing her mind—Edie wants to slap me so bad. She wants to shake off my grip and leave. But when she looks into my eyes, she can see that I will follow her. I'm desperate to sort this out.

Shuffling deeper into the passage, she backs into a corner so that no one can see us. "What is it going to take for you to leave me alone forever, Bucky Lewis?"

"First of all, I'm Sterling. Sterling Lewis. No middle name."

She scoffs, throwing back her head with amusement. "Fine. Why does your family call you 'Bucky' then?"

I tell her that I used to pretend I was hunting deer in our backyard when I was a small kid growing up; imagining one of my dad's golf clubs was a rifle. Buck hunter. Bucky. It's the wrong explanation to give Edie, not with our complicated history.

"Okay, so it's clear to me now why you are such a psycho—you grew up like that." She locks her eyes on me. I don't look away—I've got too much riding on this for me to wuss out now.

"Sure, I'm a psycho, Edie. But I'm the psycho who came to your rescue at the airport, so now will you admit we have something?"

A small shake of her head. "Nuh-uh. No way. You haven't changed. And you knew I wanted nothing to do with you, Sterling. Your anonymity took advantage of me during a vulnerable moment in my life!"

I give a soft bark of laughter. "Vulnerable! Is that what you're calling it? I suppose you could describe being bent over in the shower and begging for me to fuck you harder and deeper 'vulnerable,' but I wouldn't bet on it holding up in a court of law."

She raises her hand to slap me, but it doesn't come down. We're in each other's faces, our mouths only inches apart. I'm so aware of her breasts rising and falling under the soft silk as her breath quickens. Her one shoulder is bare, and yes, it does make her look vulnerable. I want to cherish her, protect her, and fuck the living daylights out of her.

Edie actually feels me stiffen, that's how close we are pressed against one another in the corner. Her eyes blink with an emotion I can't read, but she's not moving and she's not running away. After a quick glance over my shoulder, I slide my hand up her inner thigh.

Pushing her panties to one side, I finger her pussy. She's wet and her clit is engorged. Edie's eyes dilate as I stroke her. Instinctively, her hand reaches out for my cock. With her eyes closed, she moans softly as she feels how hard I am, and how much I want her.

I kiss her the way I know she likes it. Biting her lower lip gently as my tongue licks it. "Would it have really made a difference on the plane if you had known who I was, Edie? Would it have been enough to stop us wanting this?" My voice is deep with all the crazy things I want to do to her.

As my strokes get faster, I feel her get wetter. Her breath starts to come in short gasps as her hand grips the thick outline of my cock in my pants.

She's a few strokes away from coming when the sound of a customer approaching interrupts us. Like a startled fawn, she pushes me away from her. Adjusting her panties quickly, we wait for the woman to walk past us. It manages to break the spell.

"What decision I made, Sterling, was mine alone to make! But only when I had all the facts. And now we'll never know, will we?"

Chapter 10: Edie

I'm shaking when I reach the counter. Jack's friends try to catch my eye when I walk past, but I ignore them. Mr. and Mrs. Lewis have taken the kids for a takeout burger, but I can see Alice inspecting me as I get closer.

"How did it feel getting that off your chest? What did my big brother say?"

"N-nothing. He's anxious for us to get a fresh start, which you obviously gave him. What changed? I mean, the last time I heard you talk about Bucky, he was being a prick for blowing off the invite to your wedding."

Alice chuckles. "Yeah, thank God for that. I don't think you would have agreed to be my bridesmaid if he hadn't! But Buck has changed, Edie. He's done a lot of growing up over the last few years. I just never bothered telling you because I didn't want to bring up painful memories."

I see Sterling flag down a waiter. If he thinks another vodka martini with a twist is going to fix this raging urge inside my heart, he'll be very mistaken. Only he doesn't order a drink. Taking a black credit card out of his coat pocket, he pays for everything.

I'm so confused. Is he Jack's PA or something? Before the waiter gives him back the card, my mind is made up. "Whirly-oh, be a darling, and let me take the car back to the apartment, please? Jet lag, and all that. I've got a lot on my mind."

Of course, my best friend says yes. She shouts after me as I flee. "Keep your phone off, Girly-oh! You don't want anyone mindfucking you with messages!"

It's too late. I'm already mindfucked. How on earth can my brain be telling me one thing when my body is telling me the opposite? Go back in there, Edie, and finish what you started.

You know you want him. You know how much your body is craving for him to fuck you again with that big, beautiful cock of his....

Giving a little scream, I bury my face in my hands. This makes the driver buzz the intercom. "Everything all right, Miss Kruger?"

Nodding and smiling, I pretend I'm fine. "Just jet lag. Sorry." All South Africans apologize for doing nothing wrong. It's a national pastime. If we bump into one another in the corridor, we say sorry. If we trip over a paver on the sidewalk, we beg pardon. It's crazy. No wonder the country's like a pot about to boil over with repressed rage.

The concierge buzzes me in and uses his pass key to allow me access to Carter's floor. When the elevator door slides open, I see a massive vase of flowers waiting right in front of the entrance. I am so tempted to kick it and smash it with my foot, but I don't.

Fuck you, Sterling "Bucky" Lewis! You can beg on your knees the whole night for all I care. I'm not ever forgiving you for what you did.

Why do I reach for the card with my name print-ed on it neatly, and open it? Curiosity, I guess. Plus a little bit of vicious enjoyment at Sterling's discomfort as I read the card.

I'll make an exception for you, honey bunny. You're so hot. Come on up and visit me when you have the time—or better yet, let's go to St. Barts in my private jet and grab some sun. You'd like that, wouldn't you? I promise you'll have the best time of your life.

I'm so confused. Ignoring the flowers on the floor, I walk to the kitchen and press the in-tercom. "Howzit, it's Edie—ag, yah, you can see which apartment is buzzing. Cool. These flow-ers—?"

I say "ag" a lot when I'm home in South Africa. It's pronounced the same way the Scottish people say "och," with that guttural inflection on the g.

The voice comes over the intercom. "The flow-ers are from Mr. Cohen on the seventeenth floor, Miss Kruger. The Carters always allow de-liveries in."

Bidding the man good night after thanking him, I hang up the phone, throw the card in the recycle bin, and get ready for bed. The Carters' unit is a six-bedroom, seven-bathroom suite, with a state-of-the-art kitchen and dining-living area. I'm in the guest room.

It's very sweet but decorated in the starkly minimalist style Jack favors. The monochromatic Picasso sketch of a woman's face seems to stare at me with disdain as I slip out of the silk dress.

"Don't give me the side eye, you bitch," I scold the picture. "You would have let him finger bang you in the restrooms too if you knew him."

It's time I faced up to the fact that I am more attracted to Sterling than I was initially prepared to admit. The two emotions—intense hatred and immense desire—struggle inside me before I give up and allow my fantasies to take over.

Lying on the five-hundred-thread-count Egyptian cotton sheets, I press my thighs together before allowing my fingers to slide down my belly and find my clit. I'm still excited. I'm still wet. God, but I can't stop thinking about his touch, his kiss, his delicious taste, and smell.

I'm reminded of a quote I picked up during English lessons at school: how could my only love come from my only hate? But I don't love Sterling; I just want him more than words can say. No matter how angry he made me in the past, I can't stop the arousing effect he has on me.

As I think about us fucking in first class, I get more excited. I want to be riding him so hard right now. I wish he was here with me, holding my hips, that delicious half smile of pleasure making one side of his firm mouth tilt up.

I want to trace my finger over his handsome face. Trailing from the white scar slashing across his eyebrow to the high arch of his nose, and then along the perfect line of his jaw and chin. I want to unbutton his shirt all the way down, unzip his pants, and inspect his naked body with my eyes and hands.

We've never been in bed together. I've never seen him without his elegant charcoal black suit on. But somehow, he has been able to entrap me with his moves, his looks, and his attitude.

And don't get me started about how good he is at using his cock.... The memory makes me come. I've been circling my fingers around and around my clit, thinking about the one man in the world who is strictly off-limits to me, and I come harder than I ever have in my life.

If this is what jumping out of my comfort zone has done for my climaxes, it can only be a good thing that I upgraded my life to New York.

***

"It took three days of intermittent sleep patterns for me to adjust to East Coast time," I tell Alice as I breeze into the kitchen as my friend is getting breakfast ready for the kids. "Now, I'm ready for my first cup of coffee! I don't think I can take much more of these caffeine-withdrawal headaches."

Only after she pushes a mug towards me and I take a sip are we ready for a conversation.

"I feel you." Alice holds her back and groans, then stretches. "They gave me decaf by mistake at the coffee shop once and I thought I was coming down with the flu."

It's nice watching the dawn light filter through the floor-to-ceiling sliding doors that lead out to the balcony. Jerking my head, I ask Alice if she wants to sit outside with me and enjoy it. She shrugs.

"I can promise you that the traffic and pollution are just as bad early in the morning as it is during the day." I give her that look; the one that means "Don't be an old poop." Sighing, my friend follows me. We plonk our butts down on the all-weather patio cushions and get ready to gab.

"Can I finally tell you what your mom and dad have been messaging me?" Alice wants to know.

I take a long, thoughtful sip of coffee. "Okay. Let it rip."

She takes out her phone and begins a run-down. "I'll wrap it up in a nutshell for you. Your folks want you to come back home and try to work things out with Koos. And then they go into all the details about how I must plead their case for them." Alice puts the phone on her lap and glares at me. "It's quite a guilt trip they've put on me, Edie. I'm not going to lie."

That makes me wince. Here I am, drinking coffee and staring at the Manhattan sunrise from an elegant Upper Eastside apartment, while my parents have been left holding the big mess that was my relationship with Koos. I would feel worse, except that my dad took out wedding insurance, thank goodness.

This was not because he believed I would do a runner, however. Every wedding planner insists on working with heavy insurance cover because of all the riots, explosions, water and electricity cutoffs, and strikes that happen in South Africa on a daily basis.

"What can I say?" I shoot the question over my shoulder as I go inside for a quick refill. "I let things go too far. I need to know Koos and his family of vicious Van der Hoffs are not going to take out a vendetta on my parents' lodge. They are very influential."

"Let things go too far? That's the understatement of the year! You were one or two hours away from becoming Mrs. Fucking Van der Hoff for keeps. But don't worry about that vendetta. Stern-ling has connections. Koos wouldn't dare."

The change of topic intrigues me. "What does he do? Sterling, I mean." I would never tell Alice that her brother upgraded me all the way from Cape Town to Dubai. It's my dirty little secret.

Alice holds up one finger and pops inside for a refill. Coming out, she searches her mind for a way to describe her brother's job.

"He's like some kind of fixer. I dunno. He gets a lot of data intel from Jack."

"Well, listen to you, Ms. Thang. 'Data intel' indeed! Like James Bond." We laugh and clink our coffee mugs together before Alice leaves to get the kids out of bed.

The apartment is empty when I get out of the shower. Feeling caged, I slip on the athleisure wear I bought in Dubai and rummage around in the hall until I find the sneakers (called tekkies in South Africa for some strange reason). When I reach the lobby, I tell the concierge to point me in the direction of the park.

He grins and points forward. "Just cross the road, Ma'am. It's behind that wall. Cross at the lights and you're there." I'm about to leave when he adds. "Mrs. Carter mentioned to me that you might want directions to the pharmacy. She's added your name to her account if you need anything. Instead of turning left, take a right and left at the corner."

I thank him. Trust Alice to preempt my every need. It must be so nice to be able to have anything you want at the drop of a hat. Koos has locked me out of my cards, but I knew he would do that. And the rand-dollar exchange rate makes the currency worth nothing anyway.

My sixth sense tells me I'm not alone. Glancing behind, I see a four-wheel drive sliding alongside my shadow. The windows are blacked out, so I can't see who is following me. I'm tempted to turn around and walk back the other way, but I don't want to overreact.

Oh no! What if it's that creepy Alf Cohen from two floors up? Alice has the flowers he sent proudly displayed on the coffee table in the living room. Should I have returned them?

Two choices: I can cross the road and enter the park or continue to the pharmacy. But the more I think it might be Alf, the more I want to run back to the apartment. That's it. I turn and start to head back.

The door of the town car opens and a man steps out.

"Good morning, Sunshine." Sterling smiles at me; he's so sure of me welcoming him back into my life. "Would I be right in guessing that you thought I was your elderly neighbor?"

Chapter 11: Sterling

Edie's face clouds over the moment she sees me. "You seem to be remarkably well informed about the comings and goings of my life, Sterling."

I join Edie, walking beside her on the outside of the sidewalk after signaling to my driver he can pull away. "Just the comings." I grin down at her, hoping she'll appreciate the joke. That makes her shoot me a dirty look.

"Did Jack tell you?" Edie wants to know.

I shake my head. "Snitches get stitches." She huffs, pivoting in a one-eighty to return to the apartment building. That makes me grab her arm and spin her to face back the way we were going. "Okay. It was Noah. I took him for tutoring this morning and it was all he could talk about. I have to admit, Mr. Cohen is the opposite of subtle."

Before Edie can huff with annoyance about my uncanny inside information again, I explain. "Alice found the card in the recycling bin. You know how she is. She thought the flowers were from a woman trying to get with Jack."

We both stare at each other for several beats before bursting into laughter. "Oh my God!" Edie covers her mouth with her hand, she's laughing so loud. "How did I miss that? I would give my right arm to have been a fly on the wall and watch that accusation play out!"

"I know! Right?" I'm laughing for the first time in ages. Truly, madly, deeply laughing. It's a crazy feeling. "Why is my sister so jealous of Jack? She's been paranoid about him cheating on her since they were first dating."

Clutching my arm, Edie tries to be serious for a moment but fails. Her eyes are sparkling with humor as she asks me. "Please. I'm dying to know. Has he ever been unfaithful in any way?"

I feel her footsteps slowing down as we reach the pharmacy signage. "He has about as much interest in the female of the species as he does in the male. If it doesn't beep or accept code, Jack doesn't want to know."

She's so beautiful when she laughs, I feel a surge of some strange emotion inside me as I watch Edie wipe the happy tears from her eyes. Indicating with my head, I ask her why the pharmacy. She replies with the laughter draining out of her face. "I don't think that's any of your business."

Dammit. Why do I keep striking out? I'm looking for a way in—searching for a break—but I keep hitting a wall. "I'll wait outside, then," I concede to her need for privacy. "I don't want you getting lost on the way back home."

She smiles and nods, closing the door quietly behind her.

I lean with my back against the storefront, texting Alice. The family uses its own private app to chat with each other—one that doesn't demand access to photos, contact deets, microphone, and camera in order to function properly. Jack created it himself.

Alice works part-time in Jack's building as a customer relations consultant. Jack downplays his wife's role in running this side of his business, but he knows he's the worst person to face down his clients. Jack has all the finesse of a fucking sledgehammer.

Is Edie sick? I'm with her and she's gone into the pharmacy.

A pause and then a reply comes through. What a coincidence! Cause Edie texted me just now to tell me that you curb-crawled her when she went outside for some fresh air.

There's nothing more invincible than two women who have been best friends for over fifteen years.

My thumbs fly over the keypad. I didn't curb crawl her. I've actually got one of my guys posted outside the building. Don't pester me with questions as to why.

My darling sister shoots back fast. If you want to know if Edie's sick, ask her yourself. And stop spying on her.

Edie finishes her transaction and comes out carrying a small brown paper bag in her hand. She sees me tucking my phone back into my front pocket. "You look nice today," she tells me out of the blue. "I thought that maybe you were incapable of enjoying the comfort of casual clothes."

I look down at my faded denims and white T-shirt. I never wear sneakers in case of emergencies. Nothing lands a kick harder than a pair of freestyle army protection boots, so that's what I have on my feet. "Thanks. So do you."

She smiles serenely and points right. "I think that we have both established that we find each other attractive, Sterling. Do we turn right here to get to the park?"

Once the traffic noise fades behind us as we head towards East Drive, I get the chance to answer more fully. "What brought you out today? The need to buy something at the pharmacy or a walk in the park?"

Edie gives me one of her scrutinizing stares. "The last thing I would describe you as, Sterling, is a walk in the park." I'm about to snap out a frustrated defense against her hostility when she takes pity on me. With a light laugh, Edie continues. "Alice allowed me to use her account at the pharmacy. Okay? I'm... I'm having a bit of trouble with my cards."

This is my chance to step up and offer her money, but I can see from the look in her eyes that Edie will just shoot me down if I try. Pointing at the bag, I ask her what's in it. Her smile is wry. "Mascara. See?" Sliding the plastic tube out of the bag, she pushes it back in again and sticks it in the pocket of the black Lycra yoga pants she's wearing.

"Now that that's out of the way, Sterling," she says, back to being confrontational, "how did you know I was coming out here today?"

I don't bother lying. "Jack and Alice have a smart house. It's linked to their bank cards so that the utilities and grocery bills automatically get paid. I hacked it so I could tell from the water and power consumption when you got into the shower this morning. I used this information to hazard a guess as to when you would be coming outside."

Her hazel-green eyes get really wide with amazement. "But how did you know I would come down? I might have chosen to go two floors up and pay a pleasant visit to Mr. Cohen."

It takes a while for me to realize that Edie is teasing me. There I am standing in the middle of Central Park in the middle of a lovely late spring morning trying to persuade her to stay away from Alf fucking Cohen, before I see the mischievous look on her face.

Damn, this girl is good. "She shoots, she scores. Listen, Edie, can I please take you out for brunch? It's the least I can do after spying on your utility usage." And for me getting so hard imagining you standing in the shower naked....

We walk together to Tavern on the Green in silence and get a table for two. I can see the stress in her shoulders relax as she stares out at the trees and fountains. When compared to the harsh concrete brightness of the city, the Park often has that effect on people.

I allow my defenses to come down a little. I stop scoping my surroundings so that I can pay closer attention to the fascinating woman sitting opposite me. We both order the same meal: a pastry basket and Greek yogurt parfait, with coffee.

The sides of her nose crinkle and I know she's about to make fun of me again. "I had you down as a 'meat and potatoes' kind of guy, Sterling."

Reaching for her hand, I try to hold it, but Edie slides it away before we can touch it. It makes me feel like I'm on a wicked combination of a carousel and a Ferris wheel, her ever-changing mood toward me makes me so dizzy.

"And I thought you said you would never forgive me for shining you on about my identity during the flight, Edie—and yet here we are."

I admit I said it to needle her, but nothing can dampen her high spirits. "I've decided to forgive you for doing that," Edie shrugs, "because I had such a good time."

My heart soars. It's the weirdest feeling to get totally happy from such a small thing, but I do.

"I did too," I confide in her. "I mean, it makes sense, you have to admit it."

Our meal arrives. Edie breaks off our conversation to thank the server and beam one of her gorgeous smiles. I see a few men turn to stare at her when she asks for one percent milk for her coffee, but it's not because of her accent. They're checking her out.

Maybe it's the way Edie's hair is pulled back into a tight ponytail at the back of her head that's giving her that carefree, playful allure. Maybe it's because she's dressed in skintight Lycra with an extra-large T-shirt hanging off one shoulder. Whatever it is, men can't help but notice her when she gives a little yelp of laughter as she accidentally spills the milk.

But the second the server leaves, she focuses her attention back on me. "What makes sense?" I'm lost. So much has happened between my question and her reply that she has to fill me in. "Come on, Sterling. You said that we had a good time together and then added that it makes sense and that I had to admit it. So, what makes sense? The good time or the admission?"

I search her eyes for some clue, but she's like a cat playing with a rat. I decide to take a shot in the dark. "You and me. We make sense together. Admit it."

The air thickens between us. It's no longer an enjoyable brunch. This seems to be more like some kind of a face-off.

"No." One word. Edie torpedoes my aspirations with her negative reply and then continues to eat her brunch calmly. I have never been the kind of man to take a "no" lying down.

"No, you won't admit it? Or no, you don't think we make sense together, Edie?"

With her coffee cup held up to her mouth, I can't see if she's smiling or not. I'm still hoping Edie's going to confess that she gets pleasure out of teasing the shit out of me, and not just being vindictive. Then I see her eyes are smiling.

"I admit it. What's the use of lying? We make so much sense together, Sterling. When you fuck me, it feels like one of those—very large—puzzle pieces that just slots into place in the most perfectly satisfying way. I would have to be crazy stupid not to admit that we"—she points to me and then taps her chest—"make sense together physically."

Gesturing around the restaurant, Edie tilts her head as she looks at me. "I bet every single person in this room is thinking, 'Wow, they must fuck each other's brains out six times a night—and not that aimless ack-ack style of banging sex either—the goooood, looooong, slooooow sensual fucking.' And they'd be right nine times out of ten."

I have to stare down at my plate while she talks. The way she's talking has got me all het up. Edie rubs the side of my leg with her foot. I murmur my reply in a low voice. "So, let's get out of here and prove them right."

God help anyone who is listening in to this nice little chat Edie and I have got going. They would have to be as rock-hard as I am right now.

"No." My siren temptress shakes her head, patting her mouth delicately with the napkin. "I might have forgiven you for the deception on the flight, but I have not forgiven you for what you did to my pet, Sterling. So, until I do, it's always going to be a 'no' from me, I'm afraid."

Chapter 12: Edie

Is it my imagination, or does Sterling get incredibly grumpy after my reply? He's not exactly a ray of sunshine at the best of times, but he looks like a thundercloud after I give him the brush-off.

Am I satisfied being the reason for him experiencing the pain of rejection? Absolutely. Do I feel a tiny bit guilty? Yes. As much as I hated Bucky in the past, I must face facts and confess that my best friend's brother is starting to grow on me as an adult.

What is the word that I am trying to remember that will describe Sterling the best? Gallant. He is a gallant man. His manners towards me are impeccable and he respects every sassy reply I have ever given him—although I can always see the gears in his head turning as he looks for a way to contradict me.

They don't make a lot of gallant men nowadays. I would have to be blind not to notice that my old archenemy has turned into a bit of a super-hero; always there to save the day or help out.

He accepts my no like a real man, submitting to my rejection of him. It's the most noble way a man has ever heard a "let's just be friends" speech that I've ever seen. There's no "you're not the only fish in the sea, babes" nonsense. No pleading or anger.

He just closes up shop to his emotions entirely and switches to "polite friends" mode immediately. I love the way there is no awkwardness afterward, but goddamn it, he gets grumpy. The smiling man who walked in companionable silence with me through the park is gone, re-placed by someone who looks like he has the cares of the world on his shoulders.

One flash of his black credit card again and we're walking back to the modish cream-colored apartment building that I now call home. Sterling gives me monosyllabic responses for the most part, but when I ask him if we're cool, he smiles.

"I'd be cool if I had a time machine, Edie. But I don't, so I guess I'm stuck with the current state of affairs." We've reached the traffic lights closest to the building. He stops me walking by holding my hand.

"Are you okay to cross over and get home from here? Or would you like me to escort you?"

For some inexplicable reason, I give his hand a squeeze. I want to comfort Sterling, hug him, whisper in his ear that it's going to be alright and that we just have to work through this.

But I don't. "If I see Alf, I'm sure I can outrun him, Sterling. Thanks for brunch. Cheers!" My breezy tone doesn't let me down. And I manage to keep smiling and waving until he turns the corner.

Only then does my brow furrow.

It's in my head all the up to the Carters' floor. Alice is there with Gabby. They are off for a mother-daughter experience at the spa. Do I want to come?

I wince. "I feel bad about accepting all these freebies from you, Alice. I know you don't begrudge me for having no money, but it still hurts."

Gabby's face falls and I can see her gearing up for an "Oh please, Edie, come with us" debate, but Alice gets there first.

"Tell me how the money situation was in your relationship with Koos, please girl."

Gabby goes to get us two bottles of mineral water out of the fridge and hands one to me before joining her mother on the settee. I can see that they are genuinely interested in finding out. After cracking the bottle cap and taking a long gulp, I think of the best way to describe my dependence on Koos without coming across as a complete numbskull.

"He never liked the idea of me having my own financial independence. I get that now. I had accrued a few debts when I was a student—small stuff that all young women are exposed to when they try to build a credit score—and he used that as a way to shame me into thinking I was not money savvy."

I told Alice and Gabby that I was left with a few unpaid clothing store credit accounts during that uncertain period between graduating from university and getting a job.

"Koos leveraged my debt to bully me into opening a joint account with him once we were engaged. It made sense because everyone knew I was heading towards having kids and running the household. He went on and on at me until I handed in my notice at the Save the Rhino charity—said they were not paying me enough for it to make a difference. The moment I did that, his mask began to slip and he allowed the control freak inside him to come out."

Gabby gasped. "Edie! Even I know that a woman should never give up her power to a man!"

That makes Alice and me laugh. Alice gives her daughter a hug. "Listen to you, Ms. Gloria Steinem the Second! Damn right, a woman should never do that! But your godmother was under a lot of pressure to conform because of something called 'cultural expectations,' so go easy on her."

As we get ready to go to the spa, Gabby asks her mom what cultural expectations are made on women in New York.

"I dunno." Alice shrugs as she tightens the belt of her Donna Karan wrap dress. "Look nice. Act tough. Be smart."

I couldn't have put it any better myself. The driver is waiting for us downstairs. I can't help looking over my shoulder before settling into the comfortable leather seats in case Alf Cohen is running down the red carpet, trying to stop us.

The town car doesn't have to travel far for us to reach the spa. We just jump a few blocks over to Third Avenue. But I'm used to driving everywhere because, in South Africa, the sidewalks are reserved for beggars and muggers. Even if someone isn't carrying anything in their hands or has a bag strapped over the shoulder, criminals might want to 'redistribute' a coat or pair of sunglasses instead.

"Edie, how did it go with Uncle Sterling this morning?" Gabby asks after giving a sly smile to her mom.

Alice gives her daughter a playful smack on the leg. "Hey! No fair! I told you that in confidence."

Gabby justifies her question. "Excuse me, Mom, but Noah and I love both our godparents, so I think I have a vested interest in knowing the outcome."

Alice rolls her eyes at me. "She learns that kind of wiseacre talk from her dad."

I tell her it's okay. "I have nothing to hide, Gabs. In fact, I want to pick your brains a little bit. What exactly does Sterling do for work? Does he help Jack in any way?" I'm not about to say anything about the upgrade or tell them dear godfather Sterling has a nice sideline going in hacking their home computer, but I want to know for myself. The mysterious Mr. Sterling is still quite an enigma to me.

The car pulls up outside the spa. Alice waves her hand in a vague gesture. "I think it's international business. Sterling goes away for long periods, Edie, so you won't have to put up with him for much longer. I think he's just taking a break so he can hang around you a bit."

That gives me a lot to think about during my massage. The manicurist redoes the polish on my toes and shapes my nails, but she can see from my face that I'm not in a chatty mood. The question uppermost in my mind is this: How do I feel about not seeing Sterling for long periods?

How do I feel about him finding some other women to upgrade as he jets off for another one of his international business thingummies?

Since finding out that Spotty Bucky brat-fink bastard is actually ever-so hunky Sterling Lewis, International Man of Mystery and Awesome Sex, I haven't been brave enough to admit to myself that it was actually me who asked him if he wanted to help me delay my stopover in Dubai and book into a hotel.

And while I was chill with waving him goodbye when I believed he was blowing me off at the airport, I must reassess my reaction now, because Sterling knew he would be seeing me again soon, hotel stopover or not.

"What?" The beautician asked me a question, but my mind was elsewhere—in the shower on the plane, on my First-Class seat, outside the restrooms at Kochi—

"What color varnish would you like on the fingernails, Ms. Kruger?"

Now, that is a question I can answer. "Leave them clear, thank you. You've done such a nice job with the cuticles I may as well show them off."

I ask Alice and Gabriella if we can walk home because I want to buy a change of clothes. "If you could front me fifty dollars, please, friend?" I clasp my hands together like the "pray" emoji. "I promise I will pay you back the second I get a job."

Gabby pipes up. "If your budget is only fifty dollars, Edie, you better wait until we get home and then buy something cheap and nasty from one of those clothing websites that use slave labor." She nudges her mom. "Please can we take Edie to Saks? I love playing dress-up with her."

We laugh. Alice jerks her thumb toward the car. "Okay, everyone. Get in. Saks it is."

But Gabby and I insist on walking there. I'm dying to see a bit more of the city and look up at all those mind-boggling high skyscrapers that darken the sidewalks with their grand shadows. It's hard to describe how blue the sky is when it's contrasted against the gray outline of the city. The sharp angle of shade slices the buildings into diagonals, half-light, half-dark.

I've never seen such a great example of how life plays out. The good and the bad; the bright side, and the doomy, gloomy "can't find the will to get out of bed" side.

Our shopping spree at Saks lightens my mood a lot. While I don't go overboard with designer clothes, I am very happy with the jeans and short cap sleeve T-shirt Gabby insists I get because "they make my bum and boobs look amazing!"

After adding a week's worth of underwear to the shop because I don't want to be walking around town with no bra under my tee, it's time for us to stroll back to the apartment along

Fifth Avenue, heading uptown with our bags of tissue-wrapped lingerie. Jack is there when we step out of the elevator. Gabby ignores her dad, too busy telling me about this girl who stuck gum in her hair at school.

Jack checks out my shopping bags. "Please don't tell me that Alice allowed you to use her account for that stuff, Edie. What is it you've splurged on this time? La Perla?"

Alice bustles out of the kitchen like a bat out of hell, soup ladle poised for action. "Please don't tell me, Jack, that you just said that to my best friend! I swear to God, I'll hit you with this giant spoon if you don't apologize right now."

I see a look of deep concern on Gabby's face as she looks from one parent to the other, but Jack is laid-back. Raising his shoulders to shrug, he sticks to his guns.

"What, Alice? What did I say wrong? She's staying here for free. She got a spa day out of you. And then she goes to shop at Saks on your dime." He turns to me, his hands held up. "I'm just saying, Edie. Don't shoot the messenger.

But I would really like to know what are your plans?"

I feel myself turning beetroot red. I get a sick feeling to my stomach as embarrassment churns the acid. Stuttering, I start backing out of the living room.

"You're right, Jack. I'm s-sorry. I took advantage of Alice's generosity. I'll text my folks tonight and ask them for a ticket back—maybe I should at least be open to listening to Koos?"

Aiming for her husband's head, Alice throws the soup ladle. She misses, but she made her point. "Now see what you've gone and done, you old poop, Jack!"

Noah chuckles from his perch in front of the living room flat screen. "You old poop, Dad."

Pointing at her son, Alice articulates her complaint. "You see? Even Noah agrees with me."

Leaving them to it, I scurry off to my bedroom, but I can hear Alice coming after me. When she opens the bedroom door, her phone is in her hand. "I'm texting Sterling. He's real good at helping out with these kinds of situations."

And before I can beg her not to, Alice pushes the send icon.

Chapter 13: Sterling

I'm staying at the Grand Penthouse Terrace Suite at the Plaza. It's the closest I can be to Edie without spooking her or being tempted to drop in unannounced.

One of my guys has the Fifth Avenue building under observation. It's not because I want to spy on her, but because Koos Van der Hoff is an unknown entity, and I didn't become so good at my job without factoring things like that into the desired outcome.

The family app pings.

Stern-ling. Please be a doll and help Edie. You know how Jack gets. He wants to know for how long Edie will be staying with us. Poor girl is talking about going back to that big ape fiancé of hers in Cape Town! She's got no money or connections. I'll sanction anything you can arrange. Love, A xxx

Typical Jack. He's such a prickly customer, but he has my best interests at heart. Only my sister gets his caustic sense of humor. If the guy knows someone's weak spot, he likes to poke it. I swear he's probably upset right now for Edie not getting his "joke."

Keep this on the DL, sis. Don't tell her or else she'll reject my help. I'll catch her when she goes walking in the park tomorrow morning.

Of course, I'm excited at the thought of seeing Edie again, but I don't waste that edgy sensation pulsing inside me by jerking off. If Edie lets me in just a little, only then will I allow myself the luxury of fantasizing about her again.

I make a few phone calls and then hit the hay. The military teaches recruits all sorts of different mind control techniques for both staying awake and relaxing. Tightening and releasing every muscle one by one, I manage to regain command of my body and fall asleep.

She haunts my dreams. I'm behind enemy lines, under fire, and hiding, waiting for the chance to return fire. The field falls quiet; seeing my chance, I aim and shoot at the only moving object I see.

To my horror, it's a small antelope. I turn away from the sight, horrified at what I've done. Suddenly, Edie Kruger is in the foxhole with me. "I hate you, Bucky, you killed my pet." I reach for her, but she's gone.

Bolting upright, I wake up shouting, "No!"

Damn. There's no mind trick to help me with nightmares like that. But nothing can make me quit now. Fumbling for the phone, I call the white glove butler service. "Coffee, black."

By the time the coffee arrives, I've showered and shaved. I pull at the wet strands of hair as I stare at myself in the mirror with the towel wrapped around my hips. Wiping the steam off the glass with my hand, I inspect my body.

Letting the towel drop, I lean against the marble basin. Besides the scars I have on my face and the obligatory "Semper Fi" US Marines tat on the left side of my chest, I am relatively unscathed except for a puckered white mark under one of my ribs. I hate all that shit they show on entertainment channels about soldiers getting shot and then continuing with their lives as if nothing is wrong.

If you get shot, you're looking at a minimum of two years of physiotherapy and counseling ahead. It's a devastating injury. Fuck Hollywood for glossing over that. And don't get me started on how ruinous explosions are on the ears and internal organs.

Going out to the balcony after shrugging into one of those white toweling robes, I finish the rest of my coffee staring across at the park.

A flock of birds gets startled by an engine backfiring and goes flapping into the air altogether. Not a single bird sticks it out to face down the enemy. That instinctual flight reflex has to be trained out of people too.

I find myself continually looking at my phone, worried in case Alice texts to let me know Edie has put the kibosh on my plan. When it doesn't happen, I pull on my jeans and a clean white T-shirt and take the elevator down to the basement. Two minutes later, I've got my leather biker's jacket on and I'm riding my Harley-Davidson Road King up Fifth Avenue. I have all the permits to use two-wheel transport in the city.

I see Edie clock me the moment she steps outside. Taking off my helmet, I beckon her over. She's looking somber this morning.

As much as I can take Jack in small doses, her sad face makes me want to ride to his building and kick his butt.

"You look like a movie poster sitting astride your bike like that, Sterling," Edie says, protecting her eyes from the sun with her hand as she stands on the sidewalk to chat with me. "I've only seen pictures of Harleys before." Sliding her hand over the chrome, she nods her head with appreciation.

"You're full of compliments this morning, Edie."

She acknowledges my remark. "That I am. I gather you're here because of Alice's text?"

I've already unlocked the spare helmet that I had couriered overnight. "Less chat, more action," I hold the helmet out to her. Then I lean down and lift the spare leather jacket I have folded up in front of me. "Come on. Hop on."

After helping her to fasten the strap under her chin, I wait for Edie to settle herself into the seat comfortably before speaking. Her helmet knocks against mine with surprise when she hears my voice coming from inside. "If you want to stop at any time, Edie, just say so. We're going to the helipad, so this shouldn't take long."

"You can hear me?" Her voice is squeaky with shock, but also excited.

"Yeah. These helmets have been fitted with receivers and mics."

Thirty minutes later, we're at the Downtown Manhattan Heliport at the East River Piers. Edie's long, blond hair falls out of the helmet like liquid metal, but I can tell from her expression that she's enjoying herself.

"Do you like the bike? Or would you like to continue by car once we land the helicopter?" I don't want that sad look to come back on her face. I don't want her to regret following her heart either.

"Bike, please!" She grins, shaking that gorgeous hair of hers to knock out the tangles. "It gives me a whole new perspective on things."

We don't talk during the helicopter ride. Edie is too busy looking down out of the window and making "wow" noises into her mouthpiece. I call ahead and have another tour bike waiting for us. It's only an hour's ride to Mount Olive, but I don't want her to get jolted on a narrow seat.

The first thing Edie asks once we've cleared the main roads is what I do for a living. "I know all this fun you're giving me isn't courtesy of Jack, Sterling! So, how do you get access to such cool toys?"

I want to tell her, I really do, but I think it will sound like I'm showing off. Or even worse, rubbing her face in my wealth. "My friend, Dan Marshall, believes that fast, easily accessible travel is the future."

"Well, please tell your friend Dan that he's right!"

The way she says it makes me glad I lied. The bike eats up the miles as the scenery changes from New Jersey suburbs to green trees and thick bushes, indicating Wildlife Management

Areas. As I slow the bike down, I flick up the visor and take off my Bobster Fat Boy sunglasses.

"We should be coming up to the spot right about now...," I tell Edie.

"What spot?" she asks me, genuinely curious as to what's going on. "I thought we were test-driving this fast, easily accessible travel gear for Dan?"

Why does she always manage to get me laughing? "No, well... maybe. Actually, I'm here to bring you to your first job interview."

As I see the turnoff, she speaks loudly into the mic. "Hey! Wait! Stop, man! I'm wearing jeans and a T-shirt, for fucks' sake!"

Bringing the bike to a halt, I crane my neck around, hoping she can see from my profile that I'm not joking. "Edie. These people are my friends. They don't give a fuck what you're wearing. Please let me take you to the interview."

Her voice is panicked. "Sterling, please. The only makeup I have on is mascara. I don't even have a domestic microchip for my phone yet. They'll think I'm a throwaway, just like Jack does!"

"If anyone calls you a throwaway within hearing distance of me, Edie, I'll kick their asses. You are dedicated to saving animals. They will want you on their side because you are the best advocate an animal could ever have."

She huffs and scoffs with irritation, but she allows me to continue. I pull up outside a small shop front overlooking Budd Lake in Mount Olive. I'm bracing myself for another scolding, but it never comes. Edie sees the sign above the door.

The Wildlife Conservation Organization.

Swinging the helmet off her head with one joyful movement, Edie hunkers down to lock the wheel. When she stands up, I see tears of gratitude in her eyes. "I really hope I get this job, Sterling. Thank you. Thank you, more than words can say."

Well, I have no comeback to that. Jerking my thumb towards the door, I tell her to go in. "They're expecting you."

With so much of our workload coming from Africa, I make it my duty to keep informed about every ongoing conservation effort in the African continent. Poaching is eradicating species at an alarming rate even though safari tourism is a main source of income for many people.

In a country where crop and food production are paramount, feeding people is more important than saving animals from extinction. Not only that, but most administrations are simply worn down from the never-ending fight. Cape fur seals are dying by the thousands on the Southwest African coast, and no one knows why, but nor are they prepared to investigate the problem.

After eleven of his rhinoceroses were killed in rapid succession by a plague of poachers, a rhinoceros conservationist farmer committed suicide. The ultimate action when it comes to giving up.

But for a small handful of people dedicated to fighting poaching and illegal hunting, Africa would be a vast landscape of domesticated herds and no wildlife. What those colonial trophy hunters started two hundred years ago has mutated into a ravenous beast as wealthy idiots compete to kill exotic animals so they can mount the heads on their walls.

I know Edie's dream is to continue being one of the people fighting back on behalf of the animals. And I know she'll get this job. All she needs is a little push in the right direction to put her on the pathway to financial independence.

Edie comes out after twenty minutes, looking downcast. I run up the last few stairs to meet her. "What happened? If they are worried about your work permit and social security number, I can sort that out right now."

Raising her eyes to mine, Edie allows me to see the naughty triumph shining in them. "Ha! Got you! I did get the job, oh ye of little faith! You are looking at the official fundraiser and charity event organizer for the Wildlife Conservation Organization South African Division! Now all I have to do is find somewhere to stay close by. I am so looking forward to telling Jack, you would not believe it."

"I'm looking forward to doing that too." We walk back to the bike together. "Well, seeing as we're here, why don't we have a look at a few apartments? Maybe some car rentals?"

The words prick her bubble of happiness, and the joy fades a little bit. "The logistics frighten me, Sterling. I have to apply for so many things. I don't know anything about green cards and permanent residence applications. I don't even have a bank card in this country. All I have is the job offer."

I can't help it. I have to kiss her. Pulling her closer and tilting up her face towards mine, I ask Edie the question burning in my mind. "Do you trust me?"

She opens her mouth and I know a sassy re-mark closely followed by a rejection is bub-bling just under the surface, but Edie stops to think first. The gap stretches out for several heartbeats, but I'm not complaining. She's in my arms, accepting my close embrace.

"Yah Sterling. I do trust you. You've brought me this far, so I don't see any reason not to."

We kiss. It's only a light brush of the lips, but it's everything I hoped it to be.

"And do you forgive me?"

Chapter 14: Edie

My inner struggle is real. There's young Edie at the back of my mind telling me to stand strong and torture Sterling some more. But adult, mature Edie succumbs to his gallant charm. At least until he proves me wrong for trusting him, I really want the New Improved Sterling to be the real deal.

I have to tilt my head quite far back for him to kiss me. I'm wearing tekkies, which means he towers above me by a good eight inches. It's not a deep kiss, just a sweet caress when his mouth brushes against mine.

Still, it has so much repressed tension behind it, that I can almost taste the sexual frisson we have together. I feel his arms tighten around my waist and I know he's waiting patiently for my answer. I'm tired of fighting my intense desire to fuck Sterling again.

"I forgive you, Sterling." I breathe the words into his mouth as he lowers his head down to kiss me again, and this time it's a real kiss. His firm mouth slots over my upper lip and gives it a very gentle suck before changing to my lower lip for a tantalizing nibble.

There's no doubt that this man has some kind of a hold over me. Physically. As the blood rushes to my clit and my pussy gears up for fucking, I can hear a small voice at the back of my mind.

You're in dangerous territory now, Girly-oh. You better believe it. This is your best friend's brother we're talking about. Can you tightrope walk your way in and out of this?

That aching, desperate, physical side of me wins. One kiss is all it takes to drive me over the edge.

He takes my hand and guides me back to the motorbike where we kiss some more before our helmets put an end to it. One short ride later, we pull into a motel courtyard. I don't bother getting off the bike as Sterling runs inside and books a room.

The motel is typical of what's on offer once the big city gets left behind. Stand-alone bungalows with a parking space out front and a bedroom-bathroom combo inside. The room's interior is basic early Noughties decor.

A dark-brown blanket with a turned-down white sheet, and one of those strange decorative throws draped over the foot of the bed. An armchair in the corner next to the phone-side table and some local attractions brochures laid out on a round wooden tray. Two reading lamps bolted onto the headboard.

Sterling throws two bathroom kits he bought at reception onto the double bed. He looks at me.

"You can use the bathroom first, Edie."

Giving him a nervous smile, I move to the end of the room where I find a neat, white-tiled shower and basin. I'm hesitant to touch myself down there in case I set off some kind of a chain reaction and start coming. After using the toilet for a pee, I open the kit and use the scented wet disposable towel to freshen up.

I clean my teeth, staring at my reflection in the rusty-edged bathroom cabinet mirror. I'm really going to do this because I really want to have sex with Sterling Lewis again. It's as simple as that.

I sit in the armchair and wait for him to come out of the shower. My right knee is bouncing up and down as I bang my heel up and down on the floor. My fingers are knotted together as I wring my hands.

He comes out with only a towel on. I wish he wasn't so jacked because I'm absolutely overwhelmed at my first look at Sterling without his clothes. Nervously, I point to his heart.

"Nice tattoo. I was thinking of getting one, you know, but—"

It's useless. Without champagne and the highly strung nerves of a woman tasting freedom for the first time, I'm back to being Little Edie Kruger from the Safari Lodge. I struggle to make eye contact with him, but when I look down, I can see the long, thick outline of Sterling's cock underneath the towel.

Covering my face with my hands, I hunch my shoulders. "It's easier doing this during an up-graded flight for some reason, Sterling. My in-hibitions were lower. I'm... I'm shy."

Stepping to the jacket he left hanging at the door, he takes out his phone. Oh God! Is he calling me a cab? No. He puts on some soothing ambient music, soft enough so that we can hear each other talk, but loud enough to drown out the awkward silence.

Next, he draws the drapes, plunging the room into twilight. Then he fiddles with the HVAC and a warm breeze begins to filter into the air.

"How's that?" he wants to know, hopping into bed after pulling down the sheet, and keeping the towel around his waist. "Daytime sex can be a bit of both—daunting and exciting at the same time, don't you think?"

I nod. He looks as good as a box of chocolates waiting for me to unwrap him lying on the bed with his arms locked behind his head. Without taking my eyes off him, I remove the leather jacket, slowly followed by my jeans and T-shirt.

I see his breath catch as I stand up. I'm wearing a padded white lace bra and matching panties. The peach-colored drapes across the window turn my skin a soft golden hue. This is what true sex is all about. No alcohol, no forbidden transient anonymity, and no barriers.

Summoning up all my courage, I unhook my bra and let it fall. Despite the ambient HVAC, my nipples tighten with the change of temperature. Instinctively, I rub them to loosen the hard puckering.

The towel fabric strains as Sterling's cock automatically responds to me touching myself. Gaining confidence, I slide my hand down into my panties, not hiding the fact that I am fingering my clit, using the wetness from my pussy for lubrication. Then we make eye contact, and my inhibitions fall away.

"Get over here," he growls, loosening the towel, getting ready to expose that part of himself that I desperately need to feel inside me.

Stepping out of my panties, I crawl over the bed to get to him. Hooking one finger under the towel, I yank it down. His rampant penis rears up, rock-hard, glistening, and dripping with pre-ejaculate. Using my fingertip, I dab the transparent fluid, slathering it around his knob.

I want to jack him off a bit, but he clamps his hand around mine. "Too much. I'll come, and when I do, I want to be inside you."

I am beyond excited at the prospect of our naked bodies sliding against one another. The thought of feeling him slowly inch himself inside my tight, wet pussy is getting me all edgy too.

"Maybe it's best if we get that out of the way first," I whisper as he climbs on top of me. "So that we can explore more afterward."

"Beautiful and genius," he murmurs gruffly in my ear as he kisses my neck. "But you already knew that."

It's the way he says it that makes it so sexy. How can Sterling manage to build up my ego so well, all the while as he pushes his engorged cock deeper into me? I love the sensation as my sheath envelopes his throbbing girth.

I'm close. He knows the signs well by now. The way I moan softly, close my eyes, and frown. Why I love Sterling fucking me is that my orgasms seem to crash over me like a big wave; I don't have to concentrate or block out interfering thoughts. All I have to do is give myself over to the enormous experience.

We come at the same time because who wouldn't? The length of his cock seems to tease and tickle a part deep inside me. It's in sync with my hidden crevasse and I can feel his knob expand as spunk explodes out of it.

The music fades and the light dims as my orgasmic ripples increase, maintain, and then fade. I'm shook. And for that one brief moment, I'm in love.

Sterling moves to lie beside me so that we can chat face-to-face. Fulfilling my fantasies, he lets me run my right hand over his skin and body as we talk. Occasionally, I drop my hand to cradle his balls or make his cock stiffen again, so our conversation is, by necessity, interrupted by sex—lots and lots of sex.

"Tell me about your life. Not the boring stuff. The incidents that led up to you running away." He isn't being nosy. It's almost as if Sterling is gathering intel.

Lying on my back, I stare up at the ceiling. Life with Koos seems so very far away now.

"Koos was my first boyfriend. You know my mom and dad. They are so strict. No dances, clubbing, smoking, drinking. You name it and I couldn't do it. It was because they treasured me and stepped up to teach me the value of my purity when I was still too young to realize how special it is."

Sterling hugs me tight and lets me run my fingers over the hard pectoral muscles of his chest, curling the black ink of his tattoo. "You are special, with or without your virginity, Edie," he growls in a deep voice.

"I know." I sigh, shifting so that I can drape my leg over him. "But I'm grateful I reached twenty years old without being diddled by dirty old men or some clueless man-child. And don't get me started on how much my schoolfriends regret being drunk-fucked by random dudes from the disco when they were teens. But my innocence—no, wait. Maybe I should describe it as naivety—set me up to meet someone like Koos."

I let out the saga of me and Koos like someone lancing a septic wound. We dated for a year. When I graduated and got my first job as an intern at an anti-animal cruelty organization, I moved in with him.

When I first met him, Koos played rugby for his university. He was built like a brick shithouse; with the fair hair and skin many members of the Afrikaner race are born with. It was his dream to play rugby professionally, but a torn cruciate ligament put an end to his dreams.

With nothing in his future to look forward to, Koos began to drink. His impressive physique and blond handsomeness faded faster than a sub-Saharan sunset. Instead of seeing the writing on the wall when he started taking his frustrations out on me, I played the martyr card and "stuck by my man."

I ignored the fact that his parents scorned me because my mom was English, and I had been raised speaking that language at home. I closed my eyes to Koos's aggression and violence. It was always my fault for doing so well in my career while all he had to do was strut around his parents' vineyard and make sure the grapes were harvested on time.

"If you want to know what it felt like, Sterling, it was a bit like a rabbit with its paw stuck in a bear trap. You can either chew it off or starve. Or wait for the bear. So, I ran."

His chest rumbles as he comments on my narrow escape. "I figure it's time for you to stop running and rest with me awhile, Edie."

We've fucked so much; I can't move without leaking. Sterling is cool with sleeping for a few hours. "We can take a shower in the morning, and then I think we should try some oral. I really want to lick you out. I've been dreaming about tasting that sweet snatch of yours since forever."

That gets my interest. "Ooh, I've never done that before. And can I lick you too?"

He chuckles, already half-asleep. Slipping his arm under my neck, we nestle together. "Just you wait, girl. I plan on showing you much more than that."

Chapter 15: Sterling

I'm up with the birds, feeling dapper, dashing, and downright fantastic. Turning onto my side, I watch Edie sleep. Smudges of black mascara are smeared over her eyelids. It makes me smile to see how blonde her lashes are underneath it.

She's still my Little Edie from the Safari Lodge once the layers of black mascara are gone.

Gently sliding my arm out from under her head, I go shower. Despite the fact that we fucked half a dozen times last night, I am raring to go again whenever I think of Edie lying naked on the bed on the other side of the door.

Leaving my underwear hanging in the shower—they are stained multiple times from pre-ejaculation, and I had to rinse them out—I pull on my jeans and boots and shrug into my leather jacket, zipping it up as I step outside. Thirty minutes later, I'm back with a paper bag of coffee and muffins.

Edie's looking blearily at the door when I step inside. "Rise and shine, sweetheart," delving into the bag, I take out a muffin and coffee for her. "One percent milk, isn't it?"

Sticking up one finger in the air, Edie replies in a husky, tired voice. "Hold that thought, please."

I watch as she staggers out of the bed, heading for the shower. Her shoulder blades stick out like angel wings, but her ass looks as delicious as always—like two small apples I want to take a bite out of. When she was riding my cock last night, I noticed that I could span her waist with my hands.

The skinny, self-conscious little girl is still hiding underneath that fragile coating of womanhood. I would protect this woman with my life.

Coming out of the shower, Edie heads straight for the muffin and coffee. Indicating towards the cup as she takes large gulps, she makes these cute, appreciative noises with her throat.

"Mmh, mmh," she sighs as she drains the cup and gives me a thumbs-up. "That's so good, Sterling. Thank you."

All we have had to sustain us since we bolted ourselves up in this motel is water and a box of Tic-Taks I found in one of my jacket pockets. I'm about to ask Edie if she's feeling like exploring the oral option when there's a knock on the door. There's no way it would be the management at this time in the morning. But I already know who will be waiting for me outside.

Waiting until Edie has hidden her head under the sheet, I crack open the door.

"I brought these over as soon as I could, Lewis," the man who is acting as my courier tells me. "The work visa is temporary, but the Social Security number is permanent. I've linked the bank card—" I cut him off there. I don't want Edie to know that I've linked her bank card to one of my business accounts. She has enough issues with financial independence without me making it worse.

"Thanks, Clint. I'll make the deposit into our friend's offshore account this afternoon."

I trained Clint myself. He's an accomplished undercover operative, with countless missions under his belt. And here I am sending him to a politician's door at home last night to sort out Edie's work visa for her.

But when she sticks her head out from under the sheets when the door closes, all I can think is "money well spent."

Unzipping my jacket and throwing it down on the floor, I hook my thumbs through the belt loops of my jeans and ask her if she wants to fuck again. As I stand at the foot of the bed, I see her eyeing the sharp line of my oblique abdominals that angle down towards the root of my cock. It's like an arrow pointing to what she's going to get if her answer is yes.

Never running out of ways to surprise me, Edie asks if I can come first. Standing on one leg to pull off my boot, I ask her why.

"Well, I'm a bit sensitive down there. I feel sore and bruised. It'll be easier for me to come if you do first. Then you won't be so... it won't feel so much like an iron fist pumping me."

I tell her we can work something out. Lying back, I let her experiment sucking my cock. She's scared of hurting me at first, but I let her know I like it wild and rough. Soon, she's sucking my knob and licking my shaft like a hungry expert.

It gives me the perfect view of her tip-tilted breasts and the soft curve of her ass as she kneels. I could stare at Edie all day, and never get tired of doing it. I could fuck her all night, and never get bored. Add that to the incredibly heightened sense of protection I feel whenever I think of her, and there's the strong possibility that I might be in love.

I warn her that I'm about to shoot my load and she watches my spunk with fascination. The moment my spasming finishes, Edie mounts me, grinding my semi-hard cock into her with a satisfied moan.

Rocking slowly, tipping her hips forward so that her clit is in close contact with my manscaped pubic hair, she closes her eyes to block out my gaze. It's not shutting me out. She needs to concentrate to come.

I adore the way her fingers grip my chest as the pleasure peaks inside her. "Oh, oh, oh, yes...." I grab her ass and help her crush her pussy against me. She falls across my chest like an angel with its wings clipped as the throes of ecstasy subside.

We lie together like that for a long while, drifting in and out of sleep, despite the caffeine jolt from the coffee.

"Let's talk about the future." I open up the topic the best way I can. Stirring, Edie slides off my hips and falls onto the bed beside me.

"I have to look for a place to live close to work. I've got all of summer and most of fall to save up for a car. I can walk to and from work until then," is Edie's tired reply.

I poke her upper arm to wake her up. "No, I want to know about us. I know we've skipped over the dating part, but—"

I'm about to say "I want to lock this thing down. I want us to be exclusive. I want you all to myself." But I get interrupted by a specific call on my phone. Damn! Pushing the sheets down, I go into the bathroom.

"This better be good, Dan," I growl into the receiver. "I'm booked off for another week."

"That won't fly, Marine," Dan's voice rasps into my ear. He took a wicked punch from the butt of an AK-47 assault rifle to the throat when he was a jarhead. It totally fucked up his voice box. "I gave you fair warning. Our contact in East Europe needs you to retrieve collateral on a five-billion-dollar loan from his dear friend in Northwest Africa. Fraser will run counterpoint. Clint is due some R & R."

I'm about to say that Clint is not taking some well-earned rest and recreation at all. He's actually running around trying to sort out how to extend Edie Kruger's holiday visa with one of our pet senator's help. "When?" That's the only question I say out loud.

"Bird's waiting for you at the heliport. Clint's outside your little shack-up to give you a lift there. You honestly didn't think you could slide a freebie past me without me noticing, did you? I said Clint's due some R&R. He's not actually on it yet, is he?"

That's what Dan calls it when I have sex with a woman outside of my job—a freebie. Even though Dan is my business partner, he's old school when it comes to vulnerabilities and weak points. And that's what he calls lovers and girlfriends. If there's anyone in a soldier's life who can be used to emotionally blackmail him, then he's no good to our organization.

Holding back the anger I feel boiling inside me, I remind myself that I know the rules. Hell, I wrote the fucking rules! But that was back when I was a cold-hearted son of a bitch who shot a young girl's miniature antelope in cold blood.

"Right. Tell him I'll be out in ten."

I get a chance to see my face in the steam-rusted mirror above the basin. Yep. I'm officially pissed. I do a breathing exercise before ducking out. Green air in, red air out. Repeat until the rage has gone.

I've got to get my head back in the game. One lapse of shrewd judgment, one second of broken concentration, and five billion dollars worth of an international deal might trickle away.

"Edie," I begin, laying five hundred-dollar bills on the nightstand, "I have to split. Take an Uber back to Manhattan. If your app doesn't work, get the clerk at reception to help you."

Sitting on the edge of the bed next to her, I spread the paperwork Clint spent the night preparing on the sheet. "Okay. Pay attention."

Scooching her body so that she can lean against the headboard, Edie rubs her eyes, spreading even more mascara over her lids. "What's going on? Has there been an emergency?"

I don't waste my breath trying to explain it to her. It will only make me sound as if I'm cranking some sorry story out of my ass, anyway. "This is your Social Security card. It's already been signed, so don't worry about that."

Her thin little hand grabs hold of my arm, but I dare not look at her. "Please wait for me to get ready, Sterling. I promise I won't take long. I want to go with you."

Shaking my head firmly, I continue. "This is your bank card. Download the bank app and register the details I have printed out for you here so you can bank online. Which reminds me. Here is a new microchip for your phone. These phone deets are for the contract. Don't lose any of the paperwork. Or at least, try not to."

Getting up, I step into my denims. Edie is completely bewildered at the sudden change in me. "Who was that on the phone, Sterling? Tell me!"

Ignoring her, I pull the T-shirt over my torso and run my fingers through my hair. "Don't forget what I said about the Uber. I don't want you stuck out here. Remember to upload your contacts onto the cloud before you change out the chips."

She gives a soft huff as she swings her feet onto the floor and starts looking around for her clothes. "So, all I get for breakfast is a coffee, a muffin, and a fuck before you fuck off and leave me here, Sterling? Is that it?"

I'm backing towards the door as I reply. "Please don't think about it like that, Edie. I have to go, but I will carry the memory of what happened here with me." Shit. Is it my imagination, or is my voice cracking with emotion? It's coming out hoarse and stressed as if leaving her now is tearing me up inside.

I want to ask her to wait for me. I want Edie to say she'll be my girl. The urge to spill my guts about how much she means to me burns a hole in my chest.

But I say nothing because that's how I've been trained. My instincts kick in and tell me that I've gone soft, and the enemy will eat me alive once they find out.

Edie's hands are shaking as she hops into her denims, pulling the white baby T-shirt over her pert breasts. Flipping her hair out from under the collar, she turns to say goodbye.

"I can't believe I allowed you to do this to me again, Sterling." With her hands on her slim hips, Edie confronts me. "This is exactly what you did in Dubai. Business meeting my ass! I know an irate girlfriend checking in when I hear one! Do you think I'm stupid?"

Chapter 16: Edie

Sterling tries to justify his horrible behavior as he makes all the moves of a "fuck and duck."

"Look outside the window, Edie. There's one of my work colleagues standing there. We're taking the bikes back to the heliport together because it's an emergency."

Shaking my head, I go to wash my face in the basin with cold water, all the time speaking through the icy splashes. "So, let me come back with you. Don't let me do the walk of shame back to Fifth Avenue without you, Sterling. Please." I'm struggling to keep my voice reasonable, but it's hard to stop that note of suspicion creeping in.

Patting my face with the towel, when I go back into the bedroom Sterling has his arms folded across his chest and his black look is back. "Choose to believe me or not, Edie. If I can't change your mind from the hysterical conclusion you have reached because I have to leave now, I give up."

Like every single woman who has ever existed on the planet, I try to hurt him with my words. "Go! Go, then! I don't care. If you think you can treat me like a motel ho just because you made me come with a couple of two-penny fucks, I have news for you."

It's like I slammed a door in his face. His face goes blank, showing no emotion. "We'll pick things up when I get back, Edie. I can't handle you when you're like this. Goodbye—and good luck with your new job. You'll be the most successful fundraiser the organization has ever seen. I know it."

And just like that, he's gone.

I can't help myself. I run to the window and watch him leave. He looks spectacular as he shrugs into his jacket and the T-shirt lifts up to expose the angular sharpness of his lower stomach muscles slanting down his slim hips. Those fancy black sunglasses of his go on as he chats to the other man who's already straddling a motorbike.

Once his helmet is on, they rev the motorbike engines a few times and then back out of the parking lot. I lift my hand to wave goodbye, but he doesn't look back before the two bikes join the early morning traffic. As the loud pop and splutter of engine noise fades away, I sit down on the edge of the bed.

It seems best for me to sit and stare out into nothing for a while. My thoughts are utter chaos as I take in the rumpled sheets, five-hundred-dollar notes on the nightstand, and my white lace bra on the floor. A buzzing sound from too little sleep and too much emotion hums in my ears.

I don't know how long I sat like that, but I see the maid and her cart trundling from chalet to chalet as she checks who has the Do Not Disturb sign up. After leaning over to sweep my hair forward so that I can tie it back with the band, I shrug into the leather jacket and head for reception. Every step of crunching gravel hurts my wounded pride.

"Good morning…." I wait to see a smirk of condescension on the clerk's face, but it never comes. That makes me relax a bit. This is a motel, after all. He must be used to mascara-smeared eyes blinking at him through the thick glass. "Can you call me an Uber, please?"

"Sure thing, Ma'am! Right away. Please thank your partner for the very generous tip. Maria says she can take her kids out for supper every night of the week if she wants to."

"Maria?" I'm confused.

The clerk grins and points at the maid's cart. "Maria. The most she's ever gotten is five bucks, so to get a hundred dollars really made her day. Like I said, please thank your partner."

I was going to make a scoffing noise, but now I can't. It seems as if Sterling is kind to everyone else except me today. "Do you know how much an Uber will be to Fifth Avenue, please?" The clerk shows me the price on the app, and I go outside to wait in the parking lot.

I'm silent all the way to Alice's apartment. I feel like a heel. All I did last night was flick her a "wink" emoji and then tell her I would be back the following day.

Well, here I am, doing the walk of shame on my own, heading back, trying to think of the best way to answer my best friend's questions about me and her brother.

Fortunately, Jack is in his office when I step out of the elevator and the kids are on playdates. Alice looks up when she hears the doors slide open, but my expression shuts down any teasing remark she might have planned.

"Sterling left for work?" Her voice is kind when I come to sit next to her. Reaching for my hand, she gives it a comforting squeeze.

"Yah." I stand up. "I'm going to have a bath."

***

He's been gone for three months. I wake up every morning and tell myself that I don't mind, but it doesn't help heal the hurt.

My work consumes me, helping me recover from a bad case of the post-fuck blues. I try reminding myself that all it was ever meant to be was sex, but the memory of Sterling and me lies under my skin like a throbbing splinter. Although I don't want to admit it to Alice, I'm happier now that I have a place of my own.

It might not be much—a cute little one-bedroom place above a sporting goods shop in a strip mall—but it's private and about as far away from Sterling's family as I can get. But every hot summer night, I lie on top of the bed, naked, with the electric fan blowing on my goose-bumped skin, and all I can think about is the man who took me to heaven and hell so fast, that it left my head spinning.

Work is my salvation. I walk to the office every weekday morning and hit the phones first thing. The conversation with donors always goes something like this.

"Hi there. Thank you for taking my call. I'm calling from the WCO. I got your number from our list of kind donors. Would you be interested in buying some seats for our annual fundraising dinner?"

And the answer is always the same. "Where are you from with that accent?" I always take it and run with it. "I'm from Southern Africa. Rhinos are being poached into extinction. Elephants are running out of habitat. Human life is being prioritized over animal life, and rightfully so, but the African wildlife need their voices to be heard before it's too late."

After one month of planning and phoning, I have sold enough seats and tables for us to book a really nice rooftop and events room in Tribeca. My two workmates, Lizzie MacLean and Juan Valdez, start to get excited as the next stage of fundraising comes along—finding weekend getaways, boy toys, tech, jewelry, and other freebies to auction off during the event.

Before I leave the office Wi-Fi connection, I text my parents. Hi, guys, I hope you are both well. Lizzie got a Picasso etching for the auction today. I can't believe how generous people are when it comes to charity fundraisers. Juan says I must wait until we do Los Angeles. He says they are even more generous there. But it seems to be just a drop in the ocean. Love you lots and miss you stax, Edie.

I wait for my mom's reply. She's a real late-night owl and always stays up reading.

Hi, darling daughter. Please don't forget to try and get some donors interested in giving money to the lodge. (Three prayer emojis). We offer the best safaris in the Western Cape, but if we want to keep doing so, we need more fences, infrared CCTV, tagging equipment, and rangers. Try to keep a low profile over there. Don't stick your head above the parapets! Koos is on the warpath. Love, Mom.

Fuck Koos. Fuck Sterling. Fuck all men. I have the rest of my life in front of me to find the perfect man... and who knows, maybe I'll meet someone nice at the charity event.

***

Leaving Juan to handle the auction, I stand by the cocktail bar and look out over the room of ultra-sophisticated diners and donors. The donations and pledges poured in tonight, and I'm feeling very positive about our bottom line after the venue and caterers have been paid for.

Lizzie wanted to keep a widescreen in the corner showing rolls of dead rhinos, elephants, and lions, but I put my foot down on that. These people know, and they don't need to be reminded that the doomsday clock is ticking for wild animals in Africa. Let them have a good time and we will loosen their pocketbooks that way.

A tall, well-built blond-haired man comes to stand next to me. He offers to buy me a drink. I'm not even tempted, dammit! Sterling's face and image still haunt my best dreams.

Shaking my head and giving him a smile of denial, I shift away a few feet and continue listening to the auction.

My dress is a cheap polyester knockoff, bought out of the bargain bin in one of the clothing stores at the strip mall. Black, tight fitting, and with three garish gold gilt buttons on the bodice, I'm not really in the mood for any one of these beautiful people to get a closer look at my clothes.

Giving a little wave to Alice and Jack's table, I pretend not to notice Jack's work colleagues beckoning me over. Leaving Jack to raise his paddle and bid, Alice comes to stand with me, shaking her head when the server asks for her drink order.

"I'm impressed, Girly-oh," she mutters in a low voice. "Mr. Hot Blond on my left hasn't stopped checking you out throughout the entire event. Are you going to return his smoldering stare or not?"

We giggle together. Not much has changed since Alice and I were tweens—at least as far as how we see men is concerned.

"He asked if he could buy me a drink, but I said no. He's really not my type."

Alice gives me one of her looks. "You mean he's not Sterling."

I pout. "Ag, please. That chubby dude with the expensive suit over there has also been check-ing me out all night. He's not Sterling either. I'm just not in the mood for all that male-female chitchat. That's all."

The chubby middle-aged man in the expensive suit must have seen us looking at him. Putting his glass down on the wall ledge with a firm hand, he comes walking towards Alice and me.

"Ms. Edie Kruger. Are you the organizer of this event?"

I give him my best smile. He wants to make a donation. "I hope you had a good evening, sir. Please use the donation machines. All you need to do is tell the operative how much you would like to donate and then tap your card. And thank you for your kindness."

He doesn't move, staring at me with eyes that tell me his heart is closed for business. "I represent Mr. Koos Van der Hoff and Mr. and Mrs. Piet Van der Hoff, his parents."

He shoves an A4-size brown envelope into my hands. "Consider yourself served. You are to pay all court costs arising from this breach of contract suit. If you don't make good on the loss of earnings, and costs arising from, the wedding cancellation that my clients experienced because of your unannounced departure, you will be held accountable in court."

Alice's face is gaping with shock. All I feel is cold dread. "I don't have any money," I say the words out aloud. The tall, blond standing next to me seems to be paying close attention.

"Are you not one of the co-owners of the Safari Lodge Adventures?" The chubby man's beady eyes are drilling holes into me.

"Yes. But I don't derive any income from it—my parents...."

"Then your assets in South Africa will be seized. Or you could return to your—I can only describe him as exceedingly tolerant, patient, and good-hearted—fiancé, Ms. Kruger, and he will consider your debt forgiven. Good evening."

Chapter 17: Sterling

This is how business is conducted in Africa. I have a bandanna wrapped around my head to protect it from the sun and serious SunGod sunglasses strapped to protect my eyes from dust and glare. I was offered a helmet by the guy who hooked me up with the Jeep but declined.

No helmet is going to protect me from an armor-piercing bullet shot at mid to long-range. One glorious burst of pink mist and skull fragments, and I'll be history.

I'm not here in Nigeria to deal with rebels and renegades. Their under-the-counter currency is uncut blood diamonds, slaves, and cocaine, and I don't want anything to do with such re-pugnant trade.

I'm here to bring my Eastern European client's offer to a high-ranking Nigerian politician. But secrecy demands that I meet him in some hole-in-the-wall shithole in the bush so that there is plausible deniability if the shit hits the fan.

It won't. Not while I'm in charge, but trust is a rare commodity in Africa. So here I am, being jolted around in a borrowed 1948 Willys Jeep, and I haven't seen the inside of a bedroom or shower for six weeks. When my hair began flop-ping in my eyes during the first month, I used some blunt clippers to shave it as close to the skull as I could get.

I can still feel rough tufts when I run my hands over it. I missed more than a spot doing it with-out a mirror. My neck is sore from moving my gaze across the tall, grassed landscape. Finally, barbed-wire fencing gives way to banded walls of bush-cut grass strung between long sticks. This organic fencing structure is called a boma. It keeps goats off the dirt track road.

Vaulting out of the Jeep, I stand for a beat as I tilt my head to touch my ear to first my right shoulder and then the left. I hear the spine bones in my neck click and the tendons creak. Fucking bouncing on dirt roads—motherfucker gets me every time.

I follow my escort into the kraal. This is a traditional grass hut with a sunbaked mud-packed floor. I have to duck my head really low to gain access. Inside the air is dry and relatively cool.

The minister is sitting on a woven grass mat with one of his wives or girlfriends kneeling there to pour me a ceremonial welcome drink—Ògógóró. One of the West African tribes, called the Yoruba, brew it from Raffia palm tree sap, which is fermented and served at room temperature.

With the ceremony out of the way, I wait for the wife to skedaddle so I can chat with the boss man.

"Thank you for agreeing to this meeting, sir. Our mutual friend will place the five billion in holding at the bank in Switzerland. Once the first shipment of oil has arrived at the port, they will release the agreed amount of money—to be continued over the next five years. My associates and I will handle the paperwork and provide safe passage."

The minister wants to avoid transporting the oil through the established pipelines. That means a long, complicated route around the African West Coast with the tankers disguised as cargo ships and a cargo transfer done in international waters. I advise the client about dates. The transaction has to be completed by winter before the North Atlantic close to Arctic Circle waters begin to freeze.

Promises made and hands shaken, I haul ass back to the Jeep. The moment the windscreen is facing Lagos, I turn comms back on and check in with Dan. Only then can I restart my private life. I see I have a few missed calls from Fraser on the satellite phone. I call him back first.

"S'up," I shout into the receiver, over the roar of the engine.

"Hey, it's not looking good. She got busted with a summons. It happened right in front of me. Some lawyer fuck. Call your sister ASAP."

Thank you, Fraser. Don't mind if I do. But all I say into the phone is "Right."

I sleep at the back of the Jeep, next to the tripod-mounted Heckler & Koch MP5K on the flatbed next to me and my Uzi set to semi-automatic short fire bursts. I set up a laser point perimeter all around me first, and dine on cold, re-saturated noodles. Blocking out the sound of lion grunts echoing off the hillsides, I manage three hours of sleep before dawn wakes me.

Getting close to Lagos, I call Alice, forcing my voice to sound relaxed and carefree. "Hey, sis. How's things on your side?"

Alice lets rip. "Oh, Sterling. Thank God! Where have you been? These disappearing tricks of yours have got to stop. Edie is talking about going back to Koos again! After all I did to get her out of his meaty clutches, he goes and threatens her parents. Mr. and Mrs. Kruger gave Edie one-third of the safari lodge when she turned twenty-one, and that creep is threatening to take it. Breach of contract, and shit like that!"

I have to close my eyes. I have a throbbing headache from the heat and lack of sleep. I really want to go in guns blazing and take out Edie's fiancé once and for all, but I can't. If I do that, then Dan will get wind of how much Edie means to me.

"Thanks, Alice. Tell Jack and the kids I say hi. I'll come back via Cape Town—see if I can't talk a little sense into him."

My sister tells me that I'm an answer to prayer before disconnecting. Our family has never been big with goodbyes.

I flick a text to one of my independent connections in Cape Town. Gerrit. Meet me at CTI. I will send you my arrival time. Bring anon rental transport and one kit. Hire a rental car using one of our anonymous business cards and bring heat.

After disassembling the weapons and ditching the Jeep in one of our storage lockups, I sleep-walk to the first-class lounge. Then I use the shower facilities and fall asleep in one of the armchairs.

***

I use the Wi-Fi in first class to send Gerrit more info. He must dig up everything he can on Koos Van der Hoff. Where we can find him one hour after my landing time. Whether he carries a weapon with him. And if he hangs around with anyone who might be encouraged to come to his aid if someone is beating the living crap out of him.

Fifteen minutes after landing, I see Gerrit waiting for me outside first-class security clearance. He is ready to debrief me. Gerrit Meyer is a good soldier.

"Howzit, Sterling. Good to see you again." He hands me a fact sheet, which I read on the way to the SUV. Gerrit nods to the man sitting behind the wheel of a discreet white SUV at the Drop and Go. The guy gets out and nods back before disappearing into the parking lot stairwell. He was guarding the firearm.

I picked up some new clothes at Duty Free. A khaki-colored T-shirt with a small African-centric logo on the left-hand breast pocket, thick khaki bush pants, and hiking boots. It's winter, but it's hot as Hades outside. Back go on my

SunGod glasses as the car joins the traffic heading northeast.

"He's out in Stellenbosch." Gerrit points to a signpost as we flash past on the left. I can handle a right-hand drive steering wheel and traffic, but I want to listen to the debrief. Gerrit continues. "At this time of the day, he'll be sitting down to lunch. He's moved back in with his parents—given up the house they planned to live in after the wedding."

I grunt to let him know I'm listening. "Sounds like Mr. Koos Van der Hoff isn't that keen to get Edie back. He'd have to buy another house if she did."

Gerrit shakes his head. "Nah. He's still hot for her. Or at least he wants his friends to continue believing that she's still hot for him. The man can't stand the idea of his 'klein meisie kind'—that's 'little girl child,' by the way—having her independence and humiliating him at the same time. He's out for blood."

"He's going to get it." We continue the rest of the journey in silence. I don't like throwing my weight around. To me, violence is something

I use as a last resort to get my point across. It would be exhausting for me to walk around with the knowledge that I'm a lethal weapon all the time. So, I shelve it until I need it. Words before deeds, and all that.

The drive to Stellenbosch is scenic and beautiful—all sloping green hills with yellowing grapevine leaves fluttering in the warm wind. Lots of bends in the road and eroding tarmac as nature tries to reclaim it. The occasional guinea fowl runs out into the lane as the vehicle slides past.

Gerrit and I chat about the differences between American football and rugby, cricket, and baseball. I tell him that it's not the Atlantic Ocean that divides our countries, but the difference in sport between the colonies.

He flicks on the indicator and the SUV turns into a white-walled entrance with the wine estate's name proclaimed in wrought iron on the arch over the top. Ignoring all the signage that tells us wine tasting hours and where to find the cellars and gift shop, we continue on to the big house.

It's archetypal Dutch architecture: white-painted domed facades and wooden framed windows. Wisteria and grape vines climb the pagoda beams covering the patio. The house is quiet when we get out. No security. Nothing.

"They have guards posted at the public access areas," Gerrit explains, "but nothing in the main house. Security systems only get turned on at night. No portable panic buttons."

I nod and begin walking up the driveway while Gerrit leans with his elbow on the SUV's roof. A maid comes to the door when two large dogs begin barking inside. I already know about the dogs.

"I'm here for Mr. Koos?" I tell the maid. Leaving me outside on the patio, I hear her calling. "Baas, baas! Daar is 'n man hier om jou te sien." Boss, boss. There is a man here to see you. Crazy grammar to the English ear, but recognizable vocabulary. Afrikaans is a Creole language, after all, a mix of English and Dutch.

The squeak of a chair on flagstone floors and a large shadow blocks out the light in the doorway. Koos Van der Hoff is built like a prize bull at the State Fair. His flat, yellow hair is plastered in a side part across his domed skull. The blood-shot eyes and jowls tell me that he's already started dipping into his wine stash. The big gut drooping over his khaki cargo pants tells me that he loves the meal he must have been in the middle of scarfing down.

I don't hold out my hand. "Mr. Koos Van der Hoff. I was wondering if I could have a word. I'm here as an envoy on behalf of Miss Edie Kruger."

He might look like a half-cut silverback gorilla, but Koos is no dummy. He takes one look in my eyes and knows immediately that I've enjoyed his runaway bride in the Biblical sense.

"You fokking motherfokking—!" He's chewing the words in the same way he was chewing his lunch just a moment ago. Stepping back inside, he screams for the maid to release the hounds. I signal to Gerrit who brings out his rifle.

The command to attack dies in his throat and he tells the maid to forget it, to keep Max and Rex inside. My respect for him increases a tiny amount. You have to respect a man who keeps his dogs safe.

"What the fok do you want, jou bliksem?" He scowls at me, his large hands bunched into fists the size of Christmas hams.

"Your vendetta against Edie ends here, now. And that includes her parents. If I have to come out here again, I won't ask so nice."

He seems to mull my message over. Then he crosses his arms over his chest. I can read the negative body language. I know a challenge is coming.

"You and me. One on one. If you beat me, that's fine. You can call the shots, bru. But if I win, you fok off and leave things to play out."

Backing off the patio, I go to stand in the driveway, making sure the afternoon sun is not in my eyes. I have barely moved to the spot when Koos charges at me. He wants to catch me off guard and bring me down with a tackle. He must outweigh me by a good eighty or ninety pounds. Once I'm down with his weight sitting on top of me, I will lose my mobility, which is all I have to match against someone of his size.

I duck out of the way, like a toreador dodging a charging bull. Koos tramples past but turns on a dime and faces me. Fucking rugby players. They fight like Sherman tanks.

Gerrit stays quiet and respects the rules. I don't want to win this with an assist. I want to win this for Edie.

I want to go back to New York and see her again. I want her to smile and laugh and tell me that everything in her life is coming up roses.

Koos and I circle around one another. The way he holds his fists up with his body at a side angle, not giving me a large target to land a blow, lets me know the man can handle himself. I wait for him to make the first move. Which he does because he doesn't know who I am or what I am capable of.

Lowering into a crouch, he rumbles in for a gut punch, hoping to wind me, and then pops up for an uppercut to the jaw. I step to the side and land a blow on his ear, putting all my height and weight into it.

I step back and watch as the pain and shock hit him. He's disoriented and stumbling, but his pride makes him shake it off and continue. This time, he's cautious. He's also scared. I use it to my advantage.

Flexing my hand to shake off the bruising in my knuckles, I bend my knees and push off my heels, launching myself at him side on. I land a one-two punch to his stomach and in the middle of his chest.

For a moment there, I think old Koos is going to die on me. He folds to the ground, wheezing and gasping, no air pressure getting in or out of his lungs. Then he vomits up his lunch in a violent spew of gunk.

I wait to see if he's coming back up again, giving him a little tap on the ass with my boot.

"We good, Koos?"

Flapping his hand in a futile wave, he curls into the fetal position and lies there on the ground. "Take the bitch. I don't care."

Gerrit sits back down in the SUV and guns the engine. Hopping into the seat beside him, I have only one sentence to say. "Take me back to the airport."

Chapter 18: Edie

I wake up in my little apartment to find an A4-size envelope that has been slid under the door crack. My tummy jumps. The lawyer has found me again.

They know where I work and now, they know where I live. If I don't sort this out, my parents will lose the safari lodge. Koos wants me back, but I know it's not because he loves me. He's always been a sore loser, and while that's an admirable quality when someone plays sport, it makes for a hideous relationship trait.

Giving the ominous envelope the side eye, I make myself some coffee while flicking through messages. The usual optimistic note from Alice about please allowing her to contribute to my legal expenses so that we can fight the bastard together pops up in my alerts. I smile as I read it—my best friend is the last word when it comes to generosity and kindness, but I can't handle Jack's sarcasm.

Another box pops up and lets me know I have a message from my mom.

We just got word the case has been dropped. Is it true? Please don't go back to him, Baba. Nothing is worth a lifetime of misery. I'd rather lose the lodge than have you marry K. Love, Mom xxx

What?! I open the envelope with shaking fingers. Blah, blah, blah, legal jargon I don't understand. After taking a big gulp of coffee, I start reading again, only this time I go slower.

It's true. The Van der Hoffs have dropped their small claim and breach of contract case against me. I am no longer responsible for reimbursing them for the purchase of the engagement ring, wedding costs, canceled honeymoon, and the realtor's commission for the sale of the house.

When I look at the list of financial outlay that went into setting up my new life with Koos, I can better understand the Van der Hoffs' anger towards me. Not only did I publicly humiliate them by running away on the day of the wedding, but my cowardice cost both sets of parents a large amount of wasted time and effort.

No successful insurance claim can get that back. But after another long sip of coffee, I read the breakdown of costs on the spreadsheet stapled to the letter.

Flowers, bridal gown, attendants' dresses, and gifts, booking fees, tux rental, cake, venue, five-course meal. The list goes on and on. Did we really need all of that? Did we even want it? How much of that shit on the list was foisted on us by the wedding planner, and the expectations of those people around us?

How many things on that list are harmful to the environment or just there to enrich the already comfortably well-off players in the thriving bridal business? Throwing the paper onto the kitchen counter with a flick of revulsion, suddenly the entire wedding and bridal indus-

try comes across as incestuous and self-indul-
gent.

Not a single one of those greedy parasites
wanted what was best for me. I can remember
how my eyes would fill with frightened tears as
I was trying on my expensive designer wedding
gown or choosing a cake flavor. No one suggested I see a psychologist or talk to an advisor
who had no stake in the game of love and marriage.

They turned a blind eye to my terror as they
kept their focus on turning a profit. We weren't
proclaiming our love for one another to the
world—we were participating in an ugly display
of status and legal bondage.

Sighing, I throw the letter in the bin and text
my mom. Our nightmare is over. Now, if only I
could get back to my normal state of mind and
stop thinking about Sterling all the time.

I've stopped counting the weeks since he rode
away on his motorbike and never looked back.
Somewhere inside my heart, I know that I can
never be truly happy again—and I hate him for
doing that to me. If it wasn't for the wonderful

sense of satisfaction I get from my job, I would pull the sheets over my head in the morning and continue sleeping.

But not today. Today, I'm going to see my god-daughter, and finally, I have good news to give my friend. The Koos nightmare is over. I can definitely get enthusiastic about that!

It's the weekend, so I know that Alice likes to stay in bed while Jack bops off to work and the kids watch cartoons in the living room. I won't disturb her Kindle binging with a text message. And besides, by the time I arrive at the Upper East Side Fifth Ave apartment, it'll be closer to lunch than breakfast.

After grabbing a quick shower and brushing mascara several times over my lashes, I dress in yoga pants, a T-shirt, a gray hoodie, and my beloved tekkies, and head out for the train station.

***

The concierge greets me like an old friend and calls upstairs to let the kids know it's safe to open the elevator door when the bell rings. By the time I reach the fifteenth floor, Alice is there to welcome me back with my favorite words. "Jack's not at home today!"

We both laugh. As I step into the living room, Noah grins at me over his shoulder and tells me he's going to let his dad know that we are happy he's not at home.

"Ag, Noah, please don't." I play along because I know he likes to tease me. "I just like talking to your mom without Jack around."

Gabby interrupts. "They don't smack talk about Dad, Noah. My godmother hasn't built up an immunity to Dad's corrosive wit yet."

I ask Alice where the kids are picking up their vocabulary when I come back from washing my hands in the restroom. She blames the tutoring. "You're just lucky to catch them on an off day. We've got the kids learning Mandarin and French after school every day. They learn it from their classmates. It's a mixed bunch."

Alice's idea of a "mixed bunch" is anyone living south of E Fifty-Ninth and north of E Ninety-Sixth Streets.

Noah and Gabby say something sassy to their mother in Mandarin, which makes Alice pull a face. "Nice try, guys, but you do realize that an insult has to be understood to be effective, don't you?"

Noah jumps up and starts doing karate kicks all around the room. "I don't need words! Uncle Sterling is going to teach me how to be effective with my fists!"

After rolling her eyes to the ceiling, Alice drags me to her bedroom walk-in closet so that we can choose an outfit for her. "I've booked a sitter so we can do some shopping." She tells me as she lies on the bed to do up her skinny jeans zipper. "I thought we might walk to the park for some brunch?"

That perpetual knot in my tummy does a twist as I remember walking in the park with Sterling. Every time I think of us, it feels like battery acid being injected into my blood. But all I say out loud is "Sounds good. I've been doing most of my clothes shopping locally. One way of dodging marginally higher New York sales tax."

We experiment with a few hairstyles before I give Alice the news. "By the way, I got a letter from that lawyer pushed under my door this morning."

Alice reacts, grabbing my hand as I brush her hair back. "Oh no! They've found out where you live! Those fuc—!"

Patting her shoulder, I continue. "The Van der Hoffs have dropped the case. I'm over the moon. If I hadn't gone back for the court appearance date, they would have issued a warrant for my arrest when I go back to visit my folks or even begun asset seizure. You know how connected Koos's family is."

Alice is thrilled. We chat about how long it will be before I can apply for a credit card and take a vacation. I settle for a mermaid braid hanging down my back and Alice goes for a simple headband to hold the hair off her face.

This is how it has always been during our friendship and nothing—not distance, marriage, college, kids, or family—has ever been able to get in the way of us hanging out together whenever and wherever we can. After kissing the kids goodbye and telling the sitter where the cookies are, we head out.

We order drinks while seated at our table at the Tavern on the Green. Alice brings up the subject first. "You haven't mentioned Sterling since that day he took you for the job interview, Girly-oh..., what gives?"

The acid surges around my system once again. "Umm... nothing. Why?" I give a good poker face when it comes to hiding my emotions. I'm not going to play the game by asking Alice if Sterling is back or if he has been enquiring after me. I... don't... care.

Dunking her cardboard straw up and down her drink until it gets wet and soggy, I can see that Alice is definitely thinking about the best way how to go about picking my brain. "Well, what with Koos trying to get you back or make you pay, I would have thought you'd drop Sterling a message. You do remember when I told you that my brother is good at sorting things out?"

"Yah, but—" I'm not about to deny that Sterling Lewis can be a regular Prince Charming when it comes to damsels in distress. The problem is that he sticks around to fuck the damsel's brains out before going bye-bye. "Yah, however, I need to learn to stand on my own two feet now, friend. I want to live on my own and make my own mistakes without reaching out for help."

"But you told me about it," Alice reminds me, "and I know it would hurt my brother to learn he could help, but you didn't think to ask him."

Stretching my arms like a lazy cat, I sigh. "I could care less, Alice. Honestly. I thanked him for the job, and I think it's best if we draw a line underneath it and move on."

Staring at Alice intently, I'm about to ask her what brought about this sudden change of subject, but I see her eyes drift to the space behind my chair. It's like a horror movie or comedy; I'm not sure. Whichever entertainment uses that cliché when someone says, "He's standing behind me, isn't he?"

"Hey, Sterling. Would you like to join us?" Alice is blushing as she fumbles to push the chair out for her brother with her foot. I can see when Sterling sits down that neither of them was expecting him to overhear my remark. I can also tell that this is an ambush.

But I forget that Sterling is kind of shameless. "Draw a line under what, Edie?" He wants to know as the server brings him a glass of ice water.

My heart's beating like a jungle drum. Wiping a light film of sweat from my upper lip, I gather my courage and reply without looking at him. "Draw a line under having to feel beholden to you for a job I probably would have gotten without you driving me to the interview, Sterling. Anyway, how are you?"

"Technically, we were riding there. We took the bike, remember?"

Yes, I remember. I remember how you held me close to your chest after we kissed and touched and joined our bodies together over and over again.

"Whatevs." Picking up the menu, I try to catch the server's eye. "I'm starving. Do you want to split a salad?"

I see brother and sister shoot a look at one another over the table. For some reason, it feels as if my best friend is betraying me and taking her brother's side. The menu trembles. No wait, it's my hands. The two cups of coffee I had for breakfast are churning in my belly.

Pushing my chair back with a nervous laugh, I make the surrender sign with my palms facing out. "You know what? I think I'll go back to the apartment if that's okay. I never get to spend time with Gabby anymore. And... and I'm not hungry. Thank you. Bye."

I trip over someone's handbag on the floor on the way out. In typical rude New York style, the handbag owner clicks their tongue with annoyance. I make my exit apologizing.

"Hey! Swiss Miss," a man in the park shouts out to me as I stumble past him, "you look like a panda bear. Buy some waterproof mascara next time, Blondie."

Dammit. Sterling made me cry... again.

Chapter 19: Sterling

My sister looks worried. "I knew it wouldn't work, Sterling, the whole 'surprise, I'm back' thing. Why don't you just text her like a normal man?"

"I dared to hope that Edie would have gotten over acting like a spoiled kid, Alice. What else can I say?"

I have to act nonchalantly, but inside I'm devastated. For over three fucking months, I have been living, breathing, and thinking about Edie, and she all but ghosts me. The server comes over to take our order, but I can't speak.

Rubbing my hands over my face with a weary sigh, I hear Alice order for both of us. "Drink some water, Stern-ling," she says softly. "You're looking beat."

I am beat. I've been hiking in the Carpathian Mountains and driving across West Africa for weeks, with the only light at the end of the tunnel being the goal of seeing Edie again, and I come home to this.

"You didn't attend her first fundraiser. You go offline for ages. Frankly, Sterling, you should be grateful you're not coming back to find Edie hooked up with someone else."

"Thanks, Alice. You have a great way of comforting a man. Don't give up your day job, though."

Alice scoffs. "I need to know—do you want to smooth things over with Edie because you were such a cunt when you shot her pet? Or do you want to get with her?"

I rub my eyes and then drink water. Alice gets a look at my hands. "Ooh, okay. Who did you scrap with? I wish you would be more open with what it is you do, bro. I feel like I'm covering for you all the time."

Ignoring my sister's questions like she knew I would, I ask. "What does Edie think of me?" I may as well start from the top and work my way down. "I mean, how many bridges have I burned?"

Sitting back in her chair with her arms folded as the server brings our appetizers, Alice picks up a fork. "Edie accidentally let it slip that you flew with her to Dubai. When I pressed her, she said it was easier for you to upgrade her ticket that way. Is that true?"

"Jesus," I complain, after eating a few mouthfuls of salad. "Fine, but stop with the third degree after this, okay? I wanted to be nice to Edie so that she would forgive me for being a dick when I was a kid. And...."

Alice gives me the evil eye, so I continue. "And because she's hot. Satisfied?"

My sister is satisfied. We eat in silence until the server removes the plates when we finish. "Good to see you eating," Alice says. "You've got that whole Slavic thing going on with your sharply etched cheekbones—you've lost weight. And you could have warned me about that jarhead haircut of yours."

Giving in to my need for information, I ask my sister if she thinks Edie likes it. That makes Alice lean forward and tap the table.

"Look here, Stern-ling, and listen good. I'm not going to play middleman between you and my best friend. Got that? Use your head. If you screw this up, I'll have to take Edie's side, because you have a nonexistent track record when it comes to long-term relationships."

"Are you saying I'll screw this up?" We both sit back as the server brings out the mains. Alice thanks the man before returning to the conversation.

"I'm just saying that you might. And then I would have to kick your ass and not invite you to family gatherings anymore. Do you see the point I'm trying to make?"

I do. But there are a few things that my sister doesn't know about me. I'm a hunter at heart. And I don't need a rifle to enjoy doing it. There is something about the way Edie Kruger blows hot and then cold on me that stimulates the hunter in me.

If she had just laid back and accepted a casual fuck, things might be different. But I get the feeling that she regrets giving in to our rampant attraction to one another, and she is prepared to fight me every step of the way.

Edie doesn't want to want me. And she definitely doesn't have trouble forgetting about my existence when I screw up. This is because she still identifies me as that silly teenage boy who laughed at her young tween love, and then stood by and watched her pet die.

Alice finishes half her plate then picks up her phone and checks the time. "I need to get some shopping done," she tells me. "There's nothing like trying on a dress for real, you know. Online just ain't the same."

"I was there at the fundraiser," I confess. "At least, one of my guys was. He bought the Medieval Rus cloisonné crucifix."

We see Jack outside, heading for our table. "I asked him to make a foursome," Alice admits to me, "but I get the feeling that Edie will never sit down with me at a table for four again."

Typical Jack, he smacks my back when he comes to sit down. "Bad luck, bro. Did she take one look at that commercial carpeting haircut of yours and do a runner?"

"Is there anyone who doesn't know that I struck out with Edie?" I can't help complaining. I was hoping this afternoon would end with Edie in my arms, and now I have to slither all the way down the chute and start climbing the ladders again.

"My brother has got spies hanging around Edie. Who was the guy who bought the cloisonné item at the auction again, Jack?"

Jack shrugs. "Hell if I know. My advice, bro, is this. Hit up that spy network of yours and find out where Edie is staying now. And then head on over to Mount Olive. Don't stop ringing that doorbell of hers until she answers. Women always answer. They don't want the neighbors to hear their shit. And you're not at that toxic stage where she's going to call the cops on you either."

"Good luck if she tries that," I admit to myself that what Jack is saying interests me. "Cops love Marines. In fact, I think some of them are ex-Marines. It would be like a convention."

Clicking her tongue, Alice gets up. "I'm going to catch dessert on the fly. You boys have fun."

Jack watches her go. It's at moments like that when I can see that my brother-in-law is still crazy in love with my sister. But he gets down to business the moment she heads off.

"Okay. The oil tanker program has been hacked. When the shipment transfer happens, it won't sound the alarm at the maritime insurance company."

That's why our clients pay us the big bucks. They can mess around with tankers of oil out in international waters without the weight transfer registering on the computer mainframe. This enables poor nations to pretend they are cutting down on fossil fuel imports and exports while scoring points with net zero countries. This enables them to take out bigger loans.

Jack suggests I keep him company while he eats and orders me another steak. "You're looking a pert peaky there, Sterny—more like a Ranger and less like a Marine."

"You forget, Shorty, that I don't mind being compared to an Army guy. It's more than you ever did for your country."

"I keep national secrets for my country, dude. They should kiss my butt every sunrise and sunset, like the flag."

"Ha!" I raise my glass to Jack. "You're so skinny they could probably fold you like the flag too!"

We tell jokes and drink beer, which enables me to forget my disappointment. There's nothing like steak and beer to make a man skip over his problems. But I am troubled; I've just gotten really good at hiding it.

Splitting up with my brother-in-law, I head for the gym. While walking, I call Fraser. "What's Edie's address again?"

He tells me, filling me in on a few more details. She walks to work at seven every morning. She has her own set of keys so she can open up if she's the first to arrive. Her day consists of learning how to operate the computer system so she can access mailing lists.

Edie is a whiz kid when it comes to cold calling, making sure she has the personal assistant's name first so that she can circumvent them and ask for the boss directly. She's started a live donation feed on the website so that anyone logging on can see the name of the person who has just donated.

There's a special feed for kids that she's set up. When a dollar donation is made by a junior donor, they get access to how many days of hay or meat a rhino or lion will be fed from it. Everyone is thanked and then reminded once a month that a dollar doesn't go towards paying staff—it goes straight to feeding and protecting wild animals.

"Is she happy?" I know I'm putting Fraser on the spot, but I need to know. "I mean, how is Edie handling living alone?"

This is Fraser's chance to break it to me gently. If Edie has hooked up with someone, I want to know.

"Subject picks up supper ingredients on the walk back home. Never touches takeout and passes right by the liquor store without a second glance. Lights out at nine or ten. Wi-Fi shows a moderate amount of streaming service consumption before lights out. Some Kindle reading. Over a hundred entries on her search engine about how to fight breach of contract lawsuits in relation to broken engagements. The usual."

I wish I hadn't put spyware onto the microchip for Edie's phone, but I was desperate. About to ship out for months on end without access to communication. I'll swap it out the first chance I get. That was meant to be at lunch today when Edie used the restroom, but that was a bust.

"Thanks, Fraser. I owe you one. You can cease observation. Send me the bill for the auction."

"We square, Sterling. She was looking real sad at the event when I spoke to her. And then that lawyer came along and made things worse. Fix it, dude. She's not as strong as she makes out. That's my two cents' worth. Over and out."

I work off my frustration at the gym. Some of the guys poke my stomach and tell me to eat more chicken breast / whey powder/carbs. I laugh and tell them that a girl broke my heart so they should give me a break.

"Nice to know you have one to break, dude" is how most of them answer me back.

A cold shower isn't enough to cool me down. I'm agitated and jet-lagged. I want to know what's going on. Time to text Jack.

Should I really pay her a visit? What do you think?

Back comes the reply. Yep. She left the apartment as soon as I came in from the park. Ed's scared of me. She should be home a long time already. Go for it.

That I would see the day when my "one hundred and fifty pounds soaking wet" brother-in-law would be giving me dating advice. Calling my driver to bring the car around to the front of the gym, I tell him to drive to Mount Olive, New Jersey.

It's dark when I arrive outside her building entrance. Thunderclouds have built up into a low wall of black. As I tuck my phone into one of my pockets, a bright flash of lightning turns everything yellow and the rain starts bucketing down.

Looking up at the light in the windows, I can see the top of her blonde head moving around in the kitchen. When I lower my face, the skin is already soaking wet. The noise of raindrops pounding on the rooftops drowns out my voice as I turn around and tell the driver he can go back home.

I don't want any witnesses if I strike out. Only when the car is gone do I push the buzzer.

"Yah?" She must think it's a lost pizza delivery guy or someone from one of the other apartments.

"Edie. It's me—"

The intercom disconnects. I wait for the door to open or for her to come down and parlay with me, but all I get is nothing. The rain pummels the shoulder and back of my leather jacket, tapping and clicking on the soft fabric.

I push the buzzer again, but this time I don't remove my finger. The buzzer goes ballistic.

She answers, "Sterling—fuck off!"

Chapter 20: Edie

I'm about to take my finger off the buzzer, but Sterling manages to get a word in edgewise.

"I'm not leaving, Edie. I never would have left at the motel either, but I have work. Just like you. Why can't you respect that?"

It's a challenge. I know he's trying to manipulate me emotionally. He's attempting to put the blame on me for having a problem with his rapid departure instead of sticking to my guns about the despicable way he did it.

The buzzer goes again. "Fuck off, Sterling. Or else I'm going to—" I can't get the threat out. I'm not a drama queen. Maybe that's the problem. I bottle up everything inside me by not letting it out. "Just go, okay? This 'fuck and duck out' nonsense of yours has reached its sell-by date."

A huge bolt of lightning streaks across the black sky. I hear the thunderclap through the intercom. Why am I still holding it down?

Shouting above the noise of pouring rain, Sterling replies, "You and me, Edie, we don't have a sell-by date. What we feel for one another is fresh and brand-new. You can't deny it."

Why am I so thrilled that he has come looking for me? Why can't I forget Sterling Lewis and move on with my life? I give up. My finger slides off the buzzer button as I hesitate whether I should release the lock on the downstairs door.

The buzzer trills again. Ignoring it, I bang my forehead lightly against the wall in a slow, steady beat. Then I push the intercom. His deep voice growls over the rumble of thunder. "I'm going. Sorry to have disturbed you, Edie. Bye."

I rush to the kitchen window and see him turning away from the door and stepping off the sidewalk as he turns up the hood of his gym sweater. His broad shoulders are hunched against the rain. He doesn't seem to care that he's walking out into a storm. Two steps, and he is already drenched.

I press the release on the door. He hears it and turns, coming back to check if it's what he thinks it was. I don't bother looking at my face in the bathroom mirror or running my fingers through my hair. Opening the front door, I run down the stairs.

We meet up on the landing.

We can feel that this time is different. It's like we have climbed over mountains and crossed deep rivers to get to this point. His face is dripping with raindrops as he pinches his fingers over his nose to stop the water. His hair has been buzzcut a quarter of an inch short all around his scalp; he's lost weight; his hands are cut and bruised.

"Can I come inside?"

For the first time, I feel a strong motherly instinct towards Sterling. Who is going to be there for him next time he neglects himself? What has he been doing to look so drawn and desperate?

I reach for his face, cupping his cheek with my hand. "Yes."

But we don't. We can't. There is such an urgent need for us to forgive one another body and soul that we have to kiss and touch. We must try to heal the rift caused by our three-month-long separation the only way we know how.

He almost crushes my waist; his embrace is so fierce. I yield to him when he pulls me closer and our bodies slot together like cogs and wheels in an expensive Swiss watch. His mouth seems to want to devour me as he moves from my lips to my neck, and finally down to my breasts.

My nipples react to the damp rainy weather and his ravenous touch, turning into tight peaks of exquisite tenderness. I need Sterling to be closer. Lifting the hem of his sweater, I pull it up and expose his rock-hard abs.

His T-shirt and sweater come off in one. He lets the garments drop onto the cheap stairway carpeting as I run my hands over his chest. I don't care where we are or who might come along, I let him peel the pale pink baby T-shirt over my head and throw it down.

Kissing as we fumble with our clothes, he pulls the yoga pants and panties I'm wearing over my socks. I'm naked but for a pair of white cotton ankle socks on my feet. Sterling pushes me down on the flight of stairs leading up to my floor, his hungry gaze never leaving my body.

Unbuckling his belt and yanking the zipper of his denims open so that they don't hurt my skin, he lowers himself into me slowly. It's all happening so fast that I hardly had any time to get wet, but his rearing knob has no problem finding the hot dampness deep inside me.

One thrust and he loses control. When I feel him coming, it makes me come too. I've gone from a cold start to a hot finish in less than five minutes. And it's divine because his cock has some of the steel taken out of it now, I'm able to grind my pussy up against him to my heart's desire.

We lie on the ascending staircase for a long while, with just the din of rain on the rooftop and rumbling thunder to camouflage the soft pants of happiness coming from me. But I'm not satisfied yet. It's been too long and he's too desirable for me to want just once.

Clamping him closer by wrapping my feet around his legs, I share my little secret. "I need to come again. Don't move."

In the same way, an ocean wave crashes on the shore, my second orgasm crashes over me. I don't even have to move that much. All I need is the pressure of his enormous cock inside me and the closeness of him grinding against my clit.

I take it slower the second time by measuring my breathing and letting the urgency build up again. It's so erotic the way Sterling is whispering sexy suggestions in my ear or nuzzling my neck. He tells me how badly he needed to fuck me. How hard my tight, wet pussy made him come. And that he never wants to stop fucking me the way he knows I like it.

He thrills me. Everything about this man excites me to my core. It feels like I'm touching heaven as I hold the air in my lungs and let the pleasure wash over me. I have almost finished coming off when a vibrating sound comes two floors above.

Muffled voices can be heard and then the entrance door below buzzes and clicks open. The pizza delivery man has his phone light on so that he can see going up the stairs. But he stops confused when he sees us linked together on the landing.

My legs are wrapped around Sterling, but I let go so that he can zip up and stand. The pizza delivery guy is just standing there with his mouth open and his light shining on us.

"Yo, dude. Turn off the light. Give us a break." I can tell from Sterling's tone that he wants to laugh, but we manage to hold it in until we have gotten inside my door and close it.

"Oh my God. He is so going to tell my neighbors what he saw," I giggle, holding my hand over my mouth to stop the laughter from getting louder.

"Hey, he was probably inspired to ask for a bigger tip." Sterling is full of jokes now that we are inside. He throws his gym hoodie into the dryer and fiddles with the settings before turning around to look around the apartment. "Can I stay over?"

The air between us is electric. His body is so ripped as he stands there shirtless in my little kitchen. Jerking my head over to the bathroom, I tell him to grab a hot shower or use one of my old plaid flannel shirts for clothing. I bought the extra-large shirts to use as nightgowns when Alice took me downtown. They have lots of bargain-basement retailers around Madison Square Garden.

When he comes back, I have supper on the table. Lasagna and salad. Acting all normal, as if we haven't just fucked each other's brains out on the stairs, we eat and chat. He knows better than to ask for a beer or wine, which is strange. Not a lot of visitors would presume a household is dry without being told.

But I'm too happy to question it. We clink glasses of apple juice and laugh about all the strange places we seem to like to fuck in.

"This will be the first time we make love and sleep at home, Edie." Sterling smiles at me. "I think that's something to celebrate, don't you?"

The fork that is halfway to my mouth freezes. Make love. He said to make love as if it is the most natural thing in the world to confess. Placing the uneaten forkful down on the plate, I dab my lips with the paper napkin. Should I play it cool, or should I confront him about his choice of words?

"Ummm, what did you have in mind?" I chicken out and keep a light tone going.

The plaid flannel shirt is stretched tight over his shoulders as he leans forward with his elbows on the table. "How do you like to celebrate, Edie? I want to learn more about you. You've moved beyond Barbies and hopscotch. I remember Alice and you playing games in the middle of the dusty road under the shade of that thorn tree."

I smile wistfully. "Yah… but I've never been much of a girl for celebrating things that I can't put my finger on, you know? Fucking and having a roof over my head aren't exactly huge milestones."

Tilting his head to the side, he observes me keenly. "Tell me what you would consider a milestone for us, Edie, and I will make it happen."

Dammit! Stop putting the ball in my court, Sterling!

"Us? Good milestones would be us not fighting. Not running out on each other without fair warning or explanation. Doing normal things together, like we're doing now. Cooking, eating, chatting."

Sterling stretches like a cat, putting his interlocked hands behind his head. "All excellent suggestions. I can really get behind that. Does this mean that we can be exclusive too? Can I tell Alice we're going steady?"

I stare at my plate and nod.

Sterling comes to stand behind my chair. Sliding one arm around me, he hugs me tight and kisses the top of my head. "Suddenly, I'm in a real celebratory mood, sweetheart. What d'you say we have an early night?"

That makes me giggle like a shy schoolgirl. "It's a shower for me first, I'm afraid! You can use my toothbrush if you like, just rinse it under warm water when you are finished."

In the shower, I use a cap so that I don't have to waste time with the hairdryer or go to bed with damp hair. Wiping the steam off the mirror while I clean my teeth, I almost don't recognize my reflection. I'm glowing. I'm all lit up like string lights at Christmas.

I'm happy.

When I enter the bedroom, I see Sterling with my phone in his hands. "I'm just putting my private phone numbers into your contacts list, Edie," he informs me in his usual laid-back way. "How are those bank cards holding up?"

"How did you open my phone?" I'm curious. "No one can without my biometrics, my fingerprint."

"Thumbprint, actually," he teases me, "but your phone was already open. The screen light was on low. That's probably why you thought it was locked. I'm sorry. I wouldn't want you to think I was prying."

I forgive him, of course. This is our first night together in my home, after all. I'm not about to complain. "The card accounts receive my salary every week like clockwork, Sterling. Thank you."

Bouncing onto the bed, I snuggle into the nook his arm makes with his chest. "Now... where were we?"

Chapter 21: Sterling

I'm addicted to Edie Kruger. The touch of her smooth skin under my fingertips makes my head spin. And when her lips yield to the pressure of my mouth, I crave her even more. Sliding into her pussy with my tongue, fingers, and cock almost brings me to the edge of madness.

Last night was the first time she allowed me to go down on her. At first, she writhed her hips around, telling me it tickled and felt strange, but I managed to get it right by circling my tongue around her clit and not directly on it. After ten minutes, she was grabbing my hair and begging me not to stop, to never stop.

I can never stop with Edie. She's one habit I have no intention of kicking. I could lap at her pussy lips like a tame jungle cat for a really long time. I can't keep my hands off her or banish the image of her out of my mind. As deep as my cock rams into her tight wetness is as deep as I am falling in love.

Paper and glue. She's the glue. I'm stuck and I'm going to make damn sure I don't mess this up.

As the gray light of an overcast dawn filters in through the bedroom window, I sit up with my head against the wall and stare down at her sleeping face. The outline of her peachy ass curves under the sheet and her shoulders rise and fall as she breathes. The tumbled white gold of her hair splays out over my arm.

Her body is shaped like the most beautifully crafted violin, narrow at the waist and arching out at the hips. Edie's breasts are small and pert with no underfold. They are flat when she lies on her back, but turn into small, delicate peaks when she bends over. Her nipples are so pale, they are almost invisible against the two white triangle patches of bikini line. The small triangle of pubic hair covering her mound is blonde.

I wonder if Edie realizes that I removed the spyware from her phone last night. She'll still have the same number, but I've severed the connection that allowed my crew to keep tabs on her. It's not that I wanted to monitor her life in the first place. I just needed to know that she was safe, and that she had money to buy what she needed.

With Koos Van der Hoff out of the picture for good, I can pursue my relationship with the woman of my dreams without outside interference.

And I can still keep track of things from the bank cards I gave her. Maybe this makes me a control freak but show me a man who isn't and I'll show you a man who is either pussy whipped or careless.

It doesn't make me the same as Koos—Edie's money is her own to spend. I just want to make sure she has enough of it. She used the credit card to put down a deposit on this place and she's been paying it off at a steady one hundred dollars every month.

Stroking her cheek with the back of my hand, I marvel at how quickly Edie took back control of her life. And now that I'm her official boyfriend, I can back off on my own controls a little.

Swinging my feet onto the floor, I get up, stretch, and pad into the kitchen. The cupboards are a little bare—just the staples like salt, pepper, mixed herbs, olive oil, and ketchup—all the signs of a thrifty woman who buys fresh and cooks for herself every evening.

A quick look in the fridge tells me that Edie lives a healthy life. Probiotic yogurt, butter, and skim milk are on the shelves, and vegetables are in the crisper drawer. Including the bowl of fruit on the counter and the beverage containers next to the kettle, it's plain to see that her lifestyle is as neat and tidy as her taste.

Spooning instant coffee powder into a mug, I remove the kettle before it can build up a loud whistle and go sit in the living room. This might be only my second overnight stay, but I already know that Edie loves to sleep in.

I start making a list of all the things I want to get her. An espresso coffee machine, a tablet, a headboard—but I don't want to make too much of an impression on her life yet. However, the soldier in me wants to lock this shit down! Tie those loose ends up! Square those corners away!

My phone is on the kitchen counter above the dryer. I took it out of the pocket before spinning the hoodie. After a quick shower and a coffee refill, I pick it up and go back to sit on the settee in the living room.

Fuck. Dan wants me to check-in. He's not my boss; we made that clear from the get-go. Our business is a partnership. After costs, we split everything fifty-fifty. He handles logistics and setup while I'm the man on the ground.

For a moment, I fantasize about ignoring the message. I've been on the road or bonded to HQ for six years, moving from one assignment to the next. Moving and shaking up how business transactions and deals get done between those countries that never manage to make it to the international headlines. Where superfluous commodities can be exchanged for influence or scarce products. And where people like me are always on hand to make sure the deal goes through smoothly. In six years, no one has ever crossed me or tried to renege on a contract Dan and I have put together.

When it comes to dangerous deals, we are the best allies a politician, leader, or businessman can have—nameless shadows who get it done, no muss, no fuss.

Pulling my dry, fluffy hoodie over my head and shrugging into it, I go through to the bedroom in my socks; Edie doesn't like shoes in the house. "Babe, I have to make a turn at HQ. Is that okay? You've got my number if you want to get hold of me."

Edie mumbles into the pillow. "I hate your boss, Sterling."

Proffering her lips for a kiss, she smiles but doesn't open her eyes. I know it's because she hates me seeing her blonde lashes without mascara.

Whispering goodbye at the door, I head back to the city. The rain last night washed away all traces of dirt and debris. It makes me feel brand-new.

***

Dan is always at work early. We have a training center up in Connecticut and properties in some of the major cities too. But we don't have a permanently established office or location we call our premises. We leave that shit for all the Californian startups to waste their money on. HQ is wherever Dan happens to have an open laptop.

We move our servers around with us and use virtual satellite connection scramblers too. Dan has a fancy setup he uses to scope for hidden audio and video devices in the buildings we use. It also jams all the frequency waves: heat sensors, microwave, infrared, radio waves, sonar, everything.

Sometimes it scares clients when we tell them how easy it is for someone to spy on them. That's why so much of my job entails driving out to remote areas in old vehicles with no cell tower, satellite coverage, or tech.

Most of the time, I have to hike to a rendezvous out in the boonies. There is way more chance of something going FUBAR in the city, too many variables.

Dan has set up shop in a hotel penthouse suite. It's one of those chichi boutique hotels downtown. We did a favor for the owner whose wife was sticking it to him during their divorce settlement. A few photos of the wife riding me bronco while wearing a fascist uniform, and the wife's ask for more disappeared. Not a good look for the country club.

He looks up as I come in. "You're wearing the clothes you had on at the gym last night."

That's his first comment. I work out with a few ex-Marines, so I'm not surprised Dan knows what I left the gym last night wearing. What does irk me slightly is why Dan would think it was any of his goddamn business?

"You wanted to meet?" I keep all my communications short and sweet, and maybe a little bit corrosive. The only people who get to look behind my iron curtain of privacy are my family, and then it's only a peek.

He ignores my question. "You seem different, Marine. That's what giving away too many free-bies does to a man. It makes him comfortable; turns him into a tabby cat."

"As opposed to me acting like a tomcat on the prowl, you mean?" I laugh. "I'm thirty-one next birthday, Dan. It's time I stopped playing a young man's game."

Dan scowls. "Making female targets fall in love with you is part of the service package we offer clients, Sterling."

I shrug. "Fraser's well trained. He can take over. He's young, blond, and built like a Greek god. And for the record, I've never forced any woman to fall in love with me—I just fuck them."

"Same thing." Dan taps some keys on his laptop. "And you're good at it. Don't forget that Fraser struck out with that dame in the Philippines be-cause his male pride couldn't handle her beat-ing him at poker."

"He'll learn," I grunt in a nonjudgmental tone, settling into the chair and staring out the win-dow.

Dan gets serious. "You know the rules, Sterling. No wives. No steady girlfriends. Only temps. How can we demand that sort of commitment from our men in the field if they see you flouting it in their faces?"

Shit. He knows about my hands-on approach to getting Edie set up. The senator must have called in his chips already.

My partner continues. "We have never been a 'rules for ye, but not for me' organization. The chain of command goes both ways when it comes to relationships, Lewis. Set a good example."

"Is that why I'm here?" I gesture with my hand around the penthouse suite. "Is that why you called me in?"

Dan shakes his head. "I'm not your dad. I would never shit you out over something we both believe in—I've crunched the numbers from the diamond deal with the prince, and it came up five million short."

This is not going to be easy to explain. "Yeah. I meant to tell you. I took a diamond as part payment. From the prince...."

We stare at each other across the antique escritoire writing desk. Dan lifts one eyebrow. He doesn't have to ask me why. I start explaining. "Our share from the deal was ten mil, yes? So, I took my percentage in diamonds..., a diamond."

When Dan and I started out, we had a good notion about how much international black currency and commodities ops were going to make us—that's why we went private—but I don't think I ever imagined we would ever be talking about five million dollars as if it were a chunk of change.

My partner lowers his eyes. "Right... just so we're clear. The Nigerian oil exchange netted us half a billion, so I'm not complaining. I was curious why you have a sudden interest in high-end jewels?"

Because I saw the white band of untanned skin on Edie's wedding ring finger and the thought crossed my mind. "Investment" is all I say out loud. But it feels wrong. I want to be tap dancing on that fancy writing desk and shouting out to the world that Edie Kruger is my girl.

Dan seems to accept my explanation. He presses a few keys and then looks up. "Maybe we should start accepting cargo as payment? Only in certain cases, you know. The prince took your appreciation of the diamonds as the best kind of affirmation. He wants you to handle another deal for him down in Brazil. The country's wide open since Anglo-American pulled back."

"Is he diversifying his oil assets?" All of my clients—every single one of them—collect gold bars like Pez candy. Where there's gold production, there's always a deal to be made.

This time, it's Dan who grunts. "That's a conversation you're going to have with the prince. Saddle up. You're going back in."

Chapter 22: Edie

Sterling is waiting outside the Mount Olive office at five thirty on Monday. He answered all of my texts with thoughtful, sweet replies, asking me how the rest of my weekend was and when he could see me again. And now he's here.

"Can I meet your work colleagues?" He points at the door. I'm touched. "Sorry, Sterling. You just missed them. Lizzie and Juan have partners. No dillydallying for them. It's always straight home and dinner prep."

After turning the "Closed" sign to face out and locking the door, I join him on the sidewalk. "I—I'm walking home via the grocery store. But

I can give you my key and you can go on ahead, wait for me at the apartment?"

He declines. "Walking home with you via the grocery store sounds good."

That makes me laugh. "Really? I highly doubt that. Isn't it a bit... oh, I don't know, mundane for such a dashing man as you?"

Sterling shoots a lopsided smile at me. "No helicopters and Harleys, you mean? Nah. I'm a normal guy once all those things are packed away."

I tell him I have chicken breasts marinating in the fridge at home. We decide on baked potatoes with sour cream and salad for sides once Sterling checks that I don't want to go out for supper.

"We can't order pizza either," I tease him, "because I can't look that delivery man in the eyes! He must think I'm wanton. I'm not sure we didn't steal the idea of what we did on the stairs from a porn movie or something!"

"Is that something you do? Watch porn, I mean." Sterling looks at me with his laser-blue eyes. "I always had you down as more of a streaming service watcher."

Throwing back my head, I laugh. "Yah, I am! Gosh, you know me so well. But I didn't grow up in a bubble. I know about all those porn clichés—the television repairman and the horny housewife, blah, blah."

Kissing the side of my face, Sterling murmurs in my ear that I've just given him a great idea for our first roleplay sex game."

That makes me shriek with mock horror and pretend to hit him over the head with my shopping bag. I never knew having a lover could be such fun. Running up the stairs behind me, he grabs my ass, telling me my buns look good enough to eat.

We make love while the potatoes are baking in the oven. We didn't mean to, but it always turns out like that with Sterling and me. He pulls me onto his lap. I turn around to straddle him and kiss him. He inserts his hand down the back of my pants, hooking them down to gain access to my ass.

Then his other hand hooks under my yoga pants in the front. I rock against his fingers as he cups my pussy, using his thumb to rub my clit as his fingers dig deep inside my dripping wet hole. He knows his fingers will get me to that point, but then I want him inside me. Too turned on to strip, I take one leg out of my black Lycra athleisure wear so I can ride his big cock hard.

He's unzipped, and the veins in his shaft are engorged under his silky-smooth knob dripping with pre-cum. It's just the way I like it, especially when I get to control how deep the penetration is. Lowering myself down onto him, I look down so I can watch his thick girth get eaten by my glistening sheath.

Sterling groans, throwing his head back as he fights the urge to come. Taking his hand, I move his fingertips over my clit. I start to come the minute he stimulates me. My hands grip the back of the settee as I buck and grind on top of him.

Taking over, Sterling grabs my ass. It feels like he's splitting me in two when he arches up his hips. Every time we fuck, it gets better. We keep finding new ways to make it hotter, and more unbelievably compulsive.

We laugh and fall back on the cushions, panting and spent—and way too happy for this not to be significant. The oven timer rings. Staggering over to the kitchen with the yoga pants trailing on the floor, I bend down to check the potatoes. He's behind me, rubbing his crotch against my bare ass.

"Time for another quickie?" He wants to know. "I know you like it the second time around."

"Time for supper," I tell him firmly. "Go wash up. And if you're a good boy and finish your food, I'll let you fuck me in the shower."

Our relationship seems to be so much lighter since we surrendered to our true emotions. All the suspicion and anger have been leeched out, leaving only carefree happiness behind.

Over supper, Sterling tells me that he has to travel for work again. I'm sad but philosophical. It's not like Alice and Jack haven't warned me. Last night, I texted my best friend to tell her I was dating her brother.

A long-recorded message came back from Alice over the messaging app Sterling has installed on both our phones.

"Jack says it's about time. I'm happy for you both. I love you both, you know that. But we would be bad friends if we didn't remind you, Girly-oh, that Sterling is a hard man to pin down. Don't get me wrong—no one is a more loyal friend or godfather, but he's married to his work. You have been warned. So please, please don't come crying to us when my brother fucks off to Outer Mongolia for six months. Okay?"

But I'm so happy to be with Sterling here and now to pay mind to the warning. "Do you know how long you'll be?" I'm starving, picking the last of the salad out of the bowl and nibbling the potato skins.

He shakes his head. "Whenever I'm not with you, Edie, even one day is too long." Pushing his chair back on two legs, Sterling tentatively tests the water. "I... I've been thinking about changing lanes and keeping it local. Would you be interested in something like that?"

I'm shook. Only a couple of days ago, Sterling was asking me if we could date, and now he's talking about giving up his job for me. I don't know if I want to be responsible for him having to give up all of his expensive boy toys and global travel in first class.

"Um...." My brain is turning over slowly. I know what's happening here. Sterling wants to force our relationship to keep up with the fast pace of our sex life. "There's no rush. I wouldn't consider leaving my current job for a minimum of two to three years, at least. That puts me here, no matter where your job takes you."

"Pump the brakes, you mean?" He's not pissed. I think he's shocked that a woman has said no to him. I don't think it's a word Sterling hears very often.

I grin, giving his hand a little squeeze across the table. "Yah. You can pump me as much as you like, Sterling, just go slow with making any life-altering changes until we are on more solid ground."

He gives me that drop-dead-gorgeous smile of his. "How about that shower? Do we need to go slow about that?"

We fuck in the shower, whispering sexy, wet, and wild words to each other about how awesome it was the first time we had sex during the upgrade. As Sterling bends me over under the showerhead, driving his long shaft into me, he tells me how badly he wanted to fuck me from the first time he saw me.

I'm so in love with the way he always tells me what's on his mind. After he comes, he gives my ass cheeks a few smacks with his cock before letting me turn around. We kiss, the water pouring into our mouths and over our faces, as he fingers me into coming.

"If someone was to look up the word 'compatible' in the dictionary, Edie," Sterling tells me as he towels himself dry, "they should have a pic of us next to it."

He asks me if he can spend the night. I say yes. But then he checks his phone again and makes an irritated noise. "Ah, fuck. There's a tropical storm blowing in from the Atlantic, sweetheart.

We have to haul ass if we want to make it across the equator in time."

When he turns to meet my gaze, he looks worried. "But I'll cancel the departure if you think I'm pulling another 'fuck and duck' thing on you, Edie."

That makes me feel like a bitch. "No, go. I'll be fine. Consider it my 'thank you' for accepting that little 'pump the brakes' speech of mine without taking it personally." I flap my hand at him, like a queen dismissing someone from her presence.

Leaning over, he kisses me. "We'll be fine, you mean. Remember to use the app if you want to get hold of me. It uses blockchain technology to encrypt the words."

Sterling stops at the door. "Edie? Please can you ask the landlord for another set of keys? I'll send my guy to pick them up from you. Just so that I don't have to meet you at the office all the time."

I call out after him. "Hey, no fair! When do I get a set of keys to your home?"

His last words before he shuts the door are— "I don't have a home."

***

Sterling's last words kind of haunt me all the way to the Mount Olive office. Juan greets me as I come in for work. "Good news, Edie. Today's the day you learn how to use the accounting software." I move to stand behind his chair, looking at the layout. The UX seems very simple.

"It's pretty much the same program you used in South Africa for the Save the Rhino charity, only this allows you to check beneficiaries to the account numbers." Juan clicks a few times on the mouse to bring up donor information.

After I wheel my chair over to Juan's desk, he shows me all the columns using the cursor. "Okay. These are our donors' names. And the account numbers we are authorized to debit every month are here. Don't worry. All this info is blockchain encrypted. It was set up by a real clued-in dude. And here—" Juan brings up the charities and organizations who benefit from the money we raise. "—here are the folks we send the money to."

Lines and lines of sort codes, bank account numbers, and names scroll down the screen. Suddenly, I grab Juan's hand. "Stop! I know every single sort code for South African banks there is."

Pointing to the screen, I stare at a line closely. "I've never heard about that wildlife charity, and yet it has a South African bank international sort code."

Juan shrugs. "To be honest, Edie, we're more interested in making sure the deductions from the donor's accounts are transparent. And every single one of the charities we transfer funds to has been vetted and provided us with a legitimate charity tax number. Some are private operators—usually those who live in corrupt countries with governments that can't be trusted with OPM. But every deposit we make is acknowledged by the recipient."

"OPM?" I'm confused.

Juan grins. "Other People's Money. That's why we have to use private bank accounts. The recipients don't pay tax on the deposits, because they are registered charities, so the governments in corrupt countries can't get their greedy mitts on it."

I shake my head impatiently. "I don't know that charity name, Juan. Please believe me when I tell you that I know every single wildlife charity in Southern Africa. Hell, my parents run one, for God's sake! And that," I say, pointing at the sort code, "is not one."

Juan looks worried. "Maybe it belongs to the government? I wouldn't put it past them."

Lizzie comes over to stare at the screen. "Who should we call? We can't afford a long audit. It would kill our rep with the donors."

Picking up my phone, I open the app Sterling installed for me. I try calling, but it just rings. Damn. "Let's sit on this until I speak to my... friend."

Chapter 23: Sterling

"Where's your mind at?"

Dan slumps down to sit beside me and turns to ask the question. I've been staring off into space for the last twenty minutes. We're in transit, hopping from helicopter to seaplane to yacht, in an effort to throw off the Coast Guard.

Zoning out is a mental trick I use to pass the time peacefully. We're waiting in a small hangar in Connecticut for a seaplane to take us to the yacht. Caught somewhere between dream and meditation, I am stuck in the moment.

"Why did you decide to accompany me this time?" I hate answering a question with another question—to me, it's the laziest form of interrogation—but having Dan along for the ride is an unusual occurrence.

"Like I said, I'm thinking about diversifying our personal reserves into gold, just like the prince. I was thinking thirds: thirty-three percent into Crypto, thirty-three percent into offshore accounts, and the remainder into gold."

"And you want to know where my mind is on that decision?"

Dan shrugs. "Would be nice to have your input, yes. Once we have that locked down, maybe we could extend a hand to our own government. Go legit."

I know what Dan is fishing for. He wants me to tip my hand and spill my guts, but I'm not in a confessing kind of mood. "Sounds good."

Leaning back in his seat, Dan gives up. He knows I'm an oyster when it comes to discussing personal issues. The only time he has ever seen me with a woman is when I'm paid to be there. He had to know the party was going to end sometime.

"Hey, Dan," I have a question. "You were about the age I am now when we started this shit. Did you put a sell-by date on it?"

He doesn't open his eyes. "My old man was a career soldier—shit, he's still active in the Pentagon. My grandfather was in the Second World War and Korea. I always knew I would end up behind a desk someday, ordering troops around. But I saw the toll all that moving around took on my momma. So, don't hate me for enforcing the rules about girlfriends."

"That's not what I asked," I say gruffly, trying not to think of how Edie shut me out when I left her at the motel.

"Sell-by date, right? The problem with moving from a platoon to doing freelance work is this: there's not really a sharp transition. Both sets of work are basically the same. Maybe I'll quit once I know what I want to do next. No woman wants a man who sits around the house all day, twiddling his thumbs."

A string of swear words rumble through my mind like a convoy of freight trains. Shit. Edie definitely wouldn't respect me if I ended up doing that. "Ya think?" I'm fully engaged now because I need to pick Dan's brain a little.

"No doubt, Marine," he nods, staring off into the hangar space. "We're not here for the money. We're here for the adrenaline rush. Take that away from us and what would we be?"

Dan has me over a barrel. I like working out, but not enough to become a gym bro. I like playing with Noah in the park and taking him to school, but that doesn't happen often enough for me to do it for eight hours a day. The same thing goes with computers and coding. And I'm not that fond of my family, so making nice over the holidays is my idea of a nightmare.

The thought of being bent over a keyboard seven days a week like Jack, or having to interface with government officials, turns me numb with boredom. I have had no other commitment in my life, at least since my parents sent me off to the military academy than to succeed in my chosen field.

"Fuuuck...." I breathe the word out like a whistle.

Dan punches my arm. "Hey, if you got a girl, more strength to you. You want to jump off the treadmill, go for it."

No. I don't want to jump off the treadmill. The fucking treadmill is all I know. I love being paid by some oligarch to bring the beatdown on an Albanian rom baro who has taken the oligarch's second cousin for his teenage wife.

I love jumping out of helicopters in the jungle to bushwack my way to a hidden emerald stash. I frigging get off on setting up deals between Central American warlords and politicians. Danger has been my constant companion for fifteen years. If I had the choice between dying in an armchair or going out with a bullet between the eyes, I'd choose the bullet every time.

But Edie is my addiction. And she's good for me. I could never give her up. I want to love, cherish, and protect her for the rest of my life.

"Look, I can't bedhop forever, Dan," I think I'll go for a compromise. "So, what if I have someone steady who I'm tapping? It's not serious. And as for the whole 'going legit' thing. Hold back on that for a year or two. We don't want to leave our clients hanging. I think we should strategize an exit, but it's not urgent."

I hate myself for lying to my friend and lying behind my girlfriend's back. But I'm a dyed-in-the-wool soldier. I need time to muster out.

The seaplane pilot enters the hangar and gives us the thumbs-up. Dan nods and tells me he's going to check the flight log first before we fly to the yacht. Climbing into the plane, I leave the passenger seat in front for Dan and stretch out my long legs in the back.

Taking out my phone, I check the app before switching off. I have a missed call from Edie. I'm too tempted to ignore it. I want to hear her voice again, imagining her sitting with the phone pressed to her ear and her mouth so close to the receiver.

She answers on the first ring. "Sterling! I knew you wouldn't let me down! And I must admit, that promise you made to me about staying in contact has been verified."

God, I love the way she doesn't have any fake bullshit about her. Edie says what's on her mind and doesn't have a deceptive bone in her body. "Hey, sweetheart. We're hauling ass ahead of the storm, but I couldn't leave without checking up on my one-and-only. What's up?"

Her voice drops, but not so low that I can't tell she's clued in the other two people in the office into the conversation. "I... I found a discrepancy in the charity's accounts. I can just smell that something is hinky, Sterling. I'm not being paranoid."

"Which country?" I ask that question right off the bat. Charities in the United Kingdom, and other colonial countries, are notorious for overpaying their staff and members of the board.

They make hires with the proud declaration that they pay their staff a comfortable wage instead of relying on volunteers and interns. But they don't take into account that every cent that's spent on wages and bureaucracy takes away from the endangered species they are meant to be protecting.

Edie gives a little laugh. "South Africa. I recognized the bank sort code. But I most definitely did not recognize the charity's name. I know all of them, Sterling. I promise you the name attached to this bank account is not legit."

There's a rumble of conversation on Edie's side of the phone. "Can Juan talk to you, please? He is one of my work colleagues."

"Sure, I remember. Lizzie and Juan. They have partners they have to go home to at the end of the day."

Edie chuckles. "I'll be joining them with that the moment you come home, babe, I promise. Here's Juan."

The sound of the phone changing hands and then a man's voice. "Hey, Mr. St—"

"Just Sterling, please, Juan."

"Thanks, Sterling. Edie flagged a recipient's account number for us. She said you might be able to flick the number of an accountant over to me—but the only problem is—he will have to do it for free. Our budget—"

"Yeah, sure. I'll organize someone to pop over. Can you put Edie back on the line for me please?"

Juan doesn't realize that his problem is solved. "You see, Mr. Sterling. Sterling, I mean, we've never had to worry about tax auditing. We're a registered charity. All we do is enter the details into the software and do the transfers manually. From the donors to the recipients with a few deductions for our salaries and the rent on the office, so you can see how this has taken us by surprise."

"I hear that, Juan. Someone who steals from a charity is the lowest of the low. Can I speak to Edie again, please? Cheers, and good luck finding the culprit."

More noise as the phone changes hands. "Hi, and thank you," Edie whispers. I can hear she's hesitant to talk to me during work hours, but I don't care.

"Hi, indeed. I wish I could be there with you and sort this out myself, but the guy I'm sending over will keep me in the loop. Hang on—" I riffle through my contact list. "Have you got a pen?

His name's Gareth Symons. He handles all our stuff for us. I'm flicking you his number now." I hear as the contact share goes through. "Lean on him for everything."

She sighs with relief. "I'm really hoping that I'm worrying for nothing. Will this Gareth guy know that it's a freebie? Or will he be working for a tax rebate? A lot of our helpers lend a hand so that they can write it off in tax."

Staring out the small portside window, I see the clouds beginning to build on the horizon. It's going to be a bumpy ride on the yacht. "He's with me, sweetheart. That's all you have to know. I would never let my girlfriend stress over something, even if I'm not there to help out. I...." My world stands still as I say the words for the first time. "I love you."

A hiccup sound bursts from her mouth, puffing into the phone receiver. "St-Sterling, I don't know what to say."

"Heck, babe, don't say anything. You'll look like a fool in front of your friends in the office there." I blurt out the excuse for her. I can't bear the thought of her not returning the feeling. I'm not sticking my neck out here—I'm stating the cold, hard truth. I love Edie.

"I'll text, call you if I can," I promise her. "But please don't stress if I go offline. Remember those three little words."

Silence. I wait. I'm a patient man, and I've waited so long for love to happen to me that I'm prepared to wait a little longer.

"I will, Sterling. And thanks again."

It's not the best outcome, but I can live with it. "Be safe, darling. Over and out."

I disconnect the call. For one long moment, I stare out of the window, assessing the call and our exchange of words. I'm enjoying the warm feeling that telling Edie I love her is giving me.

Settling back in my seat, I turn to face forward, wondering when Dan is coming back from the tower.

He's back. He's crouching in the entrance with one foot on the stair and his arms folded, glaring at me.

"How long have you been standing there?" I ask him.

"Long enough, Marine," Dan snaps out the reply and then goes to sit in front with the pilot.

I shout forward. "I was just shining her on, for fuck's sake. You have to sprinkle a little sugar around to get good loving."

Dan swivels around in the seat and snarls at me. "You sound like a fucking country music lyric when you spout shit like that at me, you know that, don't you? You lied to me! You broke faith with the unit."

The seaplane begins to taxi down the runway on its tiny set of wheels attached to the floats. I'm all shades of anger. I'm seeing more than red. "After all the sacrifices I've made, I would think you'd cut me a little slack, Dan! What the fuck am I going to do on furlough, anyway? The unit is my life, but it has to come second sometimes."

We're bellowing at each other as the pilot blocks out our voices with headphones.

"Have you ever wondered if your sweet li'l floozy would be happy knowing that, Sterling? Well, did you?!"

There's a lot I don't know about locking down a serious relationship. Fuck. And there's a lot Edie doesn't know about me too.

Chapter 24: Edie

I get on the phone to Gareth Symons. He picks up on the first ring. "Hey there, Stern-ling, bro! Long time no hear. Your money's still safe if that's what y'all worried about."

I don't know what to say. Is he able to see that Sterling bought this SIM card for me? Or did Sterling already tell the man to expect a call from this number?

"Er... hi there. My name's Edie Kruger. I'm Sterling's girlfriend, and—"

"Whoa!" Gareth's voice sounds like he's busy sucking in a lot of wind. "What did you just say? You're Sterling's girlfriend?"

The question is clearly rhetorical, so I don't bother answering it. True to form, Gareth the accountant let's rip with loud laughter. "Oh, my God! I can't believe it. So, old Sterling's finally been pussy bitten? And here I was thinking he was a stone-cold cocksman. Well, Edie Kruger, you unicorn amongst women, what can I do you for?"

"Er, please hold on, Gareth." Putting my hand over the receiver, I whisper to Juan. "Maybe you should speak to him. He sounds like a frat boy."

Juan shakes his head and Lizzie swipes both her hands together with the palms facing outwards. "No fucking way, Edie. It was bad enough having to speak to your boyfriend. Please handle it."

"Hello? Hellooo?" Gareth is already yodeling into the phone. Sighing, I continue the conversation.

"Hey, yah, Gareth. Sterling gave me your number because the charity where I work might have a fake recipient in our books. We need you to find out who it is."

"No probs," Gareth sounds nonchalant. "Have you ever done this before?"

"What? Found a discrepancy in the recipients' accounts?"

"Nah. What I meant to say is, have you ever done a run-through of all the accounts and matched them up to real people."

Feeling like a fool, I ask Gareth to hold once again. "He wants to know if we have checked all the account numbers and checked if they are real people who are in the business of saving wildlife."

Juan shakes his head. "We've had a few donors close their accounts without telling us, and then our debit orders are rejected, but we trust the account numbers for the wildlife rescue and conservation efforts are real."

When I put the phone back to my ear, Gareth tells me he heard what Juan said. "Cool. Okay. Here's what I need you to do. Hold back on paying out at the end of this month. Don't stress. No one relies on donations so heavily that they will collapse when they don't get yours. Then, wait for the emails to start coming in."

"Yah, that seems a bit harsh, doesn't it?"

"A working conservation organization will email you and let you know. I want those emails so that I can check them against the deets the bank has."

I'm writing this down so that Juan and Lizzie can see. "Okay. And then what?"

"And then I'm coming to see you, Sterling's girlfriend! But make sure you have the emails first, right?"

"Can I call you back on this number?" I'm suspicious. Gareth Symons doesn't really sound like a legitimate accountant."

"Sure thing. I would never drop you in it. Sterling would kill me. Literally."

Hoping that Juan and Lizzie didn't hear him, I say thank you and disconnect the call. "Shoot, I wonder how long it's going to take for us to sift through all the organizations?"

Juan and Lizzie look at one another and then back at me before saying in a depressed tone. "Weeks."

***

Only a handful of conservation organizations have not gotten back to us. But it's been nearly six weeks since we began withholding funds, and we can't delay it any longer. I am not holding up well under all of this stress. It really gets my goat knowing that some bastard has been siphoning off funds from legit operations.

All the post-sex glow I gained when Sterling was with me has gone, but I have to admit my appetite is good and I'm sleeping well. Sterling texts me almost every night, but it's not the same as having his warm arms holding me tight.

Knowing that he loves me is like a warm blanket I put on every day. I wish I could shake the feeling that he's still a stranger to me, but Alice says I must be grateful for small mercies. She says that even though Sterling is her brother, she still thinks of him as a stranger too.

As for Mr. and Mrs. Lewis, they treat "Bucky" like one of those neighbors whom they meet on walks around the hood but keep forgetting his name. Whenever the subject of Bucky Lewis is brought up during family gatherings, they wave the reference away with an airy hand. But that goes both ways because Sterling does that too.

So, when Gareth struts into the Mount Olive office to check the email addresses, I know I'm going to pump his brains about how he knows Sterling.

He's not what I was expecting. From the way he sounded on the phone, I had an image of a skater boi wearing cargo pants. But Gareth is dressed in a sharp suit with his hair buzz-cut short at the back and sides.

He grins when he sees me and leans forward to shake my hand. "Legend. You're a legend, you know that, don't you? All of us ex-Marines from the Corps would swear blind that Lewis didn't have a heart. He's always been one cold-hearted son of a bitch, you know. But now, here we are."

I blush and step back to introduce Lizzie and Juan. "How do you know Sterling?" I ask him as I trundle a swivel chair to my desk for Gareth to sit next to me.

"The Corps." Pulling his chair closer, he edges me over so that he can sit in front of my computer. "Dan and Sterling reached out to me. They weren't one year into their business endeavor before they realized they would need an accountant. It's pretty cool, what they do, I mean. But once I left the Marines, I was happy to sit behind a desk, you know what I'm saying?"

I lock eyes with him. "Yah, yah. So, Sterling doesn't sit at a desk much?" I know I'm taking a shot in the dark here, but I've finally found someone who is happy to talk to me about what Sterling does for a living.

Gareth laughs and shakes his head. "Ha! Good joke. After they hooked up with that Middle Eastern connection of theirs, they needed to set up offshore accounts. I think Dan wants to diversify into gold now. He's already sunk quite a bit into Crypto. My job is to hide the money. They don't earn it here. They don't declare it here. It's as simple as that. And who cares, you know? They paid their dues when they went to war for their country."

I'm about to enter my password for my computer, but Gareth already knows it. "Don't worry about privacy issues, Edie. I'll set you up with a password that changes daily. Only one of you guys is going to have access to account deets after this. We can't be playing catch-up with all three members of the staff if there's a breach in the future, okay?"

I tell this to Lizzie and we both agree to let Juan be left in charge of password-protected spaces in the future. "Hey, no fair!" Juan laughs when he hears our discussion. "Don't I get a say?"

"You guys," Gareth says in an affectionate voice. "I wish all the businesses I gave forensic accounting analyses to were as honest as y'all."

I get back to our conversation. "So, how would you describe Sterling's day job? He always says it will bore me, but I like to hear about South Africa and South America, you know?" I know that he's been to those countries, so I'm on safe ground mentioning it.

Gareth opens up to me like a leaky faucet. "Well, seeing as you're one of the family now, I guess there isn't a trust issue. Sterling green flagged the number you use, which means you're allowed to be linked into ops."

"What does that mean?" Keeping my posture relaxed, I fight to maintain a neutral expression.

"We use our own comms system to keep in touch. We have a deal with that dude who owns the satellites we use, so our comms stay confidential."

"Call me a dumb blonde," I say, giving a fake laugh, "but won't that give the 'dude' who owns the satellite something to hold over you?"

"Yeah! I like the way you think, Edie, but no. Sterling and Dan helped that guy out of a big jam. His wife started divorce proceedings, and it got really messy. He was having an affair with one of his partners, and the wife found out. She was set to go public or reach out for a bigger settlement. Sterling got to her first. He was suspicious when she turned him down for sex, you know? I mean, no woman in her right mind is going to turn him down.

"Sterling set her up under twenty-four-hour obs. They found out the wife had been turned by an Eastern European asset! She was feeding him all this information, thinking she was getting back at her husband for his cheating while all the time getting her brains fucked out by a spy."

"She was being played. Poor woman."

I think I know how that woman must have felt. I feel sick. Not because I don't believe Sterling loves me anymore, but because I don't trust him anymore. He never told me that part of his job description entails seduction. "So, what happened to her? The woman, I mean?"

Gareth shrugs, his fingers flying over the keys like tap-dancing mice on speed. "Who cares? Once Sterling took out the asset, the wife thought she had been dumped—again. She found comfort in old Sterling's loving arms. That gave us leverage over her."

Gareth stops typing and turns to me. "That's worth a little satellite usage, wouldn't you say, Edie?"

I really don't know what to say. Inside, I'm screaming. I want to know how long ago this was. And how many women has Sterling fucked to get leverage over them? And how many women's boyfriends did he take out in order for them to fall in love with him?

Oh my God! Is Koos okay? He's a twat, what we call a "poes" in Afrikaans, but he doesn't deserve to get hurt or, even worse, killed.

Getting a grip on myself, I'm able to reply. "Ag, yah man. Totally." I'm hoping my smile isn't reading as fake. I crinkle my eyes in the corner to make sure it looks genuine. Gareth seems convinced.

He beckons me closer to the computer screen and brings up some accounts. "Okay, I was actually more interested in the charities who did not email you when you stopped payments, guys." Juan and Lizzie have joined us in the huddle around the screen, wheeling their swivel chairs over the floor so they can read what Gareth has picked up.

"Now, there might be any number of reasons why these few organizations aren't concerned that you have stopped making deposits into their account: they have gone out of business, they have organized more donors, or they are giving you the benefit of the doubt and trust that there is a reasonable explanation for you stopping payments."

The three of us wait for him to say "But." However, Gareth surprises us. "And then there are those accounts that have been happy to accept money from you every month because they are fraudulent. So, when it stopped, they decided they had been rumbled and went to lay low."

"How will we know which is which?" Lizzie wants to know. "Excuse my language, but it really burns my ass knowing that someone is out there, stealing money from wild animals. I mean, aren't we meant to represent them? No one else has those animals' best interests at heart!"

"I hear you," Gareth says, pushing his chair away from the desk and scooting back across the floor before neatly standing up. "But I need to get more info on these addresses and accounts first."

Giving us a cheery wave goodbye, Gareth heads out the door. I follow him. "Gareth. Thank you for all your hard work. Are you sure we can't pay you? Or give you a receipt for tax?"

He almost doubles up with laughter. "Your man is a millionaire, Edie. If I need paying, I'll bill Sterling."

I stand there in the middle of the sidewalk with my mouth open. "A m-millionaire?"

Hopping into the black Aston Martin Vantage parked on the curb after picking off the parking tickets, balling them in his fist, and then throwing the paper into the drain, Gareth laughs. "Sorry. Don't be so pedantic. I meant to say, billionaire. There, are you happy now?"

Running into the back of the office, I manage to close the toilet stall door before throwing up.

Chapter 25: Sterling

Edie has stopped messaging me. If I add this to Dan's glowering black looks whenever he makes eye contact with me, I would have to say that I am not satisfied.

Fortunately, Gareth is on the ball. His message comes in this morning.

Made a pass at Edie's office last week. She's got an eye for detail. I have a few phone calls to make. By then I should be able to narrow it down to one suspect. I called her now, and they are going to start releasing payments again.

No longer able to be stoic when it comes to Edie, I message Gareth back. How was she? Happy? Healthy?

I know that Gareth has to respect the chain of command and reply truthfully, which he does. Shy, but dedicated to finding the perp. Polite. Healthy, for sure. They fought over who gets to duck the responsibility of password keeper, so I don't suspect the staff. I asked her when I could pick up the duplicate set of keys to her apartment, but she said she forgot to ask.

That's about as good as I'm going to get when it comes to hearing about Edie. I see Dan clocking me. We're dossing in an old, corrugated tin roof shack in a Rio favela. It's paramount we keep a low profile. The clients are adamant that they don't want anyone to know they are mining gold on the DL.

The only tech I have with me is the satellite phone and two spare batteries hidden in compartments in my boot heels.

Holding the phone out to Dan, I ask him if he wants to check in with anyone. He ignores me and turns away. We both stare out at the curtain of rain pounding down outside. The weather is somehow managing to be cold and hot at the same time.

"Look, you were right. Okay? I mean, we both were right to put the rule in place. I see it now." I have to shout so that Dan can hear me over the sound of the rain. He perks up when I make my confession.

"You bet your ass we were right to put in the rule. Your mind has only been half in the game since you broke it."

I get up and walk closer, so we can talk in normal voices. "I never knew. I never knew she would have that effect on me. It was pretty much instantaneous, although I was able to bullshit myself for a few weeks that it wasn't."

Dan is beginning to look interested despite himself. "Really? I heard it was sometimes like that. But I kind of cottoned on already, you know."

That makes me laugh. "The diamond?" Dan nods, grinning. "She must be quite something for you to take your cut in the form of a diamond engagement ring after just one fuck."

I think a goofy, wistful smile must have appeared on my face as I think about Edie because Dan makes a scoffing noise. "Jesus. You're mad, you know that? But take my advice. Don't be too hasty. We can use Fraser for face ops in the future, but don't throw it all away until you know a bit more about her."

"I know everything I need, Dan. She's using one of our SIM cards, so I'm looped into her messages."

"All of her messages?" Dan is incredulous. "Shit, Marine, give the lady a little privacy!"

I get uncomfortable. "I don't use the audio function. Just the numbers and messages. In case of an emergency."

"And what happens if she accidentally drops it in the toilet and takes the phone to the shop to be fixed? How's she going to feel when the genius finds spyware comms on the device?"

Tapping the side of my head, I tell him that's not going to happen. "I have faith. She's turned me into an optimist. She makes me laugh. But she keeps me on my toes. I'll stop spying the second she tells me she loves me."

The symphony of rain drums, taps, and roars around us. The yellow dirt road turns into a river of mud and begins sliding down the nearest slope. Torn banana leaves bob and bend in the downpour. It's very soothing, but I can't relax. I wasn't joking when I told Dan that Edie was withholding her declaration of love.

It bugs me. I know she's just gotten out of a nasty relationship, but damn.

"She used to hate me." Dan whips his head around when I tell him that. As hypnotic as it is to stare out at the rain, hearing that a woman hated me is interesting news.

"Love-hate you, or straight-up hate?"

"The last one. I was a snotty li'l pissant as a teenager. That's what got the shit kicked out of me in the academy. My folks are Hamptons born and bred, so my idea of rebellion was to embrace more rural pursuits."

"You sound like a charming shithead, Lewis, but isn't that what draws the girls in?"

"Yep. She sent me one of those 'I like you. Do you like me?' messages via my sister. It was during our first African safari vacation. My parents had it on their bucket list, so we ended up at the Kruger's safari lodge."

"I think I've heard of that." Dan grunts, but I can tell that he's interested in hearing about my downfall.

"Not the National Park. That's not a commercial enterprise. Edie's parents own a lodge and the land surrounding it. They use the lodge for tourists and take them outside the perimeter to see the wildlife. Some herds are kept for game hunting. Impalas, springboks, elands, and any medium-size antelopes like that. They allow paying hunters to thin out the males in the herd during winter so that they don't starve or get injured during mating season in spring."

"Same way we do it here," Dan replies in a reasonable tone. "Let me guess—you went overboard with the hunting side of your vacation?"

I remember it all so clearly. It's deeply embedded in my memory. Alice whispering the words in my ear. Little Edie Kruger dragging her toe through the dusty soil and staring at the floor every time I came within her orbit. My embarrassed rejection of the report that Edie likes me; I couldn't get away from her fast enough.

And then the sound of her horrified scream as she saw her little pet duiker twitching and bleeding out on the sunbaked ground.

"Yeah, you could say that. I was a gun-mad asshole—and her pet miniature antelope got dropped. But I managed to turn it around, I think."

"Much good it will do you, Marine." I can see that Dan is interested in the story despite himself. "I can guaran-fucking-tee you that she will bring up that incident at every chance she gets. Won't take her dress shopping? But you hurt my deer! Won't buy her an expensive item of jewelry? But you killed my sweet li'l angel! Can't get a table at Central in Lima? I hate you because you potshot my baby pet!"

"She's not like that." It sounds like I'm trying to convince myself as well as my business partner. "She would never play the bitch—that's why we're together—Edie has forgiven me."

Dan gives a snort of derisive laughter. "Ha! Keep telling yourself that. How well do you even know her? You've left her to stew in her own juices for way too long, Lewis. One gets you ten that she's left you hanging out to dry because of some compounded infraction she believes you're capable of. You're stigmatized in her eyes—and you ain't never going to escape that."

We listen to the rainfall while Dan waits for me to take the bet. Am I willing to bet one dollar on Edie staying faithful and forgiving? Not faithful in the sexual sense, but faithful to her admission that she has truly forgiven me for what happened with Dickie the duiker that disastrous summer day.

I really want to pull out a dollar and flick it over to Dan, telling him that even without all the facts, Edie would never kick me to the curb. But I can't, because she hasn't told me she loves me yet, so all bets are off.

Taking his cue from my silence, Dan interrupts my chain of thought. "What is the one thing we use against a hate-filled woman when she's a target?"

Dan and I use the services of some of the top psychologists in the world to help us profile a target, male or female. But there are a few differences in how a woman goes about getting revenge on an ex.

Two things define a woman when she feels a man has done something wrong. We're not talking about when a husband or boyfriend forgets to take out the trash here. We're talking about deeply hurtful and humiliating incidents like cheating, beating, and lying.

When that happens, a wife or girlfriend makes an effort to ruin the man's reputation at work and with his family. And they want to humiliate and hurt him in turn. That's where I come in. I am happy to help a target get back at their spouse in the best possible way. Except it's usually the spouse himself who is paying me to do it.

"We flip the script on her before she can fulfill her fantasies of revenge," I tell Dan in a dull voice. "We take back control."

"Bingo." Dan shoots his finger at me. "So you better make sure, before you get your knickers in a knot over your old archenemy, that she's genuine. Because if her agenda is to get back at you for what you did all those years ago, you have a whole lot of heartache coming your way pretty soon, sonny Jim."

I laugh. "Now it's you who's starting to sound like a country song lyricist, brother."

I think about Edie lying in my arms as we chat about our godchildren, what we want to have for supper, and how rewarding charity work is; all the small, inconsequential things that I was denied in my life as a young adult. Is it even possible for her side of that to be false?

Digging in my pocket, I throw a dollar note to Dan. It flutters and lands on the floor.

"You're going to owe me ten dollars very soon, Dan Marshall."

Chapter 26: Edie

My dreams are tempestuous, tossing me around the bed and disturbing my peace. Something is on my mind, something big. Sitting upright and staring out into the dark, I wonder what it is.

Immediately, my mind begins to make a list. Sterling is a billionaire. Sterling uses women like pawns in a chess game. Sterling is—what is the euphemism people use for lying? —economical with the truth.

That's it. Sterling Lewis is economical with the truth. He never told me who he was when we met. He withheld vital information about his net worth. And he still hasn't told me what his job entails. It's my fault. I accepted his denials and brush-offs.

But no more. I had to hear the truth from Gareth the accountant. The man might be brash and breezy about that exclusive men's club they have going, but Gareth is definitely my only hope in finding out more.

A still, silent voice inside my head prods my back.

Compared to what he was like when you met him, Sterling has opened up quite a lot. He gave you a domestic phone number that links you to his business. He asked if you were comfortable with him leaving. He texts all the time, even though you haven't messaged him back. What more do you want?

He definitely would not be doing that if he had another one of his seduction missions going on. That kind of thing is despicable. Why would he bother getting involved in such intimate affairs?

Sterling is a gun for hire. And he doesn't seem to worry too much about what weapon his clients want him to use. So long as he's not killing any-one, why care?

All those keywords Gareth was using. Ops, leverage, green flagged, comms—they all mean one thing. And I know what that one thing is because I come from South Africa.

South Africa was at war for forty years. Russian-trained guerilla forces on the eastern border and China-backed armies infiltrating from the north were a fact of life for South Africans decade after decade. This was before my time, but I learned about it at the school where I boarded.

After finishing high school, every boy had to do two years of army service, called conscription, before they were allowed to attend university or get a job. When the war ended and conscription was abolished, there were hundreds of career soldiers left without a job. These were the men for whom two years of conscription was not enough—these were the men for whom war represented business.

Most of them went on to become mercenaries, contracting out to security details, personal protection, and guns for hire in active war zones. Staging coups, guarding illegal cargo, and hunting targets.

They had friends in high places. All over the world, it was considered very prestigious to have an ex-South African army soldier as a bodyguard, or as someone with whom they can plan a secret disinformation strategy.

It's hard to believe that kind of thing is still going on. But it obviously is, and it looks like I'm dating one of the players. He might be an American, but I have a strong suspicion that Sterling loves playing war games.

And when he's not doing that, I guess he likes playing bedroom games…, so then why am I the one game he wants to start getting serious with?

Sighing and punching the pillow to make it more comfortable, I settle down for some more sleep. My head might be in a spin about Sterling's secret life, but not enough to wake me early. My favorite way of going to sleep is to imagine myself with him again.

No matter how mad I am at all his lies, it could never turn me off the fascinating dark mystery that is Sterling himself. I'm touching his chest, running my fingers over the hard ridges of muscle. He lets me stroke him wherever I want.

Over the proud swell of his pecs. Probing the tight sinew and skin holding his stomach muscles taut, digging my fingernails into the patchwork of white scars scattered over his body and face. Fluttering down to his perfectly manscaped groin, where I try to encircle the root of his erect cock with the fingers of one hand but fail to do so.

His rampant member jerks when I touch him, dripping pre-cum as he growls with suppressed excitement. And for the first time in my life, I get to lower my mouth down and suck him. Oh God, how I remember the first time we did oral on each other.

I want to eat him up, suck him down as far as I can go, only I can't. His knob is too engorged to fit inside my mouth. That is why we always have more fun the second time around; once Sterling has come off, it's easier to fit his cock into all those places and positions I so badly want to try out with him.

All I have to do is wait for the pulsing sensitivity of his cum-soaked knob to lessen, and then I can ride him, bend over for him, and suck him to my heart's content. With Sterling, good sex is no longer a figment of my imagination. It's a real, tangible, permanent thing.

As far as sex is concerned, Sterling and I hold no secrets from one another.

***

Gareth is back. We hear him coming before we see him. That car of his sounds like a herd of wild stallions galloping over a cliff.

Juan, Lizzie, and I shoot smiles at each other. We are the little people who find the expensive toys of the rich amusing. We save up like demons to buy a hatchback. We use public transport or walk when our car is in the shop, and we dream about owning a recreational vehicle when we retire.

Gareth barges in, but we can tell instantly that something is wrong. He's not happy. The contrast between him now and the first time we saw him is marked.

"Hi, Gareth." I wave my hand, beckoning him to come and sit down. "Nice day for a change, isn't it? That rain—I thought it was never going to end!"

Lizzie prepares to put on the kettle and Juan brings up a list of new recipients for Gareth to look over.

"Edie. Can I speak with you in private, please?" Jerking his head towards the door, the accountant makes it clear that a soft, whispered conversation in the back of the office is not going to be enough for what he needs to say.

Looking from Lizzie to Juan, I don't move. "My colleagues need to know about everything related to the charity, Gareth. I don't think I would feel comfortable going behind their backs."

Sunny skaterboi Gareth disappears in a millisecond. "Drop the act. Let me rephrase. You do not want your precious 'work colleagues' to hear what I am about to tell you. Got that? Now, get outside."

Juan jumps up from his chair, ready to step in, but I gesture for him to stay uninvolved. "I'll go outside with you, Gareth, but if you think I'm going to get into that glorified aluminum roller skate you call a car with you, think again."

Gareth does not reply. He waits, holding the door for me to walk through. After shooting "don't worry" glances at Lizzie and Juan, I step out. Once we are on the sidewalk, I gear up to let Gareth have it.

"How dare you—!"

He cuts me short. "Don't be common. Shouting at someone on the sidewalk might be how things are done where you come from, but it won't fly here." He points down in front of him. "Got that? Now, where can we go and talk?"

I'm flabbergasted. No one has spoken to me in such a tone of voice since I was a kid. Scornful, yet condescending. Koos had only two gears: drunk and surly, or hungover and aggressive.

It takes every last ounce of willpower for me to stand tall and speak politely. "Can we at least be civil to one another? I hardly know you, Gareth. Why don't we walk down to the lake? Walk and talk. Whatever you have to say to me is best said out in the open, yah?"

Sticking his hands into the pockets of his dark blue linen-wool mix, custom-made suit, Gareth nods. He begins to talk the moment we reach Lake Butt. I feel more like a priest hearing his confession than I do the recipient of information.

"Ima leave it for Sterling to tell you about the fraudulent account, if that's okay with you, Edie."

I manage to suppress my eye roll. "And do you have any idea about when Sterling might be coming back? It's been over two and a half months now, and—"

"It might be longer. But what I need to know is this: Why have you stopped texting him?"

It takes a while for me to wrap my head around the question. "Excuse me?" I have to be careful because it doesn't take the sharpest tool in the box to see that Gareth is pissed. "You want to know why I'm not messaging Sterling?"

Gareth nods. "Look. I'm taking a lot of flak here. You haven't responded to any of his messages since I visited your office—you can see how that might be a little difficult for me to explain?"

"Well, before you came, I thought I was dating a salaried individual. But after your visit, I realized that I had underestimated my boyfriend's net worth by—oh, I don't know—about one billion dollars!"

He manages to keep the frustration out of his voice, but only just. "Let me get this straight. You're mad because the boss is a billionaire? Do you know how crazy that sounds?"

I keep calm by staring out across the peaceful water. "It would have been nice to know beforehand, yah."

Scoffing, Gareth folds his arms. "I don't know what you guys talk about in bed, but I believe there was ample opportunity for you to inquire about the cost of his watches, helicopters, motorcycles, jets—little things like that. It might have given you a clue. But no, instead you choose to ghost the man."

Tears come to my eyes. "What am I meant to do?! Send him a fucking text about it? Why can't Sterling open up to me!? He's sent you, his fucking accountant, to interrogate me. He should be here, next to me, in person! Not his fucking accountant!"

I burst into tears. So emotional and dramatic, I'm embarrassed as I bite my lower lip and wipe the back of my hand across my face.

Edging a bit closer, Gareth reluctantly pats my arm and then withdraws a square white cotton handkerchief out of his pocket and gives it to me. "It's gotta be me, I'm afraid, Edie. Sterling and Dan ran into some trouble when they doubled back to Brazil. Those fucking jungles are a nightmare. I told them they should have taken backup—"

My stomach drops. "Where is he?"

Gareth shakes his head. "Truck got fragged by a grenade. Those illegal mining dudes are hella territorial over their stake. Sterling caught a frag in the gut. He's okay and on the mend, but please, Edie, can I at least tell Sterling that you ghosted him because of some other shit?

I can't report back that you took away a man's happiness because he earns too much money."

The tears are back. One or two people are staring at me. One large man comes over to take a better look, just in case Gareth is the cause of my tears. A terrifying death stare from Gareth, and the man decides to mind his own business.

Getting a grip on my emotions, I swallow hard. "Tell him I'm sorry. I miss him. Messages are not enough, you know. When is he coming home?"

"Just as soon as you hand me the spare set of keys to your apartment, Edie. That would go a long way to cheering him up."

Reaching for my phone, I dial a number. "Hi there. Ms. Jankowski? It's Edie Kruger here. Please can my friend, Gareth Symons, come and pick up a spare set of keys? He will pay the deposit and show ID, yes." I see Gareth nodding. "Thank you."

After I disconnect, Gareth relaxes. "Cool. And as for all the rest of the shit, the two of you are going to sort that out for yourselves. My advice is this—don't leave the man hanging. If you think you can't stand the heat in the kitchen, then get the fuck out. But if you opt-in, remember that you are not just with a man—you're with a Marine."

Chapter 27: Sterling

It's not the first time I've caught flak from a projectile. It happened during my first deployment too. A tribesman got lucky with his rocket launcher and took out the front end of our armored vehicle. An engine screw embedded itself in one of my ribs.

I couldn't breathe properly for two years because of that motherfucker.

But in Brazil, once we got past Carajás and headed north towards the Amazon Basin, Dan and I had to rely on local intel to keep us informed about the perimeter of landmines around the illegal gold mining operation. Only they failed to alert us to the fact that the commander had told his workers to take out any outsiders with grenades if a vehicle succeeded in bypassing the protected roads.

We cut across a soybean field to access the mine entrance and avoid the landmines. Some genius decided we were not there to parlay and tried to frag us. Shock is what usually comes first. The explosion is not what gets me; it's always the unexpectedness of the noise. The air ripples as the sound wave distorts my reality.

Dan's driving. A piece of shrapnel lodges in the bicep of his upper arm. My eyes give me vertigo as the steel-plated Land Rover flips. My audio senses have gone on a short vacation. Unclipping the seat belt, I brace myself for the impact as gravity forces me to fall onto my neck and shoulders.

Groaning as I roll out of the upended vehicle, I check to see if Dan can crawl. Using his machete to sever the belt, he follows me out. Instinctually, we use my side of the Rover; the grenade thrower is situated on the left side of the road.

Scrabbling to use the roof and wheel hub as protection, I lean inside to grab a first aid kit.

"Call it in. Tell HQ. These fuckheads must stand down. We're here to set up the fucking deal, not steal their stash."

As Dan uses the satellite phone to contact our handler, I start breaking the kit for saline, sutures, and Novocain. I lean closer, about to rip off Dan's left sleeve. He shakes his head and grunts. "I'll do you first."

He points at my stomach. A small part of my upper intestine is sticking out of the taut skin of my belly. A flying frag must've sliced through the membrane protecting the viscera. Thank goodness it's not deeper, or wider. Any more, and the pressure keeping my insides would have turned to shit, literally.

All I can think about is how on earth am I going to explain this to Edie. I can't wait to get back to her. She's always on my mind.

The phone crackles and Dan cuts the call after listening. "They're standing down. One of their workers went off-script. Apparently, they've got grenades littering the mining site like candy. Paranoid and unfriendly. Not a good combo."

Now that we can relax our guard, we get down to the business of fixing each other up. Squirting saline solution over the wound site, I'm able to get a closer look as I pull disposable gloves over my hands and help Dan pull on one. His left arm is hanging useless.

"You poke the gut back in with your good hand while I suture, 'kay?"

Dan nods and we get busy. After wiping with alcohol prep swabs, I inject the skin around the site with Novocain and start closing the wound with neat stitches. Dan wields the scissors, cutting the suture every time I've looped the knot.

We can't use staples because there's a chance I will pierce the intestine. Then it's a one-way trip to blood poisoning. When the wound is closed and sprayed with iodine, Dan releases the hand he has clamped over his bicep and we sew him next after I pull out the metal fragment.

We have an audience while we do this. Some of the miners have come to watch the show. The head honcho is apologizing, saying he told his men to expect us, but Christo was in the toilet and didn't hear.

We get a double booster shot of antibiotics each. The cost of doing business the way we do. I shake my head when Dan offers me a shot of painkiller. "Gotta keep a straight head. What am I going to tell Edie?"

"Tell her you had a hernia," Dan grunts.

No. I'm tired of lies. Lying is probably the reason why Edie stopped texting me. From here on, it's only the truth going forward.

***

The only thing that has kept me going for the last week is the news that Gareth relays. Edie has given him a set of keys to her apartment to give to me. The moment I can stand up without popping a suture, I'm pawing the ground to get back to her.

"But you have to go visit the prince and give him an ETA for the bullion shipment."

"The only flight I'm catching is the one going home." Throwing the satellite phone towards Dan, I continue strapping the pressure band around my stomach. It's like a really wide elasticized cumberbund that holds my muscles in place so that the stomach lining can heal. "You tell him."

"Fine. Go. Try and get laid the best you can with that bandage contraption on and I hope you don't bust a gut when you shoot your load. I'm going to stay here and have some fun with all those fine Rio ladies."

"Is that bet still on? Because I have a feeling you're going to owe me ten bucks pretty soon."

"That so, Marine?" Dan smirks. "I doubt that. She'll take one look at you held together with field stitches and instant glue, and she'll head for the hills."

We both grin but hold back on laughing—it hurts too much.

Going undercover is no longer necessary. I fly back first class and leave the jet for Dan. The memory of Edie has the ability to both comfort me and drive me over the edge. As difficult as it is going to be for me to come with a hole in my gut, I know an orgasm is going to flow over me like warm water the moment I feel her tight, warm slit envelope my cock.

Gareth is waiting for me at Arrivals. "Shit, Boss, you should have used the wheelchair the airline lays on for you. You're as pale as a corpse."

"Nice analogy, Symons," I reply gruffly, "but can you honestly see me getting wheeled out the gate like a pensioner?"

He winks, steering me towards the VIP entrance and exit. "I dunno. Lay on some hot female flight attendant pushing me from behind, and I'm on board."

Once I'm settled in the passenger seat—everything takes longer when your guts feel as if they have been ripped out by a meat hook—Gareth throws a keyring on my lap. "The magnetic fob is for the entrance door downstairs. The other two are for her door."

"What I need right now, Symons, is a nice drive into the 'burbs. I figure a trip to Mount Olive might put the blush back into my cheeks. Right?"

"I'm not going to say no, Sterling. I have to de-brief you about the charity fraud anyway. You ready for that? Don't shoot the messenger, and all that."

By the time I get to Edie's apartment, I don't feel sure about my welcome anymore after hearing what Gareth has to tell me.

"You want me to stick around?" Gareth buzzes down the window and leans over to ask me. I shake my head. "Go on. Get out of here. You'll only make it worse. And thanks for the heads-up."

There's a bus stop on the opposite side of the road. Walking slowly over to it, I sit down. It's fall, and everything about the scenery seems to want to mock me for falling for Edie during our unforgettable summer of love.

The leaves hang on by a thread, or else fall to the ground with a soggy slap. A chill wind wants to dig deep into my collar. I should have a beanie hat covering my head, but all I can do is pop up the hoodie of my sweater. The afternoon has said goodbye, punching the clock as twilight takes its place.

And then I see her, and I'm warm all over. I stand up. I can't wave because even that small movement would cause pain. But she recognizes the broken man standing at the bus stop. Edie waits for one skipping heartbeat before running across the road.

Flinging herself into my arms, she tries to kiss me but stops when I wince. "Sorry, Sterling, sorry. I forgot. Come inside. Why are you waiting out here? Didn't Gareth give you the keys?"

So much for the hero's return I planned on doing. How am I going to convince Edie that I need to keep doing my job when all she can see standing in front of her are the downsides?

"Sweetheart, we're going to have to keep things real slow for a while. I'm not firing on all four cylinders yet."

She's like a little ray of sunshine, so happy that I'm back. "Count your lucky stars that I'm not on the top floor, Sterling. Oh God, how I've missed you so much! Come into the bedroom. Let's get a better look at the damage."

At a snail's pace, I enter her apartment and lie down on the bed. It feels heavenly to be back here. Lifting up my sweater and the T-shirt underneath it, Edie inspects the wide elastic bandage. "Can I take a peek?"

I lift up my side so she can unhook the claws holding the bandage tight. After unwrapping it, Edie takes a look at the huge, dark purple bruise covered with waterproof film dressing. "I'm so sorry you got hurt." Sitting back on her haunches, Edie shakes her head. "Let's get you undressed and into bed. I'll reheat some soup. You'd like that, wouldn't you?"

If I could move, I would jump up and start pacing! "Edie, don't tease me, damn it. I'm injured. That's all. Don't treat me like an old-age pensioner." Opening my arms wide, I beg her to hug me. "And don't worry if I groan. I promise you that it's only because I want us to make love so badly. I've missed you so much."

She snuggles close to me, hugging me around the waist, below the wound. "I've missed you too. Are you sure your guts aren't going to pop out without that elastic belt on?"

That makes us laugh. Holding my hand out, I beg her to stop, but that only makes us laugh harder. In between giggles, Edie manages to get the support brace back around me. And then suddenly, things get serious.

Standing at the foot of the bed, Edie stares at me. It gives me my first good long look at her. Gareth was right. She's looking healthy, beautiful, glowing. Her hair is lustrous. She's got her hair down now, no more summertime ponytails to keep the soft silver baby curls off her neck.

Those hazel-green eyes are bright and seductive, the way she's looking at me makes me realize how much she's missed me—and she's not afraid of showing it either. She's wearing one of those padded lace bras she keeps for when she doesn't want anyone to see her nipples pressing against the thin fabric of her T-shirt.

But when she lifts the T-shirt over her head, I can see her breasts are bigger, fuller, and far more voluptuous. When Edie pulls off her jeans, I see she's picked up weight in all the right places. Her thighs are fuller and more rounded. And her ass is perfection when she bends down to hook off her socks.

"Can I blow you first, please Sterling," she asks nicely, "so that I can ride you without it feeling like your cock is trying to push into my spine?"

"Seeing as you ask so politely, angel face...." I grin happily as she touches herself the way she knows I like it. "...yes, you can."

Once her breasts are free from the bra, it gives me a good view of how heavy and full her tits are. Gone are the little girl "no more than a handful" peaks. In their place are full globes of soft pale skin and tight pink nipples. She allows them to brush against my hungry mouth for a brief moment before sinking down to suck my cock.

Hooking her finger into the top of my pants, Edie lifts it just enough for my cock to rear up. Then she gets busy sucking it. I have taught her well, and she has the technique I love down pat. Keeping her eyes locked on mine, she licks the knob as if it's her favorite lollipop. I have to stifle the groan of desire that rises in my throat.

Still keeping her eyes on me, she swallows the head of my cock with one hungry mouthful, her tongue going in crazy leisurely circles around the frenulum as she jerks the foreskin up and down my shaft. I come like a fountainhead, squirting my load deep into her mouth. She swallows it greedily, licking her lips and purring a compliment. "Your cum tastes like apples. What were they feeding you down there?"

"Lots of cinnamon. They sprinkle it on everything. It makes cum taste nice, apparently." My eyes are closed. I am still coming down from my orgasm. I experienced the strangest sensation of pain and pleasure at the same time when the spasms hit me. If I was into kink, I could definitely get into that. I'm still panting when Edie pulls my pants down to expose me completely.

"My turn now," she whispers seductively.

Chapter 28: Edie

I have been craving the feel of Sterling's cock inside me for days. It supersedes everything else. As far as my pouting clit is concerned, the man thrusting underneath me could be penniless or the richest man in the world, it would make no difference to my lustful hunger. I have to ride his gorgeous, thick shaft before it makes me lose my mind with desire.

"Sweetheart...." Sterling is letting me do the driving, which makes me wild with the power I feel every time I feel his stroke pounding inside me. "...please can you turn around? I can't get enough of that ass of yours, and then you don't have to worry about hurting me if you lean forward."

It's a brilliant idea. I've never done reverse cow-girl before, but it feels so damn good when I settle back into the rhythm after swiveling around with his massive prick inside me. And from the way Sterling is groaning, I can tell how much he loves the sight of my pink pussy sheath wrapped around his shaft.

I grind my ass down to the root so that I can rub against his balls. There isn't a single part of Sterling's biggest asset that I don't crave with every fiber of my body. He makes me come so hard, that I collapse on his lap, panting and gasping.

He's not finished, though. Watching me bouncing on top of him must have riled him up again. "Don't move," Sterling begs me, "just keep tilting your hips like that. Oh God, yes, that's amazing." He comes again. We both lie locked together as the tidal waves of pleasure recede.

Turning around, I crawl back to lie with him. "I bet you're hungry now." I crack a joke as a way to lighten the mood. Once the thrill of making love after such a long separation ebbs away, I can see that Sterling has a lot on his mind. And I have questions that need answers.

Why does this kind of relationship 'upkeep and administration" shit always seem to get in the way of us? It's not fair.

"Can we eat in bed?" Sterling asks me. "Is that something you do?"

"I'll make us sandwiches," I decide. "Somehow it's not so bad eating sandwiches in bed, don't you agree?"

He calls out to me what fillings he wants while I make sandwiches in the kitchen. Then he says the black magic words. "Edie, we have to talk."

Carrying our chicken and salad sandwiches on two plates, I help him sit up and then place one of the plates on his lap. "Talk away, Sterling. I always have Alice to chat with whenever I want to discuss anything, but lately, I've had something on my mind that I can't share, you know? Not even with my best friend."

Chewing and swallowing, he nods. "It's been the opposite with me. You're always on my mind, Edie, and I can't stop squeezing your name into the conversation! I've told my business partner about us. He's not happy."

Taking a deep breath, I dive in, headfirst. "Gareth trusted me enough to give me some details about your past assignments... the ones where ladies are involved...."

Sterling shakes his head firmly and for a moment, I think he's going to try and lie his way out of it. But he doesn't. "That's business, Edie. And I've told Dan I'm not doing it anymore. End of story."

I try to feel a sense of relief, but I don't. "Why didn't you tell me you had earned so much money whoring yourself out to victims?" My belly gives a little flip as I dare to get sassy with him. I'm only half joking.

Sterling's pupils dilate with shock when he realizes that I can be bitchy when I'm in the mood. There's a lot he doesn't know about me, now more than ever before. "Is that your takeaway from all this?" He gestures at his stomach. "That I charged a billion dollars for some woman to frag me in the gut after she'd done fucking me?"

Shrugging, I stay nonchalant. "If the shoe fits."

Pinching the bridge of his nose, Sterling answers me with his eyes closed. "Fucking for leverage is only a small facet of what we do. You're South African, Edie. You know how it rolls. For every dollar on the counter, there's another ten dollars under the counter being wire transferred to a Swiss bank account."

He has me there. Backdoor deals are the lifeblood of transactions in Africa, and every other post-colonial or third-world country. "Please tell me you don't condone slavery or drugs, Sterling. That's all."

Making a scoffing sound, he drops his hand and gives me a "Really?" look. "I can't discuss the business parameters with you, sweetheart, but I can assure you that we leave the bad stuff for the bad guys to do. If our clients got one whiff of slavery or drugs from us, they would head for the hills."

"Well, it's nice to know they have scruples," I say, revealing my agreement.

Sterling laughs. "No, it's not what you think—governments use drugs and girls as a way to entrap people. The clients are shrewd enough to stay away from such evil lures. It's all about the assets. Pure and simple."

Frowning, I can think of only one thing to say. "It's the opposite of pure and simple, Sterling. But you've told me everything I need to know. If you're not having sex to blackmail someone, you're at risk of being killed or kidnapped, or something else horrible. You're wealthy enough to stop. And I think you should."

He stares at me with incredulity writ large on his face. "Stop? I'm only thirty-one years old! Why should I stop?"

Taking advantage of the fact that I'm mobile and he isn't, I jump off the bed. Our cozy little tête-à-tête is over. "Let's just pretend for one minute that you really meant what you said when you told me that you love me. I think you should sell your side of the business, or whatever it is you do, and get a job closer to home."

Sitting down on the edge of the bed, I run my hand up and down his arm, trying to coax him out of his outrage. "Sterling, please try looking at it from my point of view. Since... since that time you upgraded me to first class and we spent those wonderful few hours together, you haven't spent more than a handful of days and nights with me. You split for work during transit in Dubai. You disappear and reappear at random intervals during sleepovers at motels and this apartment. And now you've popped back into my life again, only this time you have been seriously wounded."

Folding his arms and looking stubborn, Sterling interjects. "Seriously wounded? No way. It was a gut shot that didn't even rip the intestine."

I give his arm a small pinch. "See? Only you would think that. Everyone else would tell you the injury was serious. At least, everyone who loves and cares for you would."

"My parents could care less, Edie," Sterling growls in a gruff voice, "and nor would my sister."

He might think he sounds tough, but I can see the damaged, unloved child underneath it all. Mr. and Mrs. Lewis were typical upper-middle-class parents, who went about solving their problem child's bad behavior by throwing money at it and hoping some of it stuck. They left the discipline for someone else to handle, and now I'm left trying to pick up the pieces.

"Don't exaggerate. Noah loves you like you're his third parent. Maybe you should think about that before you decide."

Struggling to sit upright, Sterling objects. "I don't have to decide anything. I don't plan on becoming a tame house cat, Edie, so forget it. I've given up the face jobs for you, so be satisfied with that."

"Face jobs?" I'm mad now. He's moved out of reach of my hands, but that's not all. I can feel him withdrawing from me. "Is that what you call bedding poor women with shitty husbands who want to reclaim their feminine energy? And I just told you that I love and care for you, and you just gloss over it like it's nothing!" I'm back on my feet now, shouting with anger. "Do you know how it feels for me to be told by your fucking accountant that you are worth billions? What you do for a living? If that is any indication of our relationship, Sterling, it shows me that, one, we haven't spent enough time together for you to tell me anything of fucking significance, and two, you don't respect me enough to try and see things from my point of view."

He's looking cornered. Instead of glaring at me in furious anger, Sterling's eyes are darting at the door and window as if he's planning an escape route.

"That's rich coming from a woman who withheld telling her lover that she actually loved him! You casually inject it into the conversation like some kind of a throwaway, and then the next thing you're doing is blaming me for not doing cartwheels because you said the words 'love' and 'care' in the same sentence."

We're glowering at one another like aggressive dogs, mouths turned down, eyes narrowed, breath huffing out of flared nostrils. Sterling is edging to stand up. I step closer and push him back down on the bed, taking sadistic pleasure when he winces. He has no idea how desperate I am.

"You said we have to talk, Sterling Lewis, so talk!"

This time, it's clear to me that Sterling is getting himself into a defensive position. Shifting to the opposite side of the bed, he swings his feet over the side and hunches his shoulders, ready to split.

"Ah, jeez, Edie. It's not the right time. I gotta go."

An agonized scream of frustration rips out of me. "Just tell me!"

Keeping his eyes ahead of him so that he doesn't have to look at me, Sterling fesses up. "Gareth came to pick me up at the airport. He's found out who's been scamming the wildlife charity fund."

I go cold, praying that it isn't Lizzie or Juan. Besides Alice, those two are my only friends.

"He's traced the account back to your parents, Edie. They are the ones who have been skimming money into accounts with false names. Hundreds and thousands of dollars."

Bam! My knees hit the floor hard as they buckle underneath me. Wincing and groaning, Sterling tries to get up to help me, but I hold him back with one trembling hand. "No! Leave me!"

Rolling into a ball and hugging my knees, I catch my breath. Who would believe such a thing? Staggering up, I sit down on the bed. "How can you even believe such lies about my parents, Sterling? They would never steal from wild animals. All mom and dad have ever done is look after the endangered species living around the lodge."

Reaching out for me, he tries to comfort me. "Times are tough, Edie. It's understandable."

I jerk my arm away from his touch. "You're not listening. I'll hand in my notice tomorrow. You obviously don't trust me." And I can't stand the thought of going into our little Mount Olive office tomorrow and seeing the expression on Lizzie and Juan's faces....

Sterling gives an unpleasant bark of laughter. "No need, sweetheart. Don't overreact, please. Let me sort this out. It's what I'm good at. No one else has to know."

Rounding on him, I'm spitting rage. "I know, Sterling. I know! I know you don't believe my parents are innocent. I think you should leave."

The full force of our situation dawns on his face. "You can't kick me out. I have keys. We love each other. I won't go."

Stalking to the entrance door, I throw it open and wait with my arms folded, tapping my foot. He sees that look in my eyes and folds. "Fine. I'm gone. But if you think I took some sick pleasure in giving you this news, Edie, you're wrong. It hurts me as much as it hurts you."

He closes the bedroom door so that I can't see him dressing. When I hear him groan with pain, that caring side of me nearly cries with compassion. I have to fight back the urge to run back there and kiss him better.

Because I can't. I have to make a stand. Both for me and for the baby I'm carrying inside me.

Chapter 29: Sterling

"You sorry-ass piece of shit, Lewis." Dan steps into the hotel suite like he owns the place, throwing his beanie onto the side table using his one good arm; the other one is in a sling. "Why have you gone radio silent?"

Like a bear with a sore head, I came back to Manhattan with a world of hurt to heal after my disastrous reunion with Edie. When I woke up this morning, my gut was aching fit to bust and my heart was not much better.

"How the hell did you manage to get past hotel security?" I groan, turning my back on my visitor and hugging my knees. "Go away."

Dan is having none of it. Striding to the sliding doors, he pulls back the drapes, allowing the light in. "That's better. Did it go FUBAR with the girl? In that case, I want my ten bucks."

I hate losing, but I hate losing bets the most of all. Uncurling my legs gently so that the sutures on my stomach don't pull, I punch the pillows a few times to push them against the headboard.

"I want some advice," I address Dan's back as he pours himself a glass of Orangina from the minibar. "Why do real-life conversations happen so quickly? I have no time to think. No time to strategize before the shit hits the fan. Why is that?"

Throwing the tiny bottle in the bin, Dan lifts his shoulders. "I dunno. Ask the shrinks. It's probably because we talk from the heart when we're in love, but our egos can't take it, knowing that we care for someone more than we do ourselves. So, it goes into panic mode. Hence the word-salad sentences and the undercurrent of outrage."

Shifting and groaning some more, I tell Dan that maybe he has a point. "She told me she loves and cares for me, but in a kind of charitable way, mentioning my sister in the same sentence. I have to admit, it took away the moment for me."

Shooting me a side glance, Dan sprawls out on the couch. "Getting sisterly vibes from your girlfriend is banned in the northern states, I think." We laugh at the joke together and I have to say I feel better.

"Pass me my phone, please, Dan. I want to get a bead on what Edie's texting me. She gave me the bum's rush last night."

Dan doesn't move. "So, she left you with your dick in your hand? Let her stew for a bit. Can't harm her. Back off a bit. You still have to make nice with the prince. Gareth needs to go with you so that we can put a ten percent bullion value on our services."

Everything seems so barren and useless without Edie beside me. She stopped texting me. Then she gave me the keys to her apartment. Then she kicked me out after the best sex of my life, just because I wanted to keep an open mind about her parents' involvement in a crime.

The rollercoaster of love is making me sick. "No can do, Dan. Let Gareth handle it. Give him his big boy pants to wear. He's one of our best recruits."

Reaching for my phone, I open the private platform that allows Edie and me to communicate. Nothing. No apology. No regretful, reasonable explanation. Zip.

Fuck. Using the direct line, I order coffee, two cups after I get the thumbs-up from Dan. Limping to the bathroom, I shower and shave, leaving Dan to answer the door for room service. By the time I come out, he's got a full carnivore's breakfast waiting for me on the cart too.

Choosing a rumpled pair of jeans and a comfortable T-shirt that's loose enough to hide the bandage, I reach for more coffee.

"Eat," Dan orders. "I like to have a full belly before I get bad news."

In between gulps of coffee and mouthfuls of steak, I ask him what he means.

"You're off the face ops and now you want to set up Gareth as our Dubai connection. I might not be much of a guy when it comes to romance, but it doesn't take a rocket scientist to see that she's given you an ultimatum."

Being guys, we finish breakfast in companionable silence together before I answer him. "Yep." Draining my coffee mug, I push back the chair and stare out the window. "Edie and I need to consolidate our relationship. We need to spend more time together. But don't count me out just yet. I can run HQ in the meantime. When she's loosened the leash a bit, I can go back on the road. Small adjustments, big rewards."

"You do realize that you just referred to your girlfriend using the same terminology we reserve for targets, don't you, Sterling? We make small adjustments to our ops according to the outcome we're after." Dan's eyes narrow and he looks at me from under his brows.

I'm pissed. "Of course, she's a target! She's my target. You know me, Dan. When I set my eyes on the prize, I don't give up and I don't give in. Fuck it!"

There we are, sitting across from one another—two wounded men with complicated loyalties.

"Just so we're straight," Dan replies calmly, "you want to eat your cake and have it too? Are you sure you love her, Marine? Maybe it's best if you kept this one as a sidepiece. You know, this being your first time in love and all. See which way the wind is blowing before committing fully."

What am I doing? I have more money than I could possibly spend in one lifetime. The woman I have been waiting for all of my life is willing to give me the time of day. And here I am being all ruthless about her parents.

"I need to go do some personal reconnaissance, Dan. You owe me that much time off. When I come back, I will make a decision, I promise."

Shutting his mouth in a firm line, Dan shakes his head. "No can do. Gareth needs the jet for Dubai. Fraser is facing that CEO's wife to see if she knows about his secret bank account, and Clint is in Asia, putting recruits through training. I need you here, Sterling. I can't type or use the cursor worth a damn with this arm."

For one moment, I am tempted to clock out right then and there. Then I remember Dan telling me that all my unemployed ass would have to do at home was twiddle my thumbs, nothing but time on my hands to spend... and what woman is going to respect that? So, I say nothing.

I'm in an inevitable position. The only job I've ever known runs counterpoint to being a good partner. But if I give it all up, I might miss the action and adventure. Pitting my wits against the banks, and the face governments like to show to the public is exciting—but not as exciting as having Edie lying in my arms.

When to call it a day? I don't know. I've broken the cardinal rule of falling so in love that I'm virtually unemployable at this stage of the game.

Instead, I decided to play on Dan's heartstrings. "Edie's folks have run into a spot of trouble. That's why I wanted to take some personal time. Only when I've sorted it out is Edie likely to welcome me back with open arms. I love her, so I'm going to help her parents whether you like it or not."

Dan rolls his eyes. "Jesus H. Christ! The entire family sounds like a rescue mission, Sterling. Actually, Gareth mentioned something about it to me. So, just because your girlfriend's parents are crooks, you're going to put our business on hold to go and sort it out?"

I glare at him in stony silence. Dan flings his hands in the air. "Fine! But if you think you're going to use company assets so that you can go play the white knight for your girlfriend's folks, you're wrong."

"I don't need fucking jets and shit to succeed. I can make it rain on my own."

In the hyper-masculine environment, I have lived in for fifteen years, nothing gets a Marine's fighting spirit up more than a bet against the odds. Losing his brusque manner, Dan gets interested.

"Are you saying you're prepared to go in cold? No comms. No funds. No backup? And with a hole mending in your gut?"

I have to think about it first, running a quick checklist through my head. I'm freshly shaved. I'm wearing a five-year-old pair of Left Field jeans that have pretty much molded them-selves to a vague outline of my legs while hang-ing negligently under my waist.

The fitted, medium V-neck, standard white T-shirt is new, but not noticeably so. Add a leather jacket and a pair of Bruno Cucinelli boots to the ensemble, and I'm good. I know better than to try and take one of my belts with me—I'll have to pick something up landside. My passport is in the inside pocket of the jacket.

"You have yourself a bet. Pocket change only. If the mission is a success, you let me take any po-sition I want in the company—I can be a fucking janitor and sweep the floors if I want. And you have to agree to keep an eye on Edie for me while I'm gone. I don't want her to think that I've abandoned her again."

Whistling in amazement, I can see that Dan is impressed. "Woo! I would like to see that work." Standing up, Dan leans over to shake my hand. "Take care, Lewis. Personally, I think your girl is a mess and her parents sound like psychos. Make sure they don't try and pull some stunt like feeding pieces of you to the lions. Right?"

When the door closes behind him, I'm on the phone. "Hi there, Lizzie. It's Sterling Lewis. Please can I speak to Edie?"

After covering the mouthpiece and asking Edie, a very embarrassed Lizzie comes back on. "Sterling, I am so sorry, but—"

"She won't talk to me. That's understandable. Things have been difficult for us since we found out about the scam. Please tell her that I'll be there in a couple of hours."

Just as I planned, Edie comes on the phone. She sounds beat. There's no more anger in her voice, just sadness. "Please don't come, Sterling. I have a lot to process."

"Do you love me?"

"Yes." She's not hiding anything anymore. There's no hesitation. No qualifier. Just the admission that she loves me. Edie returns my love. In that moment, she stops being a target and becomes the woman I want to spend the rest of my life with.

"I want you to know that I believe you. But the account is in your parents' name, and the IP address of the computer where it was set up pins it to the lodge. Do you know of anyone who would want to do this to them?"

Her voice brightens as she realizes I am on her side. "No. I've racked my brains, but my mom and dad run a tight ship. It's just them, and God, they've worked so hard—" Her voice breaks. "They have sunk all their money into the safari lodge, Sterling. If it gets out that they degraded the account, it will kill them. Do you think that Koos—?"

A small smile flickers across my face as she says the name. "No, babe, You don't have to worry about him anymore. And it's unlikely he got access to your dad's computer. I'm going to sort this out. I promise. Please wait for me to get this right."

"Thank you. More than words can say. I... I love you."

God, but it feels so good when she says that. "Don't stress about a thing, Edie. I got this. I love you. Goodbye and be safe."

"I'll see you when I come to visit Alice this weekend, Sterling. We can talk then. Bye."

Chapter 30: Edie

Lizzie wheels her chair over to me after I hang up the office landline. "Is he excited about the baby now?"

I'm bemused. "How—?" Lizzie grins. "You're about three months, three and a half months now, hey? Is Sterling excited?" She points at my tummy.

Stroking the small bulge under my belly button, I have to ask. "How did you know?"

Shifting closer in case I am too shy for Juan to overhear; Lizzie lowers her voice.

"Girl, your boobs are huge. Your face is round, and your ass is giving serious boo-tay. Of course, you're pregnant. It was the same for me. I think I was only two months gone when my mom took a photograph of me and Mark, took one look at how tight my baby tee was stretched over my boobs, and started screaming. I think she was the happiest out of all of us."

Covering my face, I say in a muffled voice. "Sterling doesn't know yet. I was really skinny after coming to live here, so maybe he thinks I've just picked up the weight. He... he likes it."

"Damn right. Every man enjoys that post-impregnation glow. It's their last hurrah before all the sleepless nights and diaper changes."

I don't find anything very comforting in knowing that. "He's got a lot on his mind. I think I'll wait before I tell him."

I want to tell Lizzie about the big fight Sterling and I had, but I already hashed it out with Alice the previous night.

Alice answered on the first ring. "Is he back? Tell him he's a cunt for forgetting Noah's birthday last week."

That news snaps me out of my black mood. "Sterling forgot Noah's birthday? I find that hard to believe."

Alice simmers down a bit. I hear her take a sip of wine. "Oh, he remembered to tell his fucking secretary to send over a couriered gift, but he never called."

"What was the gift?" I hear Alice hold the phone out to Noah as the little man yells into the receiver. "Uncle Sterling got me a motorbike, Edie! Just like his own motorcycle!"

Alice comes back on. "Don't stress, Girly-oh, it's one of those automated battery-operated ones. But now it's me stuck with having to take him to the park every weekend to ride it around. And Sterling didn't call—which is out of order as far as I am concerned. Birthdays should mean something to a godfather."

I'm torn. I want to tell Alice that Sterling was injured, but I don't know if I'm allowed to. This firewall between his work and his family has started to involve me. I know I was right to give him that ultimatum. I won't stand for all this espionage nonsense when the baby is here.

Laughing, I tell Alice she's been watching too many Mafia movies. "Godfathers aren't necessary for a child's happiness, Whirly-oh. I'm sure Sterling will call soon." I know I'm shining my friend on when I say it. "He loves his godson so much."

That's why I stopped texting Sterling. I was damned if I do and damned if I don't. If he never got back to me, I don't think I could stand the stress of not knowing if he was okay or not.

But what can a string of text messages on a satellite phone accomplish at the end of the day? It's not a real conversation, no matter how we try to spin it. There's no subtext, no subtle inflection of the voice, no expression, and no soul. Fuck emojis.

I decide to change the topic.

"Alice, what do you do after a fight with Jack? Is there some kind of protocol? The reason I'm asking is that I never dared disagree with Koos, because of his violent nature, you know? But maybe I'm being a little too heavy-handed with laying down the law with Sterling...."

Taking another sip of wine, Alice settles in for a nice, long lecture. "Iron out all those kinks before you guys get married. So many women get into a relationship thinking their partner is going to change, but that's wrong. You both have to change, adapt, evolve together. That's the very definition of love."

"Friend"—I'm smiling as I tell her— "That's the most beautiful thing anyone has ever told me."

"Aw shucks," Alice chuckles, "it's the wine talking. And when all else fails, throw a spoon at his head. No sharp edges."

We laugh and talk about the men in our lives. I'm in love with my best friend's brother, and it's done nothing but bring us closer together. Now, all I have to do is make sure I do the same with Sterling!

But will the baby and me be exciting enough for Sterling to get his mind off of the deadly games he likes to call work? Will a baby finally put to bed the long-held animosity I have carried around for him since I was twelve years old? Or will Sterling find it too much of a coincidence that I fall pregnant the moment I hear that he's a bloody billionaire?

Neither of us is blameless, but we have to iron things straight if we want our relationship to succeed.

I know from watching Alice and Jack that every partnership and family unit has its kinks. I'm not asking for perfection, just normalcy.

Lizzie tells me she will lock up. Giving me a wink, she reminds me that I'm eating for two now. The worst of the morning sickness is over, so I stop off at the store to buy ingredients for supper. When I step out onto the sidewalk, I struggle with the bag.

Giving a sharp gasp as the bottle of Spanish olive oil clinks against the jar of probiotic yogurt, my hands fumble. A tall man steps up to help me. "Need a hand?"

I don't look at him. I'm too busy peeking into the bag. "I think it's all good, thank you. I should be okay to carry it from here."

As I step back, I get a look at the man. He has the familiar brush-cut hairstyle I am starting to recognize when I see it. Short on the sides and back, manageable on the top. Neither fashionable nor noticeable enough to stand out.

My heart sinks. I wait for him to introduce himself. Which he does.

"Edie Kruger? Dan Marshall. I would shake, but—" He points at the bag in my hands.

Thanking my lucky stars that my fall weather coat hides my little baby bump, I nod. "Pleased to meet you, Mr. Marshall." I wait for him to tell me to call him Dan, but that moment never arrives. The bag is starting to get heavy in my arms. "Can I help you?"

"I thought it was time for us to meet, Edie. You live just around the corner, don't you? Let's walk there together."

I'm in an awkward position. I don't know if I'm comfortable with Mr. Marshall escorting me to my front door. He sees me hesitating. "You doubt the genuine nature of my visit? Take a snap of us together and send it to Sterling for all I care."

Ignoring the weight of groceries in my arms, I counter his offer. "Here's the thing, Mr. Marshall. I know the app platform I use to communicate with Sterling is linked to your company. And I have no doubt that you are capable of deleting anything you don't like off it."

He's not fazed. "And then you will also know that Sterling has the tech skills to go through the hard drive and retrieve deleted images and texts. If not him, then definitely Jack. He runs all of our software for us. You trust your best friend's husband, don't you?"

Huffing, I begin walking home, not bothering to check if Dan is following me. He is. Holding his hand out calmly for the keys, when I drop them into his palm, he swipes the magnetic fob and the first-floor door pops open. "After you," Dan says politely.

I can feel his eyes drilling holes into me as I walk up. He's polite, waiting at the bottom of the stairs until I have the door to my apartment open. Picking up the bag, I step inside and go to put it on the kitchen counter. "Come on in," I shout, hearing his heavy footsteps coming up.

He's a muscular man, but without that lean athleticism that defines Sterling's build. I think Dan Marshall is what folks would describe as built like a brick shithouse. The telltale signs of combat mark his face: broken nose, a starburst of white scar tissue on his forehead, and a thin line running across his cheek, following the curvature of his cheekbone.

He must be in his late thirties, a dyed-in-the-wool soldier for life, no matter how much he tells his Italian tailor to hide it with his superbly cut and sewed suit.

"Coffee?" I point at the kettle. He shakes his head, gingerly perching on the head of the settee as if he knows how much Sterling and I love fucking on top of it.

"You're right," he says, jumping straight in with what's on his mind. "I can hack into your comms. I thought you rumbled me doing it, which is why you went radio silent during the South America-Dubai mission. But now I know you were pulling back because you don't approve of what Sterling does for a living."

"Why would you do that? Hack our messages."
I take a small sip of filtered water. I can't drink
too much in the evenings now or else I spend
all night jumping up for the bathroom.

"In his wisdom, Sterling gave you a phone chip
that belongs to the company. The company belongs to Sterling and me. But I suppose you
already knew that he was keeping tabs on you
that way. Out of sight, but not out of mind, and
all that."

Dan watches me closely. He can see my mind
doing the calculations of what I said and did
with the phone. A wide smile spreads over his
face.

Fighting down my consternation about being
spied on, I lighten up and shrug as if I don't care.
"Hey, Mr. Marshall. My life is an open book to
Sterling and you."

When he doesn't react, I know that Sterling
must have done something to disconnect the
spyware—if he hadn't, Dan would be offering
me his congratulations by now. I bought my
pregnancy test kit online!

My careless attitude shows Dan that I'm unshakable. His face becomes a mask as he realizes that I'm reading him just as much as he's reading me.

"Serving the Corps and working for Lewis, Marshall, and Associates is all Sterling has ever known, Edie. I want to be clear here—he can't carry on doing that with a steady partner. You copy?"

Jesus. This guy is a lifer. Sterling told me about soldiers like that. The men or women who get dropped into military academy the moment they are old enough to carry a rifle without falling over, and then never leave service. Dan might have segued into black ops, but he took that lifer mentality with him!

"Ten-four, I copy," I say, cracking a joke to lighten the mood.

Dan's expression doesn't change. He's calculating but hiding it well. "You kept him dancing on the end of a wire for quite a long time while you made up your mind about him, didn't you? But don't those condom-size pockets on the inside of his customized cashmere Nice Laundry underpants bother you? The man gets around, you know."

I have to think about that one before replying. "If you knew about Sterling's and my complicated history, Mr. Marshall, you wouldn't say that."

He chuckles. "Oh, I know. Why do you think he founded that stupid wildlife charity you are currently playing secretary at? It's actually Sterling's money that got misappropriated, Edie. Why else do you think he's gone off to find out who's doing it."

This time, I'm genuinely shocked. "But the fundraisers! The donors! They're real. That's not Sterling!"

Scoffing, Dan stands up, brushing imaginary dust off the front of his jacket. "Your three largest 'donors' are accounts that Sterling set up. That's why he sent Gareth over there to do the audit. Nice gig you've got—working for the boyfriend."

Walking to the door, Dan looks back at me. "Look after my best friend for me, Edie. He's one in a billion."

Chapter 31: Sterling

Africa on a shoestring budget is not as cool as I thought it would be. I'm treated like a counterfeiter when I go to the Bureau de Change and ask them to turn my dollars into rands, the South African currency.

I have to jump through so many hoops for them to make the transaction, it might have been easier for me to do a currency swap with a local instead. But none of the local Capetonians trust me enough to accept my notes; some of the taxi drivers I approach have never even seen a dollar bill before.

After producing my passport and patting my pockets until I find the courier transit receipt, the clerk gives me a pathetic exchange rate and then adds commission on top of it. They refuse to take the quarters—notes only.

Zipping the cash into the inside breast pocket of my jacket, I step off and start looking for public transport.

I traveled to South Africa as a private courier. The company using my services was happy for me to escort several valuable packages from JFK to Cape Town International via a layover or two. No one uses the post in Africa and normal courier vans are carjacking targets.

The only way to get valuables safely transported is to use private couriers. The manager, Mr. Valdez, was curious, however. He has known me since Lewis, Marshall, and Associates first started up.

"No offense, Mr. Lewis, but you do know that this flight has three stops: Switzerland, Johannesburg, and Cape Town? That's going to put you in an economy-size seat for almost twenty-four hours...."

The man looked down at my long legs, wide shoulders, and the faint outline of a bandage under my T-shirt. "Hell, Mr. Valdez, I know that. I'm happy to courier the packages and hand them over at the stopovers. I'm doing this for a bet."

Mr. Valdez shakes his head like I'm some frat boy with a death wish. "Okay, Mr. Lewis. But please bear in mind that you will be treated like any other economy passenger. No special treatment. We value you as a customer—that's why I'm telling you this."

I assured the man I was fine with it. I traveled to and from the Middle East on Marine Corps Aircraft, V-22 Ospreys, and Bell UH-1Y Venoms as a jarhead; I should be able to handle one day of economy-budget travel.

It turned out to be the most extreme torture of my life. From the one-hour-long queue to check-in to the horribly tight and uncomfortable seat, I had forgotten how fucking terrible public transport could be. I had to factor in the discomfort of my wound as well.

The middle-aged woman sitting less than a quarter of an inch away from me kept shooting me dirty looks whenever I had to scratch the healing wound or adjust the bandage. It made me so grumpy, that I had to bite back the words I wanted to growl at her: "For God's sake, it's the shrapnel wound in my gut that I'm scratching, not my fly buttons!"

But I didn't, so she continued to act like I got cooties until she disembarked at Geneva with an angry sniff.

I could no longer flirt with flight attendants to get preferential treatment. Security personnel looked at me like I was dirt. The food outlets and shops at Duty Free were ridiculously expensive, so I had to stick with eating airplane meals. One of the staff came to me during the flight, bending over and whispering to me with inviting eyes. Did I want to move up to Economy Plus? I would get more legroom there.

I turned down the offer. I didn't want to be stuck for nine hours with someone who might want something more intimate from me in return.

After three stops, three package deliveries, and twenty-three hours in transit, I am shattered.

After the shuttle drops me off in the middle of town, the first thing I do with my rands is visit the pharmacy. "Codeine, please."

One of the best things about being in South Africa is the readily available self-medication aisles. Sleeping pills, pain pills, antibiotics—you name it. All I needed to do is find an off-chain pharmacy willing to sell it to me. This system makes sense for a country where most of the medical staff have gone to live in Australia.

I buy bottled water and swig down the two pills. As numbness floods my stomach, I zone out, which allows me to focus on the task at hand.

First up, transport. I ask the way to the nearest rent-a-wreck car rental. Presenting my driver's license and passport at the desk, I ask how much it would be to rent their cheapest vehicle. A short row of VW Beetle Bug cars and rusted Minis with original body shape adorn the shop floor.

I try hard not to imagine how uncomfortable it will be to drive such a small vehicle. But as it turns out, that's the least of my worries.

"Credit card, please."

Shit. "Er... listen, I only have cash. That should be enough to buy me two or three days, right?"

"No credit card, no rental. Or you can put down a cash deposit of ten thousand rand."

"If I had that amount of cash on me, I wouldn't be standing here, would I?! Come on. You don't belong to a chain or franchise. You're private. You can bend the rules. Give a guy a break. Do I look like a car thief?"

The man leans over the desk. "That's what they all say, bru. I feel for you, I really do, but this is South Africa. We don't trust our own mothers."

Raising my hands up, palms out, I concede defeat. "Hey, neither do I. Any idea how I can travel north from here? I need to head up towards Namibia."

The man does not recommend hiking. "They'll have that fancy leather jacket off you before you have time to stick out your thumb, bru. Try the taxi rank. And remember to zip up your phone inside the pocket."

Giving him the thumbs-up, I head out. Then I head right back inside again when my phone starts ringing—only an idiot would use their phone out on the sidewalk in town. That's just begging for a street hustler to grab it out of your hand mid-conversation.

It's Edie. I'm overjoyed. "Hey babe. Guess what?"

"Oh, Sterling. I already know you've gone to find out who's scamming the charity. Dan walked me back to the apartment last night," she adds that last bit before I can enquire. Damn. I knew Dan would try to pull a stunt like this.

"His bark is worse than his bite, sweetheart," I say, trying to ignore the rent-a-wreck man behind the desk. He's smiling at how fast I went from being a grouchy customer to polite and loveable. "He's looking after my best inter-ests—at least, that's how he probably looks at it. How are you, anyway?"

A long pause before she answers. "I'm good, thank you. But then again, it's not me with a rip in my stomach." I hear her sigh. "God, Sterling, when can we just keep still and catch up? What we have... it just seems so abnormal."

I feel that drag, the tug-of-war sensation of be-ing pulled from my old life into a new one. But

I'm not ready yet. There are still too many balls I have juggling in the air.

"I wish I could be there with you, Edie. But I have to find out who set up your parents and stole from—"

"I know it's your charity, Sterling. Dan told me."

I wait for her to carry on talking, but that's all Edie has to say. I take that as a good sign. "Hey, haven't you always had the fantasy of fucking your boss? I must say that the thought of you filing my cabinets for me gets me real hard."

I don't care if the rent-a-wreck guy's eyes almost pop out of his head, I love talking dirty with my girl.

"Oh, ha-ha. That's such a cliché. But when the boss is as hot as you are, I guess I'll make an exception. Just be careful, please, Sterling. I love you more than words can say, which is why I probably don't say it enough."

"Hey, honey, you cracked a joke. That's great. Don't worry about me. I love you too, and I'll see you soon."

Waving a cheery goodbye to the guy, I jog outside and head for the taxi rank. When I get within a quarter-mile radius of it, I know I've made a bad mistake. The public taxi rank is situated behind the train station. It's a seething mass of minivans and crowds of people looking for a way to get out of town and get home. It's utter chaos.

How come I never knew how batshit-crazy Cape Town was before? The trains barely function, and they are basically just steel tubes for crime now anyway. But the taxi minivans don't offer a viable solution at all.

Sticking out like a sore thumb as my tall frame cuts a swath through thronging commuters, I stick my head in the first taxi van I come to. "Yo. Where's the stall for Saltwaterfontein? I need to head north."

The enormous real estate absorbed by the taxi rank is divided into stalls. Poles with letters and numbers signal the different directions the taxi vans are headed in. It's spring weather on top of it all, which means a cruel mix of biting Antarctic winds and blazing hot sun.

My jacket is hot and heavy, but there's no way I'm going to take it off. The sleepy driver perks up a bit, thinking I'm like all the other American tourists who get lost in town.

"It's A-10, bru." He holds his hand out for a tip. It's an old trick. There are always accomplices hiding in the crowd, ready to scope where I keep my wallet. "Sorry, dude," I step back. "I lost my money. That's why I'm here."

He loses interest in me as I go looking for A-10. When I find it, I kind of wish I hadn't. The vehicle is hardly functional—an ancient bucket of bolts with splashy tires and broken headlights—and the driver is tweaking. Two reluctant passengers have already climbed aboard and are sitting stoically in hard seats away from the sun.

"How much to Saltwaterfontein North?" The man is jumping around in his seat, not even bothering to hide the glass "lollipop" in his hand. "For you, I'll make it eight hundred rand, bru. Stick around, I'm going to fill up fast."

"When are you leaving?" I want to know. Eight hundred rand is a ridiculously high price for a seat. I can see the other two passengers shak-

ing their heads and clucking their tongues, sig-
nifying the rip-off.

"I'm leaving when the van is full, bru." The driver
informs me. The passengers listlessly click their
tongues with disapproval again. I manage to
keep my temper. "How long before departure?"

One of the passengers puts me out of my misery. "Six hours. Maybe more, depending on how
fast we get another twenty passengers. And
then another six hours to Kliprand. You will
have to take another taxi to Saltwaterfontein
once we get to Kliprand. We travel through the
night. Buy water and food first."

They gesture towards one of the popular spaza
stores—unlicensed shacks made from corrugated metal sheets. Spaza shops sell everything
from snacks and cool drinks, to data and air-
time top-ups for phones.

A twelve-hour journey in an old van overloaded
with passengers. And it won't even bring me to
the safari lodge door. I don't seem to remember
it being this hard when I was out here with my
family on vacation. Not even the nicest codeine
buzz will be able to get me through it.

Stepping back, I wish the passengers a safe journey. I have nowhere else to go but back to the rent-a-wreck. I've actually started to think of it as some kind of office. The man behind the counter recognizes me straight off the bat.

"No luck with the taxis? It's a nightmare out there. But that is what happens when it's the weekend."

"How much to use your phone?" I give him a rueful grin. "I can afford that at least."

Pushing the phone towards me, the guy tells me it's on the house. "Seems like you've run into a spot of bother. I was just telling my wife that it's the first time I've met an American without a credit card. Even the kids come out here with them. Did you get mugged?"

"A couple of hundred dollars doesn't amount to a hill of beans once the foreign exchange has gotten its teeth sunk into it." It's quite a relief being able to complain to someone. "And you know what? I might be getting too old for this shit."

"Time to settle down." The man gives me an understanding wink.

I dial a number. I don't use my phone in case Dan is monitoring comms. He might consider one of our freelancers as a company asset, which I'm not allowed to use as per our bet. But I'm not averse to cheating, considering the circumstances.

"Hey. Is that Gerrit Meyer? Buckle up, soldier. I need you to come pick me up ASAP."

Chapter 32: Edie

I can see that Sterling has taken pains to replace his family with a cadre of comrades since he was dumped at the military academy. And while that might have been a great way to cope with the difficult transition years between being a teenager and adulthood, it is not an ideal trait in a partner.

We're back to being separated and back to speaking over the phone instead of living a normal life together. The worst thing is that I haven't had the courage to tell him about our pregnancy yet.

This is what an atmosphere of half-truths and lies does to people. I'm keeping secrets from

Sterling because he began our relationship with lies. All along, he's been my puppet master, getting some kind of a sick thrill from fucking me when I thought he was one of Jack's employees.

Yes, sure I was tempted to spend a night or two with him in Dubai. The sex was out of this world from the get-go, so I'm not going to hold it against us. But at no stage of the game did I think that I would see him again.

And I was happy to wave him goodbye forever when he turned down my suggestion. How did we get from that careless goodbye to here? Me, pregnant and alone, yet again: Sterling, my secret boss, has gone off to hunt down whoever is scamming his charity.

Like diamonds in the rough, I get flashes of light in all the darkness. I know that Sterling is one of those men who won't quit until he's worked whatever it is he needs to process out of his system.

He's halfway there; I can see that from the way he takes pains to spend time with Noah. And he is certainly a very good friend, almost to the point where they take loyalty and caution too far, questioning any new entry into their tight circle.

But does he love me enough to give it all up? I know I can't raise Baby on my own. And that means two things: either Sterling shapes up—or he can ship out of my life forever. Sterling assured me that it wasn't Koos trying to harm my parents by stealing from the wildlife fund. That means I can go back to South Africa and live with Mom and Dad at the game park.

As much as Sterling loves playing his war games, he's going to have to give it all up for Baby and me. Sighing as I rub my slight baby bump, I have to smile as I imagine the future. I never thought I would see the day when I wished for a man who played golf or obsessed about video gaming.

It's time for me to call my best friend. Alice is outside at the park. She answers the phone panting as she chases after Noah on his electric motorcycle.

"Hey there you! Wanna visit the apartment tomorrow? We can all go catch a matinée performance of The Lion King. That opening number never fails to give me a lump in my throat. Hold on, Edie. Gabby wants to say something to you."

Scuffling sounds as Gabby grabs her mom's phone. "Edie! Please come. Mom says that I'm too big to fit onto Noah's bike and too small to drive a normal one. How unfair is that?"

Laughing, I tell Alice that I will come over in the morning. But it's not only Alice and the kids, and The Lion King musical, I want to see. I want to talk to Jack.

***

There is no way that I could afford last-minute tickets to one of the most popular musicals on Broadway, so I am happy to accept the one Alice offers me.

"Still on a tight budget, Edie?" Jack shouts out from the office as he hears us getting ready to grab lunch before the matinée. I decide to play nice. "Yah, Jack. But I promise to pay my way at McDonald's."

That makes him laugh. Satisfied, I follow Alice and the kids into the elevator. "Is Jack being a—" Alice looks down at the kids, thinking of the best insult. Her vocabulary has expanded quite a bit since Gabby grew old enough to understand the vulgarities that were spelled out. "—an old curmudgeon."

Immediately, Noah's on it. "What's a curmudgeon?"

The moment Noah asks the question, the elevator doors open. Alf Cohen is standing in the lobby, a wide, welcoming smile on his face. "Hey there, gorgeous. Long time no see."

I'm surprised when Alice engages him. "Hey, Alf. Well, I know you're not talking to me! Do you mind if I just talk privately with Edie for a sec? Something I don't want the—" Alice points to the kids without them seeing. "—to know."

Alf looks as if all his birthdays came at once. He nods and waits. When Alice stands on tiptoes to whisper in my ear, I mutter. "Are you out of your mind? I'm serious about your brother!"

Hiding her mouth behind her hand, Alice explains. "Please, Edie, play along. I want you to tell Alf that he can pop in for a visit after we come back from the matinée. Tell him you want to get to know him a little better before agreeing to a date."

Murmuring in my lowest voice as I keep one eye on Alf beaming in the lobby corner, I have one word. "Why?"

"Because Girly-oh, I'm tired of that big boys club Jack and Sterling have got going. Elitist, macho bullshit, that's what it is. I want to see how soon the news gets back to Sterling."

I am so down for that. Giving Alice a little pinch to show I'm on board, we break the huddle. I'm wearing a long-sleeve cotton Henley T-shirt with skinny jeans and tekkies, enjoying my denims for probably the last time. I could hardly get the top button done up this morning, but they make my ass look amazing.

Slapping a smile on my face and giving Gabby a wink, then I sway over to Alf. "Alf—I can call you Alf, can't I? It's so nice to see you again. We hardly got to know one another before I went to live in New Jersey."

I allow him to take my hand and give it a sweaty squeeze. "Damn, girl," he begins, like all middle-aged men with too much time and money on his hands, Alf talks like a streetwise hustler, "you look fine. How long are you here for?"

"Alf, I'm going to be straight with you. If you come over for tea after we bring the kids back from a matinée performance, I could be tempted into going out with you tonight."

Alf's eyes nearly bug out on stalks. "I'll tell the concierge to buzz me when you all come back if that's alright?"

I nod and give him a look over my shoulder as I swing my hair back.

"Oh yeah." Alice rubs her hands together as we look for a cab to take us downtown. "He'll be there—and then we'll get a bead on how fast the network connects."

After a very satisfying lunch at Gordon Ramsey's Fish and Chips, we walked to the performance and then caught a cab back up to Fifth Avenue. Sure enough, ten minutes after we get back to the apartment, the buzzer rings.

"Can you get that please, Edie?" Alice is taking pics of the kids in their Lion masks to send to her parents. I must say that I'm looking forward to twisting the knife a little bit. And I'm also interested in seeing how fast the news gets back to Sterling.

He might be in South Africa trying to sort out who is stealing from his charity, but it would be nice to know if he cares enough about me to kick up a fuss. Alice and I were always pulling stunts like this when we were tweens during Lewis's first safari.

We would shake Sterling awake and tell him a lion had gotten through the boma. Or we would squeeze cold toothpaste over his face during the night and wait for him to rub it in his sleep. And then there was the incident with the fire ants—the less said about that the better.

And then in the middle of all the fun we were having, I had to go and get the biggest crush on the boy I loved teasing so much.

Picking up the phone, I tell the concierge to let Alf up to our floor. The man sounds kind of incredulous, but I reassure him that I really want

Alf to visit. Moments later, the elevator doors open, letting out a blast of strong aftershave and hair product.

"You're looking good enough to eat!" Alf launches for me, trying to make good on his promise. I manage to duck him, leading him to the living room. Noah and Gabby have been told to act nicely and not say anything rude to the visitor. This proves to be too much for Noah, especially when Alf picks up one of the toys and criticizes it.

"Are you the man who lives above us? Haven't you got grandkids of your own to play with?"

Suddenly, I feel bad about what we're doing. Alf Cohen is a lonely old man who obviously doesn't have anyone in his family close enough to tell him to stop pretending he's a player.

But it's too late. Hearing the sound of a man's voice coming from inside the apartment, Jack comes out of his office. "Alf! What's up?" The two men shake hands. "To what do I owe the pleasure of your visit?"

Alf grins. "Pleasure? Edie, of course." Turning to speak to me, Alf continues. "Once we get to know one another better over a cup of coffee, what say we get out of here and go shopping for some La Perla for you, sweet cheeks?"

Alice grimaces at me from behind Jack's back, so I play along. "Sounds good. Thanks. But first, herbal tea for me, I'm afraid. Or decaf. Gotta sleep tonight, after all."

Jack backs out of the room, saying he has work. I sit on the floor with the kids, chatting about school and their favorite toys, all the while trying to tune out Alf's cheeky remarks about how hot he thinks I am.

It can't be more than half an hour before a loud buzzing noise trills into the apartment. Before Alice can pick up the phone, Jack is there, telling the doorman to send the visitor up. Alice darts a naughty look at me, but as far as I am concerned, this joke has gone too far. Poor Alf. If he weren't such a cheeseball, I would feel sorry for him.

I feel even more sorry for him when Dan Marshall steps out of the elevator. Jack is leaning against the living room entrance and gives a small wave as Sterling's partner comes in.

"Alice, you don't know the co-founder of your brother's company, do you? But it's time you did. Meet Dan Marshall. Dan, this is my wife and Sterling's sister, Alice. Edie, you've already met Dan, haven't you?"

Shit. They brought out the big guns. Alice and I dart "This has gone too far" glances at each other. Not bothering to get up from the armchair, Alf waves a cheery hand. "Hey there! I live upstairs. Just came over to grab a drink, then we're heading out, aren't we, sweetie?"

Alf grins at me, his wrinkled face completely unaware that he's probably signing some death warrant.

Dan squats down next to me on the rug and compliments Noah on his toys. "This manufacturer did a limited production of Aston Martins, sonny. I'll see what I can do to get you some." Then he stands up and holds his hand out to me. "Come on. I'm here to drive you home. It was nice meeting you, Alice, Gabriella."

I stand up meekly. I have to use Dan's hand as leverage because my jeans are too tight for mobility. My time to pull tricks and play jokes on people is over. And I can't say that I went out with a doozy!

Scrambling to his feet too, Alf objects. "Hey, fella! Didn't you hear me? The lady and me are going out just now."

Dan gives Alf that patented Lewis-Marshall and Associates death stare: eyes narrowed, mouth pressed into a firm line, jaw jutting out just a fraction, one arm held slightly away from the torso with the hand clenched into a fist.

Chapter 33: Sterling

I'm in the bakkie with Gerrit when Dan calls me back. A bakkie is what South Africans call an ordinary pickup truck. They are the biggest targets for carjackers in the country, but I have one of Gerrit's rifles clamped between my thighs, so I don't expect too much trouble.

"Dan," I answer the phone short and to the point. I just about hit the roof when I found out from Jack last night that Edie was getting ready to go out on a date with the only other billionaire she knows. All I could do was ask Dan to sort it out before going back to sleep. We had an early start this morning because the roads going north are treacherous.

Full of potholes, and in some parts just plain dirt tracks, leaving the city of Cape Town and heading off to the rural areas is not something to be undertaken lightly. Reaching a top speed of thirty-five miles per hour at best and traveling under a scorching sun for the most part, that part of me I grew to hate as a youth manages to get a word edgewise into my brain.

Why are you putting yourself through this? What are you trying to prove? This is just plain old ridiculous. I'm tired. I'm in pain. And I've just about reached my limit. I have a home to go back to now. I don't have to keep running anymore....

"Sorted, Marine. No worries. Go do your thing."

Suddenly, I'm invigorated with new strength. "What the fuck was Jack on about then? He told me that knobhead was planning on taking Edie shopping for sexy lingerie or something." A particularly deep pothole makes my neck jerk like a marionette. I give a yelp of pain as my sutures pull.

"Rough going, hey? The roads are always the first thing to go when corruption takes over. I'll tell you what happened—take your mind off the discomfort for a beat."

I press speaker on the phone because a story from Dan is always worth sharing. Gerrit and I have wide grins on our faces as we squint out at the bush trail road.

"I got to the apartment as quick as I could and Jack buzzed me up like he said he would. Found the mark settled all comfortable in an armchair, watching Edie with eagle eyes—an eagle with one thing on his mind, if you know what I mean."

Immediately, I'm grumpy again. I'm stuck out here in the bush while Alf bloody Cohen sits comfortably in the living room with my girl.

Dan continues. "I met the kids and your sister. They are a nice bunch. Jack's a lucky guy."

Putting my thumb over the receiver, I whisper to Gerrit above the noise of the engine. "That's high praise coming from Dan."

"I've placed an order at the factory in Chinghai. Got to get some Aston Martin miniatures for your godson. Noah will like that." Dan interjects into the story, before getting right back on top-ic. "So, after I suggested to Edie that we leave, she seemed on board with that. Got up off the rug where she had been playing cars with Noah, ready to go with me. No complaints."

"None?" I want to know. Dan expands on it. "The mark complained. Wittering on about Edie agreeing to go out with him that evening."

My hands clench involuntarily. "That hound. He's been dogging Edie since she first stepped through the building's doors."

"Yep. He's got a real inflated opinion of his charms. Ended up with me holding on to one of Edie's arms and him grabbing hold of the other one. She didn't like that at all. Told the mark that the date was off. When he didn't let go—he was standing there all upright and bristling like a bantam cock—I pushed the back of his knees in when he was not expecting it; I had to use my legs 'cause my arm is still out of commission. He went rolling over the rug and ended up sprawl-ing against your sister's Chinese vase—the big blue and white one in the corner."

"Did it break?" Gerrit and I are so busy stifling our laughter, that we forget the misery of traveling for a moment.

"The old tomfool or the vase? The vase just tottered a bit. Alice chewed us out and then told us all to leave. But I could see she was tickled pink about the whole thing."

"And Edie?"

Dan grunts. "Hmm. Edie is a minx. Turns out she and Alice played us all for suckers, using the mark to get our attention." I groan. That is exactly how I remember the two of them during the safari holiday, taunting the hell out of me with a whole bunch of tricks and japes.

Dan isn't finished yet. "I left her at the Mount Olive apartment. Edie didn't invite me in—she could tell I was pissed about the con. She's put on weight. Looking rosy. Maybe you two should spend time apart more often. It suits her." Before I can explode with outrage, Dan tells me he's joking.

"Tell Jack thanks. And I owe you one, Dan."

The call disconnects. It was just what I needed to get me through the last couple of hours of hellish driving conditions. We have to get off the roads before nighttime; that's when all the antelope and smaller mammals come out onto the roads.

The last thing I need is an eland or kudu bull through the windshield when I have less than one thousand rand in my pocket. Even with an almost twenty rand to one dollar exchange rate, I'm pressed for cash.

***

I remember the lodge and game park so well. This is where it all began. This is where I met Edie Kruger and set the course that the rest of my life would take.

Mpo, the lodge's head tracker, comes loping over to the bakkie when we trundle through the gates. He's completely unfazed by the heat and dust. Of course, he doesn't recognize me. I was a spotty asshole with dyed blond hair when I was last here.

"Hey." I reach over to shake his hand. "Sorry, I don't have a booking, but I'm actually here to see the Krugers."

Mpo grins and indicates for us to bring the bakkie around to the back of the lodge where the living quarters are. The main part of the lodge is divided into a wide raised porch overlooking the waterhole, a pool and bar area, and a dining room for guests.

There are ten thatched-roof self-service chalets and four guest rooms inside the main house. But every single one of the guests who pays to stay here wants to see animals when they venture outside the boma walls. That is what the Krugers are struggling to provide.

No matter how successful the lodge is, it will fail if the online reviews begin to say there was no wildlife to snap pictures of.

I groan and swear like a trooper when Mpo opens the door for me. He calls for the housekeeper inside to come and help me. If I look half as bad as I smell and feel, the Krugers might think twice before inviting me in.

"Marion! Deon! There's a man from America to see you! He's not lekker, hey."

Lekker is one of those Afrikaans words that can mean anything: fit, happy, sweet, kind, friendly. In this instance, Mpo means I don't look well.

I don't feel well either. Stopping off at the kitchen for some water, I drink two more codeine pills. Gerrit asks the housekeeper to show him to one of the guestrooms. "You can pay for it when you get back Stateside, Sterling." He grins, leaving me to make my own introduction.

Mr. and Mrs. Kruger invite me into their private parlor. It's heavenly, with an air conditioner cranked full blast and a bar fridge full of ice. Slumping down on the couch, I manage to groan out.

"It's me... Sterling Lewis."

Like magic, I'm shown to a guest room by Mrs. Kruger while Deon asks Mpo to find some clothes that might fit me. After a shower, a toasted sandwich, and three bottles of cold water, I sink down onto the mattress and allow Mpo to tuck me in. Lights out.

***

I sleep until breakfast. Gerrit has departed by the time I wake, leaving a note to say he will be on standby if I need him. Mpo has left a faded T-shirt with a soccer logo on the front for me to wear. My fancy New Laundry underpants have been washed and dried. I feel ashamed in case Mrs. Kruger saw the stealth condom pocket I have custom sewn into all my underpants. She's going to be family one day, I hope.

I never use condoms with Edie. She had a contraceptive injection before she planned her wedding to Koos, and we are confident the injection is the right form of contraception for us to use for now. We might have to look into the long-term health benefits of it, though, because I don't believe in the woman having to shoulder all the responsibility.

Dressed and refreshed, I walk to the private breakfast room. I have a lot on my mind because I don't know how I'm going to break the news about the charity scam to them.

The Krugers have Edie on speakerphone. I recognize her voice as she says hello to her parents. It must be nearly midnight East Coast time. Just hearing Edie, I feel less grumpy. I hang back at the door, not wanting to make a disturbance.

"Hi, sweetie. You'll never guess what—" Mrs. Kruger is going to tell her I'm here, but Edie butts in.

"Mom, Dad, I've been keeping a secret from everyone—I'm about fourteen weeks pregnant."

My feet glue to the floor with astonishment. I couldn't speak, even if I tried!

Mrs. Kruger doesn't miss a beat. "That's wonderful news, Baba! How is your health? You were so skinny before the wedding."

"It's a lot easier now that the morning sickness has gone, Mom, but now I have to buy a whole new wardrobe."

Marion Kruger sips her coffee. "Yah, but maybe some of those yoga pants will stretch as you get bigger? Don't go over the top with buying stuff.

Big tees and stretch pants should be enough. I'm so excited for you, darling. When are you going to break the news to Sterling?"

Her voice goes muffled as she speaks. "Oh God, Mom. I don't know. Dad? Are you okay with this? It's not like I was careless or anything. We took precautions."

Deon Kruger is old-school. "You'll be running away from one marriage straight into another one, Edie. You know that it will kill your Ouma if she finds out you want to have a baby without being married."

"Ag, Dad," Edie laughs, "you always put what's on your mind out there and then pretend it's granny's idea. All I want is a healthy baby. Everything else is gravy."

Deon turns and sees me standing there. "Sterling has just walked in, Edie. Say good morning to him and then go to sleep. I don't know much about eating for two, but sleeping for two can't do any harm."

Her voice thick with emotion, Edie says, "Dad! I haven't told him yet!"

A long silence stretches out tighter than Edie's yoga pants. "Sorry, Edie, Sterling," Deon begins to say, but Edie pretends the line is bad. "What? You're breaking up. Love you. Bye."

Only Marion is okay with what just went down. "Come and sit down, Sterling. My, but you certainly filled out, didn't you? I hardly recognized you when you arrived yesterday. I think I still have some old digital photographs on USB of when you were a little boy."

"Mr. and Mrs. Kruger—," I start to say, but Marion flaps her hand. "I think we're a little bit past that by now, don't you, Sterling? Please call us Tanie and Oom."

Tanie and Oom. Auntie and Uncle. Everyone is called Tanie and Oom once they reach the age of twenty-one. It's the South African equivalent of what ma'am and sir are in Texas.

"Thank you, Tanie. I have one thing to do before Edie and me can be together—"

Deon cuts me off. "That's my little girl you're having a baby with, Sterling. What on earth can be more important?'

I explain how someone has used their charity details to steal from the wildlife fund. That takes their minds off the baby for a beat.

"Yah. We applied to the fund, but we never heard back. We presumed that our application had been turned down. Marion has been talking to Edie, trying to get her to sort it out, but I guess now we know why she was so vague about how things are run there."

Marion butts in. "Sterling, you have to understand how bad things are here. The lions, rhinos, leopards, and cheetahs—they are being culled by poachers! Not a month goes by without us losing one or two animals. This can't continue."

I wanted to tell them that what happened at the game lodge fifteen years ago was what made me start the fund in the first place. I hate taking credit for such things.

But now it's time to set the record straight.

"Tanie Marion... I think you should know what really happened last time I was here...."

Chapter 34: Edie

I'm late to work the next morning. I end up dithering around so much that Lizzie makes me a doctor's appointment and tells me to va-moose. "Go on, head on out, Edie. Make use of the amazing medical insurance we have and go get checked by the doc. Once you have a nice pic of the baby in your hand, I can promise you that everything else falls into place."

Keeping the information about why we have such good medical insurance to myself, I thank Lizzie and Juan for being so understanding and head out.

At the surgery, the doctor refers me to an OBG-YN and somehow, I manage to spend the whole day having blood tests and ultrasounds while the specialist hands me pamphlets and warns me not to get my pre- and post-natal baby advice off the internet.

There is no way I am ever going to stick the word "baby" into my search engine, not after Dan tried to drive a wedge between Sterling and me by telling me about the spyware.

And as it turns out, Lizzie was right. When the curling black and white sonar scan image is placed in my hand, it's as if a light has been switched on in my heart. I feel so protective of that perfectly domed little head. After measuring the baby's length, the doctor tells me I'm closer to fourteen weeks pregnant.

That night in the rain, on the stairs, with the pizza delivery man....

While Sterling was getting grenades thrown at his head, he was already a daddy. I knew I was right to demand that shit must end. As nice as it is to know I have an army at my disposal whenever I want it, I don't want our baby exposed to such ruthless aggression and back-alley deals.

There is no way that I want to say all of this over a video call. South Africa has no public telephone system in place anymore worth speaking of, and cell phone calls are notorious for breaking up or disconnecting. There's nothing for me to do except reach out for my best friend's help again.

"Hello there, Whirly-oh." It's best if I just get what I need out in the open without any ums and ahs. "Or should I say, soon-to-be Aunty Whirly-oh?"

It takes a while for the news to sink in, but when it does, Alice is over the moon with joy. "Oh my gaaad, girl! No way! I'm so happy! Have you told Sterling?"

"That's just the thing, Alice," I explain. "I want to go tell him in person, but he's with my parents at the lodge, sorting out something for them. And I was wondering if you could be so kind as to lend me the money for a ticket over there, but please don't tell Jack. I don't think I'm strong enough to handle another one of his sardonic diatribes."

Laughing, too happy to say much except make burbling noises and talk about all the cool shopping we can do together, Alice flicks screen snaps of her credit card details over to me.

Smoothing my baggy T-shirt over my bump, I open the search engine app and tap "Flights."

***

I plan on hiring a rental to take me up to Saltwaterfontein—I have some savings on my card that I can use to pay for it because the rand-dollar exchange rate is so favorable. But it turns out that I don't have to.

A man is waiting for me outside the arrival gate with my name written on a sign.

"Edie? Hi, I'm Gerrit Meyer. Dan sent me to take you to the lodge."

After shaking his hand and handing my hold-all for him to carry, I say two words. "Did he reconnect the spyware to my search engine?"

Gerrit laughs while keeping his eyes focused on the exit leading to the Drop and Go parking.

"Dan can be very protective when it comes to the unit. I guess this makes you one of us now. There is no way he's going to fumble the ball, not on his watch."

"Am I the ball or the game?" I ask in a dry voice. A man hops out of the large white bakkie and goes around to the passenger side to open the door for me. After I get in, he disappears into one of the side entrances.

Gerrit sees me watching him and explains. "We always travel with at least one other crew so we can leave our firearms in the vehicle. And so, we can use temporary parking."

I notice that Gerrit didn't answer my question, but he does explain about the bet Dan and Sterling have going. "Sterling is doing this without recourse to company assets. Dan bet Sterling that he couldn't knock this problem down on his own. Frankly, my money's on Dan. There is no way Sterling can find the perp without help."

"What kind of help are we talking about here?" I'm munching on handfuls of biltong as we drive. Biltong is a special kind of spiced jerky that is the national snack. I think the baby has fallen in love with it because I can't seem to stop eating it. I see Gerrit look at me out of the side of his eye.

"You miss it? The biltong, I mean." He continues talking after I swallow and nod. "The unit is not just about the skillset of the staff. It's also about us boys with our toys! High-powered laser point rifles. Black-ops comms. Code-cracker software. I could go on. Take that away from Sterling, and he's just another man with a plan."

The drive is as hellish as I remember it to be. Most of the lodge guests choose to be transported to the lodge by light aircraft; my parents maintain a landing strip a few miles away from the lodge so that the planes don't disturb the wildlife.

Before dropping me off outside my parents' side of the main house, Gerrit let slip a bit of information I'm sure Sterling didn't want me to know. "Actually, you know what? Sterling might be in with a good chance if it comes down to hand-to-hand combat. I was privileged to see him in action when he took on that dickhead ex-fiancé of yours. Koos Van der Hoff has your typical rugby player build, a cross between a mountain and a truck. But Sterling wiped the floor with him. I've never seen anything like it. So, maybe he has a chance at winning the bet."

Thanking Gerrit for the lift, I enter the kitchen door. Like all the other times when I know Sterling is close by, a frisson of excitement begins to build up inside me. It's like a switch has been flipped, and my body gears up for sex.

No matter how pregnant I am, I know that the urge to be with Sterling will never fade. He is the embodiment of the ideal man to me. He's tall enough to handle my "five feet nine and a half inch" height. And don't even get me started on how perfect his body is; the man is a natural athlete, but with muscle bulk that makes him look just a little bit formidable.

As a youth, he was a pretty boy, but whatever happened to him during the fifteen years we were separated managed to knock some rugged handsomeness into him. I've never been a size queen—and I have five years of being intimate with Koos as proof that I am not! But I adore the way it feels when Sterling slides the full length and girth of his cock inside me.

And that is what I am looking forward to the most right now.

Only it's not going to happen. When I finish hugging Mom and Dad, they break the news to me.

"Sterling has gone out with Mpo to track the poachers, Edie. But come and sit down. We have a lot to catch up on. Only then are we going to talk about the baby."

Following my parents inside, I can tell they are bursting to tell me everything. When I am settled in an armchair with a cool drink and a bowl of biltong, my dad repeats Sterling's story.

***

"Tanie Marion, Oom Deon, I was a troubled kid, no doubt. My mom and dad raised me knowing that I was a mistake and that they never meant to have me. They were really young when I came down the chute, and Mom kept reminding me that it was my fault that they had to settle down and start a family in their early twenties.

They wanted to trek around the world and pay off their student loans, but instead, they got me. Alice was the favorite child, planned, loved, and given all their attention because by that time my dad's business had picked up and my mom had inherited a bucketload of cash from her own dad.

It bothered me that three years made such a big difference in how they thought about their kid, you know. But I was never any good at showing my emotions—so I internalized all of it and soldiered on.

And then one of our family vacations brought us to you. As far as Alice was concerned, it was a gift from heaven to meet Edie. Alice was always telling me how Edie and she went together like peas and carrots, how she loved Edie like the sister she never had. She wasn't lying, but all their close friendship did for me was make me even more of an outcast.

So, I set about making my own friends during the family vacation. And that was when I met Tjoepie. Tjoepie Du Plessis, one of your game warden's sons. He could hardly speak English, but we managed to bond over all that archetypal boy stuff—rifles, catapults, machetes. Anything that could maim or injure, Tjoepie and I liked to mess around with it.

Mpo tried to get us interested in other things; apparently, Mr. Du Plessis, Tjoepie's father, wasn't big on stressing how lethal weapons can be. I wish I could say Tjoepie and I were typical boys, but I would be lying. Our games took an insidious turn pretty quickly, starting with birds and ending up with—

I hate remembering the day Dickie the duiker died, but I have to tell this story straight.

Tjoepie, me, and a few other local boys were getting a rifle lesson from Mpo. He was always so kind to us, but he reached his limit with Tjoepie and me after finding yet another dead bird. And we had used the machete to chop its head off.

Apparently, that's how Tjoepie got his name—long before I came along. He liked to chop off chicken heads, caterpillars, and worms; any living thing he could lay his hands on. Hence his family graced him with the moniker 'Choppie' in Afrikaans.

So, I split, leaving Tjoepie to take the flak from Mpo. But I ran straight into my sister who wanted to tell me that Edie liked me.

Me, being a fifteen-year-old jerk with a class full of girls my own age waiting for me back in Manhattan, I could only laugh at the suggestion that I go steady with a pre-pubescent kid.

I ran away, around the back of the boma, where I had left my rifle leaning against the wall. Running was the only way I could think of to escape Edie's young love. No one had ever said they liked me before—I didn't know how to handle it.

I decided to go back to rifle practice with Mpo. But Tjoepie was waiting around the corner for me. He was angry because I had left him to take the blame for the dead bird.

I'll never forget how it happened in slow motion. Tjoepie took aim, firing the rifle at me, and then running away. I heard the crack of the bullet as it missed me. The squeak of the little antelope as the air left its lungs.

I don't think I would have survived the horror of it if I hadn't gone into shock. Surviving that incident, and how my parents punished me after-wards, is what made me as hard as woodpecker lips. Never again would I trust someone who had not earned it. This might read as grumpy to some people, but I never let my guard down until I met Edie again."

"So, you see, Baba," my mom finishes the story, "Sterling didn't shoot your pet duiker. Tjoepie tried to murder him! That psycho. If we knew that, we never would have allowed Tjoepie to work for us."

Feeling weak after what I just heard, I manage to gasp. "You had Tjoepie Du Plessis working here? What the f— Mom, Dad! Are you insane?"

Dad interrupts. "Never mind all that because it's easy to criticize in hindsight. Listen, you must go meet up with your man. I've asked Mpo to send us the coordinates of their camp."

I hesitate. "How did Sterling take the news of the baby?"

Mom shrugs. "You know how Sterling is, Baba. You can never tell what he's thinking or feeling. A picture of Sterling Lewis should be in the dictionary next to the word 'Pokerface.'"

Chapter 35: Sterling

Hopping behind the wheel of the Jeep, Mpo tells me he's heading back to the lodge. "Don't forget the thorn trees, Sterling. You're going to need them. And if there are any problems, call on the walkie-talkie—Deon keeps a receiver open next to the bed."

After waving him goodbye, I take the machete and start chopping. I need to encircle the camp with a thicket of thorn bushes because my fancy laser beam alarm tech is in Manhattan. Now, the only thing standing between me and all the wild animals who want to eat me out here is the thorns.

I knew it was Tjoepie Du Plessis who was scamming the wildlife fund from the moment the Krugers told me he had left their employment at the same time the monthly payments stopped. Instead of writing an email to ask why the donations had been delayed, Tjoepie tendered his resignation, knowing he had been rumbled.

He had set up his own account for the money to be paid into, and then monitored the scam using the Kruger's own computer system. With the rand-dollar exchange rate being what it is, he must have scored millions of rands over the last five years, because I made it clear that I wanted Kruger's Safari Lodge to be one of the primary beneficiaries of the fund.

I started up the wildlife fund the day my Swiss bank accounts and offshore savings cleared the fifty million dollar mark. I always wanted to make it up to the Kruger family for what happened with Dickie the duiker. Although I thought that no one would ever believe my innocence, I still wanted to make good on the debt I felt I owed.

Poking some green leaves into the flames to make smoke to keep the mosquitoes at bay, I settle down to boil water. It's going to be noodles and biltong for supper tonight. I need to be up early in the morning if I want to make headway against the poachers.

I hear the Jeep rumbling back up the dusty trail but couldn't be bothered getting up. I'm kind of hoping the Krugers have sent Mpo back. He's way better at tracking than I am. I might not be able to catch Tjoepie Du Plessis and get my money back, but I can sure help the Krugers bring the pain to the poachers who have been culling the wildlife.

The sound of the Jeep reversing and leaving again interrupts my thoughts. Damn, I forgot to leave a gap in the perimeter of thorns! Jumping up, I pull out one of the branches to make a hole. All the thorn tree trunks face inwards so that no one else can pull them loose.

The sun sinks fast in Africa. Already, the strange cries of animals have begun to witter in the twilight. A slim silhouette is walking towards me. I would recognize that beautiful outline anywhere.

Letting the thorn branch drop, I run to catch Edie in my arms.

"Damn, Edie, you look good enough to eat! I've missed you, sweetheart."

I feel her body relax against me. "So, you're not pissed about the baby? We must have miscalculated how long the injection lasts...."

Holding Edie at arms' length, I show her how overjoyed I am at the news. "I would never consider our baby a miscalculation, Edie. The moment I heard the news, I knew this was what my life had been missing for all these years. I love our baby now, and you can bet anything that I will love the baby after they are born!"

Staring up at me with her gorgeous hazel-green eyes, Edie blinks back the tears. "Promise you're not just putting on a brave face? Because... I don't think I would want you to go off on those secret missions of yours after Baby is born."

Leading her back to camp and pulling the barricade of thorns closed after us, I hug Edie from behind as we watch the sunset.

"Consider this to be my last mission, darling. My last hurrah. And I couldn't think of a better way to do it—hunting down the bastards who have been hunting down endangered wildlife."

All around us seem to be waiting for the shoe to drop. As the crimson sun hits the horizon in a burst of red, the shadows begin to lengthen and narrow all around us. Craggy boulders become black, bulky shapes; trees stick out of the tall grass like spindly warning signs.

As the last of the sun dips below the hills, the sky turns purple, and the stars blaze out. The bush starts to come alive as the wildlife heads for the waterhole. All the nocturnal animals must be flexing their muscles, tuning up, and getting ready to prowl and hunt.

Tourists only get a hint of how bush animals live when the safari vehicles drive them down to the waterholes at dusk and dawn. But the real action happens at night.

Hearing a hyena's cackle, Edie asks me how many rifles Mpo left behind.

"I wouldn't let you stay here if there was even the faintest chance of something happening,

Edie. Mpo left two rifles. That should be more than enough to allow us to sleep through the night."

She turns, sliding her arms around my neck. "Actually, Sterling, who said anything about sleeping...?"

It's the first time I hesitate when it comes to taking up the offer of hot sex from the woman I love. "What about—? I don't want to hurt the baby."

Giving a cute gurgle of laughter, Edie's eyes twinkle as she looks at me. "Are you worried about your size? You forget that we've already had sex when I was pregnant, and nothing bad happened. I'm nearly four months pregnant now, Sterling, so don't stress."

Then she does the hottest thing imaginable. Sliding her hand over my crotch and caressing my already rampant bulge, Edie stands on tip-toes and whispers in my ear. "You know how I love to blow you first anyway. And I can't wait to wrap my mouth around your cock and lick you until you shoot your load. The second after you've done that, I'm going to climb you like a very tall tree."

Forgetting all about the sunset and stars, I drag the sleeping bag out of the tent and place it next to the fire, where the smoke is billowing up to the sky. I don't want my darling Edie's ass bitten by mosquitoes.

It is the first time that we are truly alone, without anyone nearby to listen in or knock on the door. Edie kneels on the ground and unzips me. God, it's so hot the way she makes sultry eye contact with me as she frees me from the confines of my underpants and begins to suck my cock.

Locking her gaze on me, she works the shaft with one hand and plays with my balls with the other. This is the first time I get to watch her take as much of me into her mouth as she can. I groan, biting the side of my lower lip as I try to make it last.

Then Edie sticks her hand down the front of her panties, fingering her clit as she jerks me off, licking and sucking my rock-hard knob. It's too much. My cock jerks as I squirt into her mouth. The sound of our panting fills the night.

But we've only just started. Stripping naked, we fall onto the sleeping bag with the feverish need to fuck. I don't even have time to kick off my boots and socks so that I can remove my jeans before Edie has straddled me.

She looks so beautiful as she rides my cock in the moonlight. I have always loved keeping my eyes open when I fuck Edie, but this time it almost blows my mind. Her breasts are heavy and full, and her hips and ass are so soft and curvaceous, as she digs her fingers into my pecs while grinding her pussy onto me.

We are both primed and ready to go. It's been too long since we were able to show one another how much we loved one another with our bodies. I can't resist caressing her nipples with my fingers, giving them a soft pinch, and feeling the thrill inside my cock when she groans and tells me she loves it.

I could lie here and watch her ride me all night, but I have to come again. There is nothing else on earth I love more than when Edie and I come together. Leaning forward so that my rigid tool can't hurt her, Edie allows her breasts to tickle against my mouth.

I suckle at them with a desperate craving and come—just as she gives a soft moan and begins to gyrate with intense pressure. I thrust up, spasming and jerking deep inside her warm wetness. The sensation is so strong that I almost pass out from all the blood ramping up inside my cock.

Collapsing against my chest, Edie goes silent. All she can do is groan softly, but I'm used to her little ways after we finish making love, so I don't worry.

Spitting some of her hair out of my mouth, I manage to crack a joke. "I saw stars that time, sweetheart, but I'm not sure if it was just because my eyes were looking at the sky or because you are my very own personal sexual superstar. Can I take off my boots now?"

She giggles and we make ourselves more comfortable by opening the sleeping bag zipper all the way and spreading it out. I remove my boots and take off my jeans too.

Edie has that postcoital glow as she watches me in a sort of trance. "I always seem to forget how big you are. It gets me every time... feeling it and seeing it."

"Hey, I'm proportional," I remind her. "I have long, thick muscles everywhere else on my body too, not just there."

"You would have broken me in two if you tried to get with me when I was in high school," Edie muses, half to me, half to herself. "I was skinny as a rake and willowy. Zero sex appeal. I only began filling out in university. I must have had delusions of grandeur to have believed you capable of falling in love with me when I was twelve."

Falling on my knees beside her, I grab her hands. "Edie, don't say such things. I was a grumpy young fool then and a grumpy old fool for a long time after I got you that upgrade. I couldn't see what was staring me in the face for the longest time—no amount of excitement and adventure can compare to what we have waiting in front of us."

And for the first time, I stroke her tummy and then kiss it.

She makes a little mewling sound, running her hand over my short hair and then kissing my head.

"I'm happy to be a tame house cat with you, sweetheart," I dare to tell her, "because I want our little kitten to grow up knowing they are loved. I never knew what it was that I wanted until you helped me see it. Let's get married."

Edie nods her head and smiles. She has no more doubt, and nor do I.

We lie under the stars together, wisps of smoke and the crackle of flames creating our own cosmos. The rest of our night will be spent planning our future and making love.

And when dawn starts to break, we will make our way to the waterhole to watch the wild animals come to drink and graze. Then we will begin planning how to catch the poachers.

Chapter 36: Edie

Waking up with the pale pink light of an African sunrise in my eyes is one of the best feelings in the world. I lie there quietly for a beat, watching the purple sky fade away and turn orange. The twittering of birds takes over as the rustle and grunts of nocturnal animals die down.

The warm feeling of love washes over me as I remember where I am and whom I am with. So, this is what it feels like to love and be loved. And have a small life growing underneath my heart, waiting for the chance to share the love.

Sterling has got the kettle boiling on the gas hob. He's nowhere to be seen. The cold space where his body had been keeping me warm all night is what woke me up. Sitting upright and stretching, I step through the gap in the thorn hedge and go to the track to look for him.

I can tell from the smell in the air that the Land Cruiser safari truck hasn't brought lodge guests to the waterhole yet, so I'm fine to walk around naked. The acidic scent of diesel fumes can be detected a mile off, never mind the grinding of gears and crunching of wheels.

The only way wildlife sightings can be guaranteed during a safari is to get out before dusk or dawn and watch animals congregate at the waterhole. Especially in spring, when most of the herds and flocks have calves and chicks to care for.

Sterling swings down from a marula tree branch, binoculars hanging from around his neck, as I wander over. He looks as gorgeous as ever. His jeans hang down, low enough to show the hair growing in a line down the middle of his lower abdomen—his own personal stairway to heaven.

His skin glistens in the early morning light, slick with a thin film of sweat. The pressure bandage from his waist is gone, leaving the angry blemish of bruise and sutures of the wound on show. It's at moments like this when I realize that Sterling is a man who has experienced so much pain in his life that a little more doesn't have the power to hurt him anymore.

He's my own personal Tarzan in this vast grass-land wilderness. If I didn't feel so funky and sticky from all the sex we had last night, I might be tempted into a little bit of early dawn delight with this stunning hunk.

I must look pretty strange—naked with tekkies on my feet. But this is the only time of the day it is cool enough to enjoy the still, temperate air wafting over my body.

"What exotic animal is this?" He pretends to be an astonished Victorian gentleman hunter. "Can I shoot it with my rampant rifle, lick its skin, and stick its head on my... wall? Or should I just fuck its brains out?"

I push him away as he tries to kiss me. "No, Sterling. I haven't cleaned my teeth. I need you to lift that water tank for me. It's too heavy."

Walking back to the camp with me, I can see he has more of the same as what happened last night on his mind, but I'm not in the mood. "And if you think I'm going to let you shoot me, skin me, and stick my head on the wall before I've washed, you can just go climb back up that tree."

The kettle is boiling when we get back to camp. Sterling makes coffee as I take a bottle of water behind a thorn tree and wash. I come back in a marginally better mood. Sterling's eyes follow me.

"It's phenomenal how your body is changing, Edie. It's like before you were a little girl, but now that you are pregnant, you're all woman."

"If there's a compliment hidden in there," I say, smiling at him, "I'm sure it's designed to make me feel better. But you only brought caffeinated coffee, Sterling, so forgive me for taking my frustrations out on you."

"Shit," he acknowledges the mistake, "how about I radio Mpo and your dad to drive the Land Rover over here? They can bring you some of that herbal tea you like."

"Red bush tea? Yah, that sounds good. Thank you." Red bush tea, called Rooibos tea in Afrikaans, is a brew the indigenous people used as a beverage for thousands of years. The thin, spiky leaves are dried and chopped, before being steeped in hot water until it turns red.

You can't turn a corner in South Africa without seeing a toddler making the transition from breastmilk to a bottle of sweetened, milky rooibos tea somewhere. That is the reason why there are so few cases of allergies and food intolerance in the local population. Kids are raised on bush tea because the health benefits are undeniable.

"What are your plans to catch the poachers?" I ask Sterling after he finishes his conversation with my dad.

He jerks his head. "Better get dressed, sweetheart. I don't want all the bridges I've been able to mend with your parents to go crashing down again."

After carefully checking the items for spiders, ants, and scorpions, I slip my clothes back on. Sterling has one of my dad's old maps on the ground. He's committing the terrain to memory.

"What are those red and yellow crosses for?" I ask him. Someone has drawn dozens of colored crosses over the outline of the game park boundary.

"Red crosses mark poacher kills, and the yellow ones are maimings—antlers and horns. And the orange ones are caged hunts."

Caged hunting is the most evil poaching practice. The poacher pretends to be a tracker and lures in hunters from overseas. Once the poachers find out which wild animal the hunter wants as a trophy, they send out one from their own team to track the poor animal down and shoot it with a tranquilizer gun.

Once the lion or leopard is too doped to move, they drive the hunter to the spot and tell him to shoot it. If the poachers can't afford a tranquilizer dart, they set a tether rope trap for the buck or big cat. When the buck is caught with his hoof in the trap and can't move, the hunter is called to come take his shot.

Where is the sport? Overseas hunters don't care. All they want are the bragging rights that go with having that head mounted on the wall. And then they hand over millions of rands to the poacher, which just encourages them to continue the practice.

Sterling and I hear the Land Rover approaching. We can smell the diesel fumes from the exhaust too. Like Mpo says to all the game farm hunters who come to visit us and refuse to bathe or clean their teeth in case the scent alerts the animals to their whereabouts: "Sir, the animal is going to smell you whether it's sweat and dirt, or toothpaste and soap. That's why we always approach the herd downwind."

If the wind blows the scent of humans away from the herd, there's a small chance a five-year-old buck can be bagged. But if any animal gets a whiff of a foreign aroma in the air, they will scatter like leaves in fall. The trick is to always feel the wind in your face.

It is not hypocritical for my parents to offer game-farmed antelope for hunting. Too many young male bucks can injure each other during mating season. A dominant male antelope can gore another buck who tries to muscle in on his herd, and without horns to defend itself or an injured leg, a buck becomes vulnerable to starvation and disease.

When a herd begins to fracture because of too many bucks fighting, we allow hunters to pay to participate in the cull. The beauty of the system is this: if the hunter misses the shot, they still have to pay. And if they injure the buck, they have to pay double for professional trackers to hunt down the injured animal.

My dad tells me that one hunter has been coming back to kill an ancient male kudu buck for the last fifteen years! And each time, he misses. Kudus are notoriously large antelope, with the uncanny ability to blend into the surrounding bush.

But this particular hunter has paid almost a million dollars trying to bag a male kudu for the bragging rights. My parents bought a lot of tag trackers and high-tech monitors with that money.

Suffice it to say that legitimate hunting helps safaris and game parks feed animals during times of drought. The costs of tagging and satellite tracking the animals are exorbitant too.

Every newborn has to be tagged and tracked so they can be monitored. If a tag doesn't move or goes offline, then my dad and Mpo go in to see if the animal is all right.

Stepping outside the circle of thorn bushes, I watch as the Land Rover bumps over the track, kicking red dirt dust into the air. Bless my parents—my dad has brought us a packed brunch my mom prepared for us.

"Mpo is bringing the Land Cruiser to pick me up once the guests have been dropped off back at the lodge," he tells us as I hungrily open the basket and riffle through the contents. "So, you can take the Land Rover. It's got a tracker in it, so I'll be able to find you wherever you are in the game reserve.

Sterling has a few questions. Glancing over at me as I pour a large serving of red bush tea out of the flask, he asks my dad what frequency the tracker transmits on.

Tuning out the men as I eat the food, I only get to hear small parts of their conversation. Suddenly, I begin to pay attention. "Do you think it's possible for the poachers to track the animals via the tags too? That's impossible! No poacher has that kind of tech knowledge." I might have a bellyful of food to make me content, but I can't stand the thought of those bloody poachers using our hard work to kill more animals.

Sterling tries to calm me down. "It's just a suggestion we have on the table, Edie, a working hypothesis."

Dad looks at me before replying. "Sterling has a point, Dogtertjie." My dad likes to speak Afrikaans when my English-born and bred mother isn't around to click her tongue at him; he's calling me "little daughter."

"The only time we manage to spring a surprise on the poachers is when we come across them while we are driving. And we can only do that because the trackers on the vehicles are on an app. But we have to consider that there might be a way to hack the tag tracker. It's the only explanation as to how they know where to find the herds and herd predators. It's not like they are hanging round the waterhole with rifles—we have lookouts posted there, beside the lodge guest tours coming in at dawn and dusk every day."

Sterling explains further. "The poachers only ever manage to hunt down tagged animals. Your dad is taking this seriously, sweetheart. We've already started capturing animals when they come down to the waterhole and removing the tags."

I get dizzy with frustration when I hear that. After all Mpo and my dad's hard work, we have to stop the tagging program.

Running his hand up and down my back, Sterling comforts me. "We're seeing positive results from removing some tags already, babe, and that's all that matters.

Turning to my dad, Sterling chats about hiring more trackers for detagging and CCTV cameras in trees.

"Can't we leave some of the tags on the animals that aren't endangered, or put the tags on rodents instead?" I'm hugging my knees and drinking my fourth mug of red bush tea. My brain is working overtime, thinking of ways to catch the poachers. "I hate those illegal hunters so much, I want them to run around the bush, wasting their energy."

Chapter 37: Sterling

Deon and I stare at Edie with our mouths open. "That's actually a very good idea," I say to Deon. "Edie can set up camp for us down by the waterhole while I keep my eye on one of the tags at the locations where the poachers like to hit. With so few tags still up and running, they are bound to take the bait."

"Hey," Edie exclaims, smacking my upper arm, "it was my idea, so why should I be stuck down at the waterhole, keeping the camp nice and clean?"

I let her father field this one. Deon shakes his head. "There is no way you are running around the bushveld when a group of lethal poachers are out there with rifles, Edie." I know what bushveld means—it's how the Afrikaaners describe the vast expanse of grasslands that sweep large parts of the country.

I drive the point home. "And you are so quick to shit all over me going out on projects now that I have you and the baby to consider, so this is me, paying you back in kind. You must promise to stay in the camp or you can go back with Deon right now."

Edie sulks a bit and pouts a lot, but she looks cute doing it and she can't keep it up for long. Her bubbly personality won't allow it. "Fine," she says, unfolding her arms. She starts digging in the brunch basket again. "But please take the sightseers to the opposite side of the water-hole, Dad. I don't want to wake up with a whole bunch of folks staring at me through the window."

We have a lot of logistics to discuss. I want to run with the idea of sticking tags on rodents and letting the poachers think that the animals are scattering, but Deon nixes the plan. "These guys are pros. They'll be able to detect the different movements and grouping patterns."

"I hear you." I grab a sandwich while Edie gets stuck into the plastic tub of strawberries Marion packed for us. "Then we need to find an animal that stays quiet and still during the day. Your least mobile antelope, happy to just sit and graze in one spot. But one that a poacher is going to place a high value on for what it can yield on the black market."

Deon and Edie say the word at the same time. "Kudu." Deon continues. "Yah, my dogtertjie is right. The kudu bucks can stand for hours in one spot, the only movement giving them away is when they bend their necks to graze. They are impossible to find in the grass because they are the same color. They don't even budge when the birds sit on them to eat the ticks."

I'm about to rally the troops and begin strategizing with Deon about how to place the rangers to intercept any roaming kudu bucks, but I guess he can see the light of the hunt in my eyes.

"This is something you are going to have to do on your own, Sterling. Why do you think Marion, Mpo, and I have let this slide for so long? Our main priority is the safari lodge. That's what pays the bills. We might have been able to erect electrified fences around a wider perimeter using funds from the wildlife charity, but that was a bust."

Deon seems to let his anger get the better of him. "Damn it! If our bank account isn't being hacked, the defenseless animals in the park are being poached! Sometimes, I hate Africa so much."

The three of us sit in silence for a long while as we think about how hard it is to make a difference on a continent where life—all life—is held so cheap.

"Mpo and I will need the Land Cruiser to bring sightseers to and from the watering hole, but you can have the Land Rover and sleep in the back. Then just keep the doors closed if you don't want to set up a thorn tree perimeter—got to keep out the leopards. They are curious animals if they smell supper scraps. If they come too close, shine a light on them. Edie knows the drill." Deon explains to me the best way to capture the oldest kudu.

"The buck will come down to the waterhole this evening. I don't have to tell you how to use a tranq dart. We don't allow hunters access to the watering spots, so the animals can relax and play there. The guests like to watch them from the patio."

"How many days do you think it will take for the poachers to take the bait?" I'm imagining Edie and me sleeping in the back of a Land Rover for weeks on end.

Deon chuckles. "Relax. Once Mpo and you have set the trap, we'll drive away the herds and predators to the outer perimeter so that any transmitter can pick up the kudu buck signal loud and clear. We should have you back at the lodge before the mosquito season starts up with a vengeance."

***

Our plan goes like clockwork. I feel bad as the enormous kudu buck collapses to the ground with my tranq dart in its hind quarters, but with Mpo's help we have the animal on the back of the Land Cruiser using the pulley and winch, and he's tethered to the ideal poaching spot half an hour later.

Edie makes sure the kudu has an old barrel of water next to him, and we watch as the buck staggers to stand up. After tugging his tethered hoof a few times, the animal simply gets back to grazing quietly, completely invisible amidst the long yellow grass and thorn trees.

Giving us the thumbs-up, Mpo tells Edie that her mom wants her to come back to the lodge with him. "Tanie Marion says you must leave arresting the poachers for Sterling to do, Edie. They are bad men."

Edie scoffs. "Pah! Please tell Mom that I'm not scared of a few skinny men with secondhand rifles. Sterling can shoot a raven at midnight with his eyes shut."

As pleased as I am to hear Edie's high opinion of my shooting skills, I have to warn her. "Go back with Mpo, sweetheart. I'm an excellent shot with a Barrett M82, but all your dad keeps in the house are old .22 rifles that haven't had the sights checked for years—and that's the only kit I get to use here."

She refuses, and I think I know why. The sex that we have been having out here in the bushveld has been wild. As grumpy as it makes me, whenever Edie puts me in a position against her parents, I make a judgment call.

"We're half an hour's drive away from the bait here, Mpo. I'll set up a hide in the morning and wait for the poachers to rise to the lure. Just make sure to scatter the animals far once they have finished at the waterhole so that the kudu buck's tag is the only one within the radius. Edie will only be a few yards back from the water's edge, out of sight from the tourists. We'll be fine."

"But there's only one walkie-talkie," Mpo points out. "And you have to take that to call it in once you have a bead on the poachers."

Edie huffs. "I'll be fine! If I need anything, I'll walk around the lake and head home."

Chuffing and shaking his head, Mpo heads back to the lodge.

"You should have gone back with him, Edie." I can't help but get grumpy whenever she doesn't take my advice. "Maybe living Stateside has made you forget how fucking ruthless people can be when money is involved."

"Like you, you mean?" Edie replies in a sunny tone. "Don't you feel great being on the good side for once?"

I stop cleaning the .22 rifle Mpo left for me to use. "I'm always on the good side."

She holds up one finger. "Wrong. You're always on the winning side. There's a difference."

I know she's trying to rile me, but I bite anyway. "Please explain to me how helping global leaders acquire assets is wrong. This one has too much oil, and they are prepared to sell some of it for gold bars or diamonds or Bitcoin. Who's getting hurt in all that? I mean, besides the people who try to get in my way."

"It's backhanded. And you didn't just do that. You were king of the bedroom leverage too."

I have the grace to hang my head. "I'm a man, Edie. Please let me go through life seeing things from a man's point of view."

She accepts that, but I can see she's not ready to let the subject drop. "Okay, then give me an example of when you used that particular skill set of yours for a woman's benefit."

"Our organization is strictly limited to male circles, Edie. We can't let it be known how we operate. All you need to know is this: if you steal from your partner or try to blackmail him for more out of a divorce settlement, it's only fair that he gets to fight back in the way he chooses."

Edie concedes. "Fine. So, tell me an interesting story. Something out of the ordinary."

I have to think hard. "A wealthy Hollywood tycoon hired me to find out if his partner was cheating on him and not using protection. That was pretty interesting. I had to find out all sorts of ways to get proof without actually getting to the point where I would have to bed him."

"Him!" Falling over with laughter, Edie shows me props with a high five. "How did that play out?"

Shrugging, I load a bullet into the rifle chamber. "Simply showed him my equipment and told him I like to ride bareback. Caught his enthusiastic agreement on film—didn't even have to get hard."

I can see that Edie is tickled pink from hearing these stories, so I tell her more. I've never had anyone who wanted to listen before, but now that I'm spilling the beans, it feels good to let it out.

"Let me see... there was a high-class Eastern European prostitute who tried to get something to blackmail her client after smuggling a framed photograph of his wife out of the couple's house. The mark thought he had theft covered because his bodyguards searched her purse and clothing before she left, but she had it hidden inside a condom in her anal cavity. He called the unit the minute he missed the item. We chased her down and got the photo back... eventually. It's not always gold and diamonds we have to go mining for!" More hilarious laughter. I think I'm getting the hang of this sharing thing.

"And then there are numerous ex-girlfriends and mistresses who threaten to go public with ill-advised text or answering machine messages, but that stuff has gotten rarer as clients cotton on to the game. I could go on."

"You're a regular Mr. Fix-it, Sterling," Edie purrs as she crawls over to me. "But please tell me that I am more interesting than the long weapon you have in your hands."

After carefully propping up the rifle against the Land Rover, I make a lunge for her. "My long weapon is strictly for your hands only, sweetheart," I growl in her ear, "so tell me, do you want to load it and make it shoot?"

She does. I don't think Edie ever gets tired of sucking my cock. In all our time together, she's never seen it soft, because the second I know she wants to fuck, I almost come in my pants. It's this way she has of licking her lips and locking her eyes on mine; it gets me so excited every time.

We keep our clothes to a minimum all alone out here as we are. With the slanting sun rays warming our skin, as we lie under the marula trees on a blanket, we have the time to take pleasure in each other's bodies. She allows me to suck her breasts, teasing the nipples into peaks with my tongue. Edie strokes my cock with her hand, spreading the pre-cum around my knob.

Moving down her softly rounded belly, I flick my tongue over her clit. Immediately, she lifts her mound to tell me she wants it harder. That's my sign to bury my face into her pussy and really eat her out with my tongue. When she's dripping wet and writhing with excitement, I drive my stiff prick into her.

Throwing back her head to expose her neck, Edie stares at the stars and screams as she comes.

Chapter 38: Edie

I open my eyes just a fraction when I hear movement in the dark. By the light of the moon, I see Sterling strapping the rifle behind his back. He must have borrowed some of Mpo's clothes because he's wearing a faded khaki shirt with sleeves that allow a good two inches of his wrist to stick out at the end.

His khaki bush pants are tucked into the worker boots he always wears. Somehow, he manages to make the ensemble look dashing, especially when he tilts a Stetson over his eyes.

I don't want to wake up. I've always loved to sleep in late in the mornings, but since I fell pregnant that lazy feeling keeping me under the covers has only increased. And besides, I don't want Sterling to kiss me goodbye when I'm all crusty with sleep.

So, I just watch him from under my lashes as he stalks away through the tall grass. Like a jungle cat, he doesn't make a sound....

I don't know how many hours later I wake up. It's as if my body tells me that I've reached my sleep limit and turns off the "doze" faucet. Sitting up and rubbing my eyes, I yawn and stretch, doing all those things while imagining what it's going to be like in five months' time when the baby is due.

Clambering down from the Land Rover, I check the camp. Being the gentleman that he is, Sterling has left a plastic basin of water for me to use. He knows how much I hate walking around all muggy with the smell of sex clinging to me.

First, I wash my face. After a beat, I dunk my whole head into the basin and wet my hair. It's the only way I'm going to beat the heat as I wait for Sterling to come back.

I don't have long to wait for his return. Not even poachers stalk animals after ten o'clock in the morning. It gets too hot, even in springtime the temperatures can soar into the upper nineties. The animals hunker down in the grass and under—or on top if it's a leopard—thorn trees.

That's why we tethered the kudu in the shade of a tree. One night and half the morning of grazing with a barrel of water nearby won't terrify such a large antelope. It simply mimics the animal's own behavior patterns.

Using a small towel and wetting it, I wash all those parts of my body that Sterling loves so much. He can get so ravenous for sex; I can't help worrying about what it might be like after Baby is born. I want to satisfy my man but wonder if I might experience a dip in my passion levels once I have a little soul to care for.

Looking around the camp, I can see no trace of Sterling. It's as if he walked out into the bushveld and disappeared. Then I see it. He left the walkie-talkie for me to use.

Damn it, Sterling! I'm safe, next to the Land Rover, within walking distance of the lodge. If anything bad happens, all I have to do is wait for this evening when Mpo or my dad come down to the watering hole with more sightseers.

I'm not the one stuck in the bush, waiting for a group of poachers to come popping out of the grass! For one moment, I'm tempted to go looking for him. I don't have a watch. Cell phones are of no use out here because there is no reception.

Cell towers are a luxury that only cities can afford. The lodge has satellite Wi-Fi, but one of the main attractions the safari offers is the unplugged experience of completely disconnecting from the outside world. The no-device policy is encouraged, but not enforced.

But it makes me sad to think how many kids are not sent outside to play make-believe instead of sitting in their rooms with whichever app they are currently addicted to. I don't think Alice and I would be such close friends today if all we had to bond over as kids was a screen and a video game!

From the faint warmth coming from the sun, I reckon it has to be close to eight o'clock. The lodge guests will be having breakfast out on the patio after having come back from wildlife watching from the hide platform overlooking the waterhole.

Sterling would be lying under his hide since four in the morning. The dawn hours are the best time to catch a big cat prowling home after hunting or find a large antelope nibbling the dewy grass.

I know the chances of the poachers coming to look for the kudu are slim, but all I want is for one of them to stick their head out of the grass and come face-to-face with Sterling's rifle sights. And as for the people who buy rhino horn powder, lion pelts, and trophy antelope horns, I pray there's a special place in hell for them.

I am so tempted to drive the Land Rover back to the edge of the waterhole and then walk over to the lodge to have breakfast, but I can't risk having Sterling return to the camp and find nothing here. It's setting up to be a hot day, so there's a big chance that he will cut the kudu free and head on back early.

I settle for eating a peanut butter and jelly sandwich from the picnic basket Dad brought. We stay away from deli meat and mayo out here because warm sandwich fillings in Africa are a one-way trip to the emergency room with food poisoning. The thought of that happening makes me instinctively cradle my stomach.

I start packing up the bedroll and sleeping bag and kicking out the smoldering fire. We don't need the smoke anymore to keep the mosquitoes away. I have a lot on my mind, but they are all good, positive thoughts. Where will we live as a couple? How will Sterling spend his days at the Lewis, Marshall, and Associates office? Should I trust him to keep his thirst for adventure to a minimum?

At no point could I imagine the two of us ever wanting to be apart for a long time in the future. Sterling and I are about to embark on the biggest adventure of our lives—being parents. And that's a full-time job.

I decide to roll the Land Rover canopy down. We won't need it once we return to the lodge....

Suddenly, it dawns on me. What is Sterling going to do if the poachers come to kill the kudu buck? He never discussed his strategy with me. They have rifles, he has a rifle—but then what?

My ears strain to listen, worried that if I hear the crack of a rifle, it might signal the end of my happiness. But no, I'm overreacting. He'll be okay. He's always going on about how well-trained Marines are, so telling a couple of skinny poachers to stick their hands in the air and drop their weapons isn't going to be too difficult for him.

I'm overwhelmed by the need to check up on him, but I know better than to go trekking into the bush on my own. After shading my eyes and looking at the squashed grass from the tire tracks, I decide to use the walkie-talkie to contact Dad.

Climbing into the front seat, I search for the walkie-talkie on the dashboard. It's not there. But I could have sworn I stuck it in the front of the Land Rover when I was packing up the camp. Did Sterling cut back while I was dithering around and come and fetch it?

Seriously panicked now, I am determined to get back to the lodge—only the keys are no longer in the ignition. This is no longer a joke or me having one of those forgetful pregnant women moments I have read so much about. This is ominous.

My only hope is that a monkey or baboon sneaked into the camp when my back was turned and took the items, but the food is still in the basket and that's the only thing monkeys ever bother stealing.

I have no choice but to walk back down to the watering hole and head back to the lodge. It's my worst nightmare. Alone, pregnant, and stranded.

After sticking on a bush hat and spraying on sunscreen, I follow the flattened grass track leading back towards the lodge. I know Sterling will forgive me for chickening out. I must look after Baby, first and foremost.

I haven't gone ten steps before I know I'm not alone. I hear a rustling sound coming from the grass and my stomach turns to water. For one bleak moment, I pray that it's Sterling returning to camp. But he would not be coming back from this side, because the hide and kudu buck are positioned to the north.

Oh God, please don't be a lion, please don't be a lion. I'll do anything, anything, but please don't be one of the dangerous animals.

It's almost unheard of for a predator to hunt during the heat of the day, but if the rule is broken, then it will always be a rogue lion who breaks it. A weaker male lion cast off from the pride will often hunt prey during the day while the rest of the pride are sleeping off their heavy meals in the shade.

But what about snakes? Cobras can grow to be over seven feet in length and can slither and strike faster than a bolt of lightning. And baboons are hideously territorial, with the male baboons hunting in packs to protect their turf.

Wildebeest love to trample unsuspecting bushveld hikers. Rhinos and elephants too, especially when they have their young to protect.

What if a bloat of hippos has set up in the waterhole? We try to keep them to the river over ten miles away, but hippos have been known to break away to find new homes near water.

All of this flashes through my mind as the swishing and trampling sounds get closer. My best hope is to freeze and pray the wild animal ignores me.

The tall grass parts just enough to show me the long, black barrel of a rifle. And then I hear the last voice in the world I want to be listening to.

"Howzit, Edie. Long time no see. It was really kind of you to send out that smoke signal so that I can find you."

And Tjoepie Du Plessis steps out of the tall grass bushveld carrying my walkie-talkie and car keys in his hand.

Chapter 39: Sterling

I don't need a crystal ball to tell me that our plan is a bust. I've been lying underneath a sniper camouflage net since 4:00 a.m. and not a single sign of life has been seen. Other than the kudu buck occasionally raising his head when he hears a bird cry, there has been no movement.

I check the sun. It's heading for nine in the morning. Shrugging off the netting, I stand up. Hidden by a thicket of thorn trees, I creep forward and cut the tether. Once the loop loosens, the halter around the kudu buck's leg will fall off.

The kudu senses my presence. The enormous ears, shaped exactly like radars, swivel around. Giving one hoarse bark of alarm, the buck heads off into the bush, using the species' distinctive rocking horse galloping motion. He's got his horns tilted backward so that they don't catch on branches.

The horns must be almost six feet long with two and a half twists. I would have sworn a poacher or two could have been lured to see if the unmoving tag yielded anything worthwhile shooting, but I was wrong. This is not a quick-fix situation.

Time for me to regroup and brainstorm with Mpo and Deon.

Shouldering my rifle after breaking down the hide, I head back to camp.

I see the boot prints one klick out from camp. I don't bother counting how many differently sized boot prints there are, I immediately double back the way I came. The prints are fresh—I can tell from the way the imprint is still crisp and no dust has fallen back into the grooves. Prints get shallower the more time passes—and someone passed by here less than ten minutes ago.

Leaving a wide circumference of space between me and the camp, I decide to make the approach from the waterhole. Could be someone from the lodge sent one of the rangers looking for me and they gave up, heading over to check on Edie instead. But just as I'm naturally grumpy and taciturn for the most part, I'm also a naturally suspicious man.

Hauling the camouflage net out from my pack after taking a few small sips of water from the water bottle, I drape the netting over my body and then continue pushing through the grass. It's a long, slow process because I can only walk when the wind blows the closer I get to the camp.

If an unwelcome visitor is there, they will pay no mind to the sound of the grass hissing in the wind.

Keeping the small lake of water on my right, I do a U-turn back to the camp from the south. Whoever is there will know that no one from the lodge will approach from the south until the next load of sightseers head out for a spot of sunset game-watching.

I duck low, crouching over almost double so that I can't be seen. The wound in my stomach aches when I move, but my training allows me to disregard it.

If an incident has arisen at camp, all I need to do is to trek east so that the person has the glare of the sun in their eyes. Keeping my eyes on the ground, I can't spot any more bootprints.

This is both good and bad news. It means that whoever was walking to camp ahead of me never made it this far, which means that they definitely stopped to speak to Edie. But it also means that they have all left the thick grass to go stand around the camp, which puts them in my sights.

They are sitting ducks either way, even when I don't know who they are and what they are doing walking around the game reserve as if they own it. But I am not about to relax my guard because I think I know what I am dealing with now.

Poachers. What better way to get around the sudden loss of tracking tags than to go and hunt animals where they are bound to congregate twice a day: at the waterhole. It is the most revolting trick a hunter can do—to sit and wait by a body of water to hunt an animal when it has its guard down. Only primitive predators like crocodiles and boa constrictors hunt like that.

And just like that, I go into kill mode.

First, I need to identify that they really are illegal hunters. To be a poacher and risk being shot or imprisoned by an irate ranger, usually means the person has to be desperate. But these guys are slick. They have hacked the lodge's tracking device, and obviously have a sophisticated method of hunting of their own.

Crawling slowly to an incline of boulders that will give me a better vantage point to overlook the camp, I set up to observe first. The netting camouflage helps me blend into the gray tufts of grass and small shrubs growing between the boulder cracks.

What I see makes my blood boil. Edie is being made to sit cross-legged on the ground with her hands clasped behind her head. I'm too far away to see the expression on her face, but I have a good idea what it might be—because a thickset man with white-blond hair has his rifle pointing at her stomach.

Fighting down the instinct to start shooting, I figure I should scope out the surroundings first. There are four of them: three skinny guys with the kind of build that allows them to jog through the bush for hours at a time without flaking out through thirst or cramps.

They look like they could handle themselves in a fight—scrappy little guys like that can be surprisingly resilient when it comes to ducking and weaving—but land one punch or kick, and they will be out.

I can tell from their body language that the three guys are not on board with what is going on. I already have a plan about how I am going to handle them, but when I use the rifle scope to observe the perimeter of the camp, I change my mind.

There's another blond guy standing guard about thirty yards out. He's taken cover in a tree by scaling it and lying out on one of the branches. And he's doing exactly what I am doing: using his rifle scope to watch for anyone coming.

Only he's doing a shit job of it. Instead of keeping a methodical sweeping motion from left to right, up and down, he's jerking the scope all over the place, choosing random spots to focus on. No wonder he missed seeing me.

The lookout's got to go down first before he can sound the alarm when I make my move. His focus is toward the lodge, so I'll have to loop east and take him from behind. Ducking down behind the boulders, it hurts my soul to take my eyes off Edie, but the sooner I fix this, the sooner I can hold her in my arms again and make sure nothing bad happens to the baby and her ever again.

Using the wind to hide the sound of my movements, I cut through the veld, going around to the back of the lookout's tree. When I part the grass a fraction to check my location while lying on the ground, I see the scout is less than four yards ahead of me, sitting casually on the branch with one leg hanging down as he scopes the horizon in front of him.

I play out my moves in my mind before launching into action. But I have to wait first because the lookout has a walkie-talkie hanging from his belt. The two-way radio crackles to life.

"Ranger Two. Any sign of activity coming from the lodge? Over."

Reaching lazily for the radio, the scout answers. "Ranger One, this is Ranger Two responding. No sign of foot or vehicle traffic. Over."

Another crackle. "Keep this channel open, Ranger Two. I just might have more bargaining power than I thought. I reckon Old Dee-Dee Kruger will hand over any number of lions and leopards if it means he gets his daughter back. Over and out."

I can tell from the lookout's accent that he's South African, but not Afrikaans. And there is something strangely familiar about Ranger One's voice coming over the radio. There's only one person I remember whoever called Deon Kruger by that strange name. Everyone else called the safari lodge owner Oom Deon or Oom Kruger, everyone except Tjoepie Du Plessis.

Thinking back to the white-blond hair and overfed physique of the man in the camp, I can detect traces of the boy who tried to shoot me but didn't blink twice when he shot Dickie the duiker instead. And then left me to take the blame.

Making sure that the wind is blowing into my face so that the scout can't smell me, I step forward a few paces and then grab his leg. He hits the ground hard, face first, rifle spinning away in the air.

Before he knows what is happening, before he can spit the sand out of his mouth and rub it out of his eyes, I have the scout in a headlock. He can't breathe.

For a moment, he can't believe this is happening and thinks I'm going to let him go, that I'm playing a joke on him. I'm not going to waste my breath telling him not to struggle. At this distance away from the camp, no one is going to hear his boot heels scrabbling on the dry dust.

A few seconds go by as he tries to look at who it is squeezing the life out of him. Then a few more seconds pass as he realizes he hasn't got any air in his lungs. He starts kicking and scrabbling at my arm in earnest, but it's as ineffective as any other move he makes. The rock-hard bulge of my bicep and sinewy strength of my forearm are lethal weapons.

All he manages to do is claw at the skin where my sleeve doesn't reach down far enough to the wrist. Rasps turn to soft whimpers. He goes limp and silent after a few minutes—standard time for the brain to get the message that no more oxygen is coming in during this lifetime.

It's rough, but he played the game and lost. I can't be bothered tying him up, nor can I risk him regaining consciousness and coming looking for me.

After checking his rifle—it's a bolt action Nosler 21 with a low kick carbon fiber synthetic stock—and deeming it superior to the one I'm carrying, I bend the barrel of my rifle so that no one can use it and take the lookout's rifle instead. I leave the walkie-talkie on. It's not likely that Tjoepie will call anytime soon.

It's going to be alright. I can feel it. Ducking down a couple of dozen yards away from the camp, I crawl on my belly until I have Tjoepie's back in my sights. Luck is on my side. He has wandered over to the Land Rover to check the gas gauge. Probably wants to use it to make a clean getaway. But it means that Edie is no longer sitting in front of him.

Casually taking the key fob out of his pocket, he leans over to stick the key in the ignition. He will never know how much gas is left in the tank. Because when he straightens up, I shoot a round through the back of his skull.

The noise is deafening. Birds fly squawking into the sky. The three scrawny sidekicks bolt into the grass as if the devil himself has appeared in front of them. Instinctually picking up the spent shell casing, I shrug off the camouflage netting and run to Edie.

She's stunned, completely unaware of what just happened because I dropped the body on the other side of the vehicle. When she sees me, she bursts into tears.

"Sterling! Sterling! Watch out! The poachers are shooting! Don't come any closer!"

Crouching down beside her, I sweep her up into my arms. "Sweetheart, my darling. Please tell me that you are okay?"

Edie is in shock. "Sterling, that boy—Tjoepie—he's here. The shooting...."

I hug her close, soothing her and stroking her hair. "Hush, darling. Didn't I promise you that I would take care of the poaching problem for you?"

Chapter 40: Edie

I have never seen my dad so invigorated. It's as if he's got a new lease on life. Since Mpo, Sterling and my dad were able to track the three remaining poachers' footprints back to their encampment and arrest them, there has been a real spring in my dad's step.

Or maybe it's because today is our wedding day. Sterling and I are getting married. We want to keep the ceremony short and sweet, with only close friends and family attending. Mr. and Mrs. Lewis still have a way to go before Sterling forgives them, but I have no doubt our baby will help mend those fences.

Mom and Alice chose my dress for me. Alice brought it with her from New York.

"No shame to your South African designers, Girly-oh," my best friend says when she breezes into the chalet holding the delicate lace creation in her arms, "but this latest Luz by Watters bridal gown was too gorgeous for me to say no to when I saw it."

Alice knows my style so well, and the floating floral embroidery that dances from the halter neck bodice down to the wispy gossamer skirt panels does an excellent job of hiding my baby bump. Not that I'm ashamed of being pregnant, but I want to be the one who chooses when to tell Baby about how they made my wedding day just that little bit extra special.

Needless to say, the "Marshall and Associates" part of Sterling's circle of friendship is not here. But Jack volunteers to step up and be the best man.

"I left Sterling and Jack in the gun room," Alice informs me, "eating biltong and talking about what to do with the three prisoners."

Because there is no functional justice system in South Africa, the men are having a field day thinking up ways to punish the poachers for the years of misery and death they inflicted on the wildlife in the game park.

Jack suggested that we fly them into the middle of the Serengeti in Kenya and leave them there when a stampeding herd of wildebeest is expected. Sterling wants to try and re-educate them. Deon wants to force them to work on the game farm erecting the electric fencing we are buying when the charity funding is recovered.

But ultimately, it's my dad who decides. "I'm going to have tags implanted into the bastards, and then I'll dump them back into the countries they come from. If they try to come back across the South African border and back to the safari park, I will shoot them."

Two of the poachers are from Zimbabwe, one from Zambia. Those countries are even more corrupt and devastated by bankruptcy than South Africa is. As Sterling says, Africa can be one of the most difficult continents to try and understand in a compassionate way when it comes to the elite who rule over the poor and mostly illiterate citizens.

"And my brother has got that forensic accountant of his to track down the missing payments," Alice informs me in a triumphant voice, "because they found all the equipment and tech at the camp."

I'm only paying scant attention. The smell of hot hair fills the room as Alice begins to curl my blonde ringlets into soft spirals. Mom has gone outside to cut long grass stems for my bouquet. The smell of smoke and fragrant wood comes from the boma where the staff are preparing the wedding feast.

Mpo has asked two of his family to beat out a serious rhythm on traditional hand-carved hide drums as I walk to the patio in bare feet holding the cleverly twisted bouquet of dry grass in my hands. It seems as if I am walking on air as I see Sterling standing there waiting for me.

And there, in front of our closest friends and family, with the view of the waterhole at sunset in the distance, I become Mrs. "Bucky" Sterling Lewis for the rest of my life. And the kiss Sterling gives me after placing the impressively large ten-carat flawless orange cushion cut diamond surrounded by twelve blue-white round diamonds platinum ring on my finger is everything I hope my wedding day kiss would be. Intense, with just a touch of the passion that is still to come....

***

Leaving the men to prepare the braai—the traditional South African way of cooking meat over firewood—Alice and I talk about the future.

"Where are you going to make your home?" my friend wants to know. "But before you both make up your minds, please know that Jack will have a hernia if I have to take a private plane from Cape Town International Airport once a month to visit you. Noah and Gabby are going to want to see their kin growing up, after all."

"We've decided we want Baby to have the benefit of an American passport, so you can expect us to set up base Stateside for at least a year.

But I know Sterling has a fire lit in his belly to take on poaching, so we'll be here a lot too."

Jack and Sterling have promised my parents that they will help them fight illegal hunting with high-performance tech hardware and software. They have plans for long-range sniper rifles mounted on helicopters, infrared sensors for nighttime vision, hidden CCTV cameras, and motion-sensor tripwires.

"It seems as though my husband wants to bring the war to poachers. How do you feel knowing about what Lewis, Marshall, and Associates really do, Whirly-oh?" I ask Alice. She recently found out that Jack's side gig is writing code for her brother and his network of undercover operatives.

To say that Alice was surprised when she found out was an understatement. "Jack really pulled the wool over my eyes, but I had a vague idea what was going on, especially after that stone-cold grump came over and kicked poor Alf Cohen across the living room! But knowing that my darling Jack is involved in international black-ops stuff has done wonders for our sex life."

We laugh together and clink fruit juice glasses.

***

I don't eat much at the braai. I'm too excited, thinking about our honeymoon night. All I manage to do is push a few forkfuls of salad around the plate and then eat some fruit. My tummy is experiencing a bad case of butterflies as the local tribal dancers sing and dance around the fire.

Then Sterling comes to whisper in my ear. "You look so beautiful with the glow of the fire warming your skin, I don't have the words to describe it."

I can't resist brushing my lips against his chin. It always turns me on the way his scruff tickles my mouth. "Funny you say that Husband, because you know that I have always preferred your body language."

True commander that he is, Sterling stands up and raises his glass toward the guests.

"Good friends and family, thank you for being here for the happiest day of my life. And to all our absent friends and family—" Sterling did not invite his parents. I guess there are some things that are going to take more time to process. "All I can say is that they are most definitely not in our thoughts!"

Lots of laughter and cheers follow the speech. I can hardly recognize the gruff, uptight man who upgraded my seat so that I could sit across the aisle from him all those months ago in my smiling, relaxed husband. He dressed casually for the wedding ceremony in jeans and a thin cotton V-neck long-sleeved T-shirt, but then again Sterling has never needed clothes to make him look hot.

I give a little jump when he holds out his hand to me. This is it. Our honeymoon night is here. My parents have given us the honeymoon suite as a wedding day gift and this will be the first time I see inside the rondavel chalet.

The circular room seems to be one giant bed. The thin lawn mosquito net hanging from the ceiling is like a soft white cloud in our own personal sky. The ceiling is a high thatched grass dome held up with thick varnished logs. There are grass mats on the concrete floor, in keeping with my parents' eco-tourism commitment.

Taking me gently by the hand, Sterling leads me to the small shower bathroom outside. We are completely isolated from the rest of the lodge, shut off by a tall boma grass fence. Under the moonlight, the waterhole laps and glistens.

The water is warm, naturally heated by the hot daylight sun. There is no need for words as he unclips my halter-neck wedding gown from behind my neck and it falls to the ground, its work done.

We stand locked together under the warm waterfall. Moving to stand behind me, Sterling lathers his hands with soap and begins to massage the bubbles over my body. I ache for him. I can feel his hard cock pressing against me as he strokes the slick wetness between my ass cheeks.

Closing my eyes, I give myself over to the experience. The water cascades over my hair and breasts, drawn between my legs with his fingers. I lean back against his firm muscles, opening my mouth for the water to fall in. I'm drown-ing in love and desire. I can't hold back any longer.

As Sterling works my clit with his fingers and massages my full breasts with his hand, I come, long and hard.

But this is just the beginning. Padding back barefoot to the rondavel after shutting off the faucet, we fall down onto the bed. The king-size bed perfectly matches my king-size lover. As the mosquito net falls around us, we lay our heads on the pillows, face-to-face, heart-to-heart.

"I need to know something," I whisper as I gently caress his lower lip with my thumb, "when did you have the time to get that diamond ring made?"

He grins, nudging my cheek with his chin be-cause he knows I adore feeling his beard scruff. "It's called a Fancy Vivid pumpkin orange dia-mond. One of a kind. I've had the stone since that time we fucked during the upgrade, Edie. I knew pretty much immediately that I wanted you forever. Jack was kind enough to have it set for us. He's known that I wanted to marry you from the time you went to stay at the Fifth Avenue apartment."

I'm not surprised. As Alice would say it's "the fucking boys club" the men in our lives have got going on.

"If you had run from me, Edie, I would have hunted you down. Not because you are some trophy, but because you were always destined to be my wife."

We kiss, and this time there is a strong desperation in our touch. We want to show how much we love so badly. And yes, that tween-age crush I had on the pretty blond boy with the major attitude problem is still there, but now that tween is all grown-up and pregnant with his baby—and oh-so-happy.

I am more than ready for when Sterling slides his erect stiffness inside me, so wet that my pussy juices leak out as his girth takes up all the space. For one glorious moment, we lie interlocked together, not moving because one thrust will tip us over the edge.

"I love you, Edie Lewis," Sterling growls, "and don't you ever forget that."

He knows I have loved him and hated him for most of my life, but now there's only love to come.

We kiss as I let the heavy weight of his body press against my clit. My clit swells as I get wetter, making the urgent sensation rise up inside me like a wave of heat. My husband can tell I'm close. Giving one hard thrust, we orgasm together.

And all I can do is scream out how much I love him....

Printed in Great Britain
by Amazon

38510367R00274